KIMBERLY DERTING

THE TAKING

An Imprint of HarperCollins Publishers

To Amanda, Connor, and Abigail.
My favorite real stories begin and end with you.

The Taking
Copyright © 2014 by Kimberly Derting
All rights reserved. Printed in the United States of America. No part
of this book may be used or reproduced in any manner whatsoever
without written permission except in the case of brief quotations
embodied in critical articles and reviews. For information address
HarperCollins Children's Books, a division of HarperCollins
Publishers, 195 Broadway, New York, NY 10007.
www.epicreads.com

Library of Congress Control Number: 2013958342
ISBN 978-0-06-229361-9

Typography by Andrea Vandergrift
15 16 17 18 19   PC/RRDH   10 9 8 7 6 5 4 3 2 1
❖
First paperback edition, 2015

PART ONE

The moment you look away from the sky,
a shooting star will appear.
—Murphy's Law

PROLOGUE

WE KILLED THEM.

Crushed, to be precise. Crushed to the point that the other team left the field in tears, like a bunch of five-year-olds, falling into a defeated huddle in their grass-stained blue-and-gold uniforms and offering one another the lame consolations of runners-up. They did their best to avoid making eye contact with us as they had to go down the line and slap our hands, congratulating us on our win on their way to their dugout. On our massive, season-ending victory.

We, on the other hand, had hoarse voices and couldn't stop jumping up and down and grabbing everyone within

1

arm's reach and gripping them to our filthy, sweaty selves as we screamed into their ears, again and again, that we'd done it. We'd done it. *We'd done it!*

Cat caught me in her tough, wiry arms and squeezed me so hard she nearly crushed the breath out of me. "It was all you, baby! All you!" She didn't bother keeping her voice down, and everyone heard her. I could feel the dampness that soaked her uniform all the way through.

My face blazed in the wake of her comment, and I giggled nervously. She never seemed to understand the whole "there's no *I* in team" that Coach was always drilling into us. As far as Cat was concerned, *I* was the team. "Shut up," I insisted, shoving away from her.

"You saw him, didn't you? The scout?"

I didn't have to answer her or try to explain that I was sure he wasn't there just for me, because we were caught up in another round of cheers and congratulations, and after a moment I forgot all about scouts and embarrassing best friends and focused solely on the fact that we'd just won the championship.

That was how Austin found me, still wearing my ear-to-ear grin as I nearly walked right past him on my way to the parking lot to meet my dad. It had taken almost half an hour to finally disentangle myself from my teammates, and another ten minutes for Coach to stop congratulating us, and herself, and then us some more, before excusing us so we could get on the buses to meet up for the victory celebration. Of course, my dad had asked Coach to make an exception.

To let me ride with him instead of the rest of my teammates on the bus. He had *things* he wanted to discuss on our way to the pizza party.

Austin was propped against the fence, offering me one of his signature smiles. It was a smile I'd known almost my whole life, and in it I could picture our entire summer spreading out before us. Long days spent on the riverbank as we stretched our damp towels over sunbaked rocks. Climbing through his bedroom window after his parents left for work so we could sleep till afternoon in his cramped twin bed with its worn Batman sheets that he should've outgrown years ago but that he still hadn't parted with. Late nights at the drive-in theater, staring up at the stars instead of watching whatever dollar movie was playing on the giant screen as we talked about our future and all the things we would do together once we were free of our parents and high school.

And kissing. Lots and lots of kissing.

Austin pointed playfully at my chin. "You got a little something. . . ." Then he grinned as his finger flicked downward to indicate the rest of me.

My eyes followed as I smiled wryly. "Ya think?" I was practically wearing the softball field: grass, dirt, chalk.

He reached for me, his fingers twirling around the orange and black ribbons, our team colors, wound through my hair. "You sure you don't wanna catch a ride with me? I promise I'll take you straight to the Pizza Palace so you can celebrate." He leaned close, his Tic Tac–fresh breath tickling my cheek, and I only briefly wondered if I smelled as ripe as

Cat had; but I knew he didn't care. He never cared.

Glancing past him, I saw my dad watching us from in front of his silver Prius, clutching a stack of shiny new brochures in his hands. He didn't wave me over with them or anything, but I could see it in the way he looked at me—the hurry-up look. The I've-got-something-to-show-you look.

I closed my eyes before answering but gave the only response I could. I pressed my cheek against Austin's, transferring some of my grime to him in the process. "How 'bout you meet me there?" I leaned against him meaningfully. "*We* can celebrate later."

My dad is probably my number one fan. He could outshout any peppy cheerleader when we were winning and could outscream any ump when I got a bad call.

My dad was definitely a bigger fan than my mom, who often worked too late, like tonight, to make it to my games. Apparently, an escrow closing on a foreclosure was more important than your daughter's championship game.

"He gave me some pamphlets," my dad announced from the front seat.

Pouting might be immature, but every sixteen-year-old girl has mastered some form of it: the silent treatment; crocodile tears; eye rolling; the fake, nothing's-wrong response. The list goes on and on.

For me it was sullenness. Not pretty, sure, but effective.

Sullen sometimes forced a sixteen-year-old to banish herself to the backseat like a little girl. It was worth the payoff, I decided as I avoided his eager gaze in the rearview mirror.

But my number one fan wasn't about to give up that easily. "It's a great school. Big Ten. He was talkin' full ride."

I crossed my arms. We'd had this discussion. More than once.

My dad stiffened, sensing, if a little late, that I was digging in my heels. Again. "You don't have to stay in-state, Kyra. You have more options than anyone else on that team. Hell, probably more than anyone else in this town. A good pitcher is hard to come by. A great one is damn near impossible to find." I knew what he was doing. My dad, who knew me far too well—better maybe than anyone else—was searching for the right thing to say, something that would coax me into seeing his side of things.

Gritting my teeth, I turned to stare out the window. It was dark outside, so there wasn't much to look at, but it was better than catching my father's hopeful glimpses staring back at me.

I heard him sigh, and then there was a silence—not long and not short either—and then he added, "I don't know why the two of you think you have to go to college together."

That was it. He'd definitely found my hot button. "It's not your decision," I snapped as if I hadn't said this a hundred times before. "We've already decided where we're going. I don't know why you keep talking to these scouts. Stop encouraging them."

"Oh for chrissake, Kyra. College doesn't have to be a

'we' thing. It doesn't have to be a joint decision. It wouldn't be the end of the world if you and Austin went to different schools for a few years."

My fists clenched in my lap. "You and Mom went to Central Washington. It's a good school. Why do you have such a problem with this?"

"Your mom and I didn't go there together; we met there. And I don't have a problem with the school. It's just that you can do so much better."

I met his eyes now, daring him to lie to me. "Are you talking about the school, or about Austin?"

He held my gaze for only a split second before turning back to watch the black ribbon of road that stretched out ahead of him. "Both, I suppose." Before I could let the gravity of his words sink in, he tried to explain. His voice was softer now. "It's not Austin. You know I like him. Hell, he's practically family. It's just that you've known him your entire life, Kyr. You've never had a chance to meet anyone else. To know any different."

This was new, this argument against Austin and me. It was no longer about my education; he was talking about my future . . . my real future. The one Austin and I had been planning forever.

I blinked hard, not wanting him to know how betrayed I felt by the sting of his words. "Stop the car," I stated, and hated the way my voice cracked when it finally cleared the barrier of my throat.

"Kyra . . ."

"I mean it. Stop the car!"

We were in the middle of nowhere, on Chuckanut Drive, still miles away from Burlington. My dad slowed but didn't stop, his tires crunching on the gravel on the side of the road. "You're not getting out. There's nothing out here."

"I'll call Austin," I insisted. "He'll pick me up."

The car was still moving, but only barely, as his words tumbled into the darkness, finding me in the backseat. "I just don't want you to settle. I want you to experience the world. To go big." It was one of my dad's catchphrases: "Go big or go home."

Only this time he was wrong. I didn't want "big." I didn't want to live a catchphrase at all, none of them. I wanted to live my life.

And I wanted out.

Opening the car door was easy, and even though the Prius felt like it was moving in slow motion, the road I stared down at looked as if we were racing in the Grand Prix. I thought of what breaking my ankles might mean to my dad's precious full-ride scholarships, and suddenly I didn't care about scholarships or scouts or full rides.

"I said stop!" I yelled at my dad, and when I heard the screech of the Prius's tires skidding to a complete stop, I leaped out of the car.

By the time my feet hit the ground I was already running, but I was moving too fast, and I was crying now too. I couldn't see where I was going, and I tripped on the unforgiving asphalt.

I barely registered my dad's voice coming from behind me, and I definitely didn't feel pain, at least not yet. But I knew from years of sports' injuries that adrenaline could mask the initial discomfort, and you would always feel it later.

I was still getting up, brushing away bits of rocks and gravel from my uniform, and from my hands, which had taken the brunt of the skidding part of my fall, when everything around me went white.

White, like blinding white.

It came in a flash, all at once, from somewhere that seemed both far away and right on top of me at the same time. In that moment I couldn't see anything, but I heard my dad.

He was screaming this time. Screaming and screaming. My chest felt tight, and my eyes burned as I tried to find him, tried to see through the light that scorched my retinas.

All I knew was that one moment I was in the middle of a deserted stretch of highway, arguing with my dad about scholarships and boys, and the next minute my limbs were tingling and I felt weightless and dizzy.

Then . . .

. . . nothing.

CHAPTER ONE
Day One

MY HEAD WAS POUNDING. BUT NOT LIKE A HEAD-ache. More like someone was using it as a basketball against the pavement. Or for target practice.

That was it, I realized, prying my eyes open at last. Something was hitting me.

There was still too much light to make out anything clearly, but after blinking several times, I was at least aware of shapes around me. I dug my fingers into the ground beneath me and recognized the gravel and sand and asphalt at my back. All around me the smells of oil and gasoline lingered with something sickly sweet—like the smell of warm rot—sparking my gag reflex.

Another hard thing pegged me in the side of the head again, and I flinched, lifting my hand to try to shield myself from the assault.

This time I heard a sound. A giggle, maybe?

I squeezed my eyes, blinking harder, willing them to focus.

It was daylight that blinded me, which seemed wrong for a reason I couldn't quite put my finger on. But it wasn't just that—this whole situation seemed wrong. And now it wasn't just my head that was pounding; it was my heart too. My brain felt scrambled as I grappled to make sense of where I was and why I was waking up here, outside, instead of at home in my bed.

The silhouette of a little boy stood above me, shadowed by the glare of the sun behind him. I blinked harder, still trying to sort it all out, and I could see his expression then, a look of delight. He held one hand behind his back.

Spread out like marbles in front of my face, I saw an array of brightly colored candies that looked suspiciously like gum balls or mini jawbreakers.

"What are you doing here?" the boy asked, the hint of a slight frown shifting the planes of his freckled face.

I searched for an answer, and when I couldn't find a suitable one, I asked one of my own, "What are *you* doing here?"

The boy looked back over his shoulder. "Waiting for my mom." Past him, I saw the gas pumps and a small convenience store behind them. I squinted against the sunlight and read the sign: GAS 'N' SIP. A woman was at one of the stands, filling the tank of her red minivan.

What the—the Gas 'n' Sip, really? How the heck had that happened? *When* had that happened? I shoved the base of my palms into my throbbing eyes, trying to crush the pain away. Eyeing me curiously, the boy absently popped a piece of the candy or gum into his mouth from the hand behind his back as I struggled to sit upright.

It wasn't easy. Apparently, I'd slept outside all night. And behind a Dumpster at the Gas 'n' Sip no less. That panicky feeling shook me, and I glanced around uneasily, wincing as I realized that the rotting smell had been garbage.

"Robby!" The woman yelled, and the boy's head whipped around.

"Gotta go," he whisper-told me as if we'd developed some sort of bond and I required an explanation for his departure. "You want these?" He held out his hand, palm open to reveal his remaining candies: three red ones, a green, and four yellows.

I thought about turning him down. They looked sticky. But my mouth tasted like I'd just licked home plate, so I nodded instead.

He held them toward me, and I accepted his gummy offering as they peeled, rather than dropped, from his skin. "Thanks," I said before he skipped away.

I popped the candies into my mouth, letting the sour jolt of them awaken my saliva glands and wash away the tang of dirt that seemed to cling to my tongue.

As always, I got impatient and bit down on one of the

candies. Despite their gooey outer shell, inside they were rock hard, something I discovered the moment I felt a chunk of my right-side molar chip away.

Cursing, I spit the rest of the candies in a messy wad onto the ground and ran my tongue over the new, rough edge of my tooth. I'd just been to the dentist last week, something I hated doing, and now this would mean I'd be forced to see him again.

Fishing my cell phone from the front pocket of my uniform pants, I decided it was time to call for backup. I still couldn't believe I'd ended up behind the Dumpster of a gas station last night. My parents were probably freaking the hell out. *I* was freaking the hell out.

Not to mention Austin . . .

I dialed him first, not caring that my decision was sure to set off another round of arguments when I got home.

I held the phone to my ear and waited. After a moment I pulled the phone away and inspected it.

NO SERVICE, the screen read.

No service—how was that even possible? I knew exactly where I was. I'd been at this gas station hundreds of times; it was maybe a mile from my house—well within our coverage map.

Whatever, I thought, getting tentatively to my feet and waiting till my legs felt steady. I did my best to ignore the headache that continued to pulse behind my eyes. The walk would probably do me good.

★ ★ ★

I wasn't sure how much good the walk had done me, but at least my head had stopped throbbing. I still felt off and couldn't quite pin down what, exactly, was bothering me.

I had this strange sense of déjà vu that clung to me. It was like a wet second skin, all itchy and maddening, making me glance, and glance again, at everything I passed. It all seemed familiar yet *not* at once. Like I'd been here before but was seeing it all for the very first time.

Considering I'd been born and raised in Burlington, Washington, a town that barely rated a dot on most maps and definitely not worthy of a mention by name, I was chalking it up to the fact that I'd spent the night outside and still had no memory of anything after the fight with my dad.

Why I'd decided to camp out behind a Dumpster was beyond me—I was claiming temporary insanity, because there was no other feasible explanation.

Going home was sure to play out one of two ways, the way I figured it. My dad was either gonna be super sorry about our argument and the fact that I'd gotten out of the car in the middle of the road and just . . . disappeared.

Or he was going to be massively pissed at me for being so dramatic that I'd decided to stay out all night, even though I had zero recollection of making that decision at all.

Either way, I was still trying to decide how to explain the part about having no memory of getting from there to here. That's why I'd been hoping to talk to Austin first. He was good at those kinds of things. Good at talking me off the ledge and trying to see my parents' side of things. He was reasonable and even-tempered in a way that I didn't seem to be capable of when it came to them.

When I saw my house, on the same block I'd lived on my whole life—right across the street from Austin's house—that sense of déjà vu returned full force, nearly buckling my knees. For a moment I just stood in front of it, running my tongue over the sharp edge of my chipped tooth. I studied the gray-blue paint that my mom and dad had agonized over when they'd had to repaint the house last summer; and the azalea bushes out front, which suddenly seemed bigger and bushier than I'd remembered them; and the place in the sidewalk where I'd pressed my hands in the wet concrete when I was four and my mom had written my initials with the end of a stick: KA. Kyra Agnew.

I turned to glance at the house across the street. If Austin's car had been parked out front, I would've gone there first. I was suddenly nervous about going inside my own home.

But his car was gone, so I was on my own.

Walking up to the front steps, I tried the door, but it was locked. I reached up to the top of the doorjamb, stretching because I wasn't really tall enough unless I stood on my toes, and felt for the spare key we kept there. My fingers fumbled along, slipping over the grit, and all the while my pulse felt like it was choking me, it was beating so fast, so hard. But no matter how many times I checked, and double-checked, there was no key.

I searched around my feet, thinking it must have fallen,

but it wasn't there either. Maybe my parents had decided to teach me a lesson for my tantrum. Maybe they'd locked me out to force me to face them at the door before letting me back inside, which of course they would. To show me that they're still in charge.

Finally, when I couldn't think of anything else to do and when I couldn't put it off any longer, I knocked. My throat felt suddenly too tight, which seemed silly. Of course they'd be mad, but they'd forgive me too.

It was an accident, my staying out all night. Somehow I'd have to find a way to explain that to them. To make them believe that I didn't know exactly what had happened the night before.

I shifted nervously back and forth as I waited, thinking of a million ways to say I'm sorry. The seconds seemed to stretch and bend and last an eternity, and just when I was about to give up, when I was sure that neither one of them was home, I saw the curtain on the other side of the door— the one above the couch in the living room—part.

A face appeared.

A child's face.

I was confused, startled by the appearance of the toddler.

I was an only child—the product of parents who'd spent my entire life doting on me, and only me. I was the center of their universe. *Their sun and their moon and their stars,* as my dad liked to say when I was little.

The little boy lifted his hand in a motionless wave, pressing his chubby fingers to the window and leaving a steamy impression around them. I thought of my mom, and the way she'd always told me not to touch the windows because it left fingerprints.

But when the man appeared behind him, I physically jolted. I looked at the door again; a sense of dread filled every crevice of my being, like I'd made some terrible mistake and gone to the wrong house. Like there was some other blue-gray house with my handprints forever imprinted in the walkway.

My panic subsided somewhat when I saw the worn gold numbers running alongside the front door: 9-6-1-2.

My address.

My house.

My home.

I was definitely in the right place. So who were these people? These strangers staring at me from the other side of *my* window?

I glanced back, but they were gone, the curtains fallen back in place. The only reminder that they'd been there at all was the outline of the boy's hand. I felt sick, still dizzy, when I heard the door.

I looked up just as it opened, and I found myself staring into the man's intense brown eyes. He didn't say anything, just gave me that look that people give you when they answer their doors. The look that says, *Can I help you?*

Suddenly indignant, I took a step forward, reaching for a door handle I'd turned a million times before. "Are my parents here?" I'd meant to sound forceful, but my voice had a wavering quality that made me sound nervous instead.

I'm not sure it would have mattered, though. He'd stopped me anyway. "Who are your parents?" he asked, and that uneasy feeling settled deeper.

I looked once more at the numbers, double-checking, triple-checking them. "This is my house."

The little boy appeared between the man's knees. He had messy blond hair and round cheeks covered in what I could only imagine was jelly. He reminded me of a smaller version of the boy from the gas station, except that this boy didn't have freckles. Or pants. His chubby legs were white, and his bare feet were wide, looking vaguely like flippers.

The man moved, pushing the boy back inside and positioning himself between me and the toddler. Like I was a danger, a threat. "Who are your parents?" he asked again, his voice slower now.

His patronizing tone rubbed me wrong. I pursed my lips. "What are you doing here?" I asked, unwilling to give him too much information, and suddenly worried that there was a strange man in my home. *Where were my parents anyway?*

The man's eyes narrowed, and I couldn't decide if he was studying me, or suspicious, or both. I saw him reaching for his pocket, and my stomach tightened. Behind him, the boy was clamoring to get around his legs. "Me see . . . me see . . . me see . . . ," he kept repeating.

When the man's hand emerged, he was holding a cell phone. "Do you need me to call someone for you?"

This time when I reached for the handle, I was faster

than he was. "No!" I was nearly hysterical now as I managed to push my way past him. The little boy jumped out of the way of the swinging door. "I need you to tell me what you're doing here!" I searched the entry frantically. "Mom!" I shouted. "Dad!"

I'd made it only one step before the man had ahold of my arms and was dragging me back out the door. I heard his phone fall, clattering on the tile floor. He wasn't gentle, and my heart was racing, slamming against my ribs, bruising them. I didn't know what he planned to do to me. The little boy was crying, but the man didn't release me as he hauled me down the steps. I tripped over my own feet as he pulled me along the walkway until we were standing on the sidewalk out in front.

"I don't know what your problem is," he hissed, trying to keep his voice low, his eyes shifting back and forth from me to the screaming boy with no pants at the front door. "But this is my house, and you're scaring my son. If you need help, then call 9-1-1. I can't do anything for you." He released my arm but didn't leave right away. He just stood there looking at me, waiting for some sort of acknowledgment that I'd heard what he'd said.

I had. I'd heard him. I just couldn't make sense of it.

His house?

Is that what he'd said? His house?

But that wasn't right. This was my house.

My house.

I tried to find something in all of it to cling to, something

18

that would clear things up. I replayed the last few minutes, when I'd burst through the front door, and tried to recall what I'd seen.

It was the same house I remembered. The same, but different.

How could that be?

Tears burned my eyes as I looked, too, not at the boy, but at the house in front of us. The house I'd grown up in.

The man gave me one last piteous look before shaking his head and going back to his son. The boy raised his arms to his father, who scooped him up and carried him back inside, closing the door without looking back at me.

I wanted to explain what I was going through, to tell him who I was and who my parents were, but all I could manage was "But I . . . I live here."

The house across the street was almost as familiar to me as my own, which right now wasn't entirely reassuring. The pounding in my head was back, starting behind my eyes and radiating down the back of my neck. FML.

Despite the past few minutes, I wasn't hesitant as I neared the perfectly edged grass and tidy flower beds, because it was all so familiar. All so comforting.

Everything was exactly as it should be.

Even the car in the driveway—Austin's mother's—the same as always.

Austin would know what was happening. He'd clear things up for me.

I checked my phone again and saw the same NO SERVICE message blinking at me from the screen. If Austin's car had been there, I would have gone to his window. Instead, I went around back to the kitchen door and rapped softly.

When Austin materialized on the other side, peering at me through the panes of glass that separated us, I leaned forward, sagging against the door as relief loosened the knots in my chest and the tension in the back of my neck. I pressed my hand against the glass, the same way the little boy had in my house when he'd waved to me through my living-room window.

Austin was here!

Everything would be fine now. Austin would make everything okay.

The door opened, and I moved with it, tumbling inside as I fell into him. His arms opened, catching me before I could fall all the way to the floor.

"Thank god," I mumbled against his chest, the only place that felt safe. I no longer cared that I was still wearing my uniform, dirt and sweat stains making it rank. "Thank god you're here. I've had the strangest morning. The strangest night. I have no idea what's going on."

The arms around me tightened, but only slightly, and then I heard his mother's voice, so achingly well-known to me that tears brimmed in my eyes. "Tyler? Who is it? What's going on?"

I hadn't noticed Tyler, Austin's kid brother, but it was a relief to know I was no longer alone, that I was surrounded by familiar faces when everything else was so out of whack.

I drew back from Austin so I could see his mom. "It's just me," I told her. "I just came over because—" I wasn't sure how I'd planned on finishing my explanation, but I never had the chance.

Tamara Wahl dropped her coffee mug. The ceramic shards became projectiles as it shattered, sending pieces flying in every direction. Coffee pooled at her feet, but she just stood there, staring at me, her mouth gaping.

"Mom, it's Kyra . . . ," Austin said, and for the first time I realized that this was all wrong too. I looked down at the arms, still at my waist, and noticed the wiry hairs on them. They should have been flaxen, closer to blond than brown. Even the arms, the skin, seemed somewhat too pale, as if this version of Austin hadn't just finished his annual lifeguard certification—something *my* Austin had most definitely done.

His voice, too, was not right. It was deep, yes, the timbre just shades away from Austin's.

I was almost afraid to look at his face.

And that was when he caught me for the second time. The moment I realized that he wasn't Austin at all; he never had been.

This was Tyler Wahl. Tyler, who looked far too much like his older brother—my seventeen-year-old boyfriend— in looks, in stature . . . and, most of all, in age.

Tyler, who, the last time I'd seen him *just the day before*, had been only twelve years old.

CHAPTER TWO

"KYRA, ARE YOU SURE I CAN'T GET YOU SOME-thing?" Tamara Wahl asked, her disembodied head looming out of the darkness as she peered into the bedroom.

I wasn't sure how I'd gotten here, but at least I knew where I was. Or thought I did. Everything felt topsy-turvy at the moment.

"No. I don't think so." I shifted on the Batman sheets that I'd laid on almost as many times as my own. "No. I'm okay."

I glanced around at a room I had memorized. I knew right where the poster of Mark Spitz (the Olympic swimmer

Austin idolized) was—the one with the preprinted autograph Austin had tried to replicate above it when he was eleven in scribbly purple marker. The furniture was arranged exactly the same as always: his bed, his dresser, his corner desk plastered with a mishmash collection of sports and music and bumper stickers he'd collected.

But despite the sameness of it, it was missing his everyday clutter. His overflowing clothes hamper, the discarded Coke cans and water glasses on top of his dresser, messy homework piles on his desk. Even the bed was too neat, the sheets too fresh and smooth, as if they'd just been changed.

As if I were inside a diorama of Austin's room. A perfect, unused replica.

His mother had tried to explain things to me, but nothing she'd said made any sense. It was like she'd been speaking gibberish.

Five years, she'd kept saying. It had been five years since anyone had seen me last.

She was wrong, of course.

Wrong.

Wrong.

Wrong.

It hadn't been five years. It had been one night. I knew because I had been at my softball game. The championship game.

I knew because I was still wearing my uniform, and it still smelled like grass and sweat, and I still had the ribbons threaded through my hair.

23

One night, I kept insisting while my head and my throat ached. My dad and I had had an argument, and I'd run off to have a few minutes to myself—that was all. I must've wandered until I'd fallen asleep. At the Gas 'n' Sip. Behind the Dumpster.

One damn night. Not five long years.

But she'd given me some time alone to absorb it, to let it sink in before coming back to check on me.

She patted my hand now, her voice cautious, as if I were held together by wishes and hopes. "Well, your mom should be here soon. Maybe she'll do a better job of explaining things than I did."

I shot upright. *"My mom?"* My throat constricted around the anticipation. "She's coming?" My words barely made it through my airway, and the last one came out as a squeak. I didn't want to cry, but just hearing that my mom was on her way made everything better somehow, and there was no way to stop the tears.

And then Austin's mom, who I couldn't remember *not* knowing, had her arms around me, comforting, reassuring, holding me in the way only a mother knows how. "It'll be okay, Kyra. Everything's gonna be okay now."

Waiting, the same way I used to do when I was a little girl and I knew it was time for my mom to come home from work, I was standing at the window when I saw her pull up. She was driving a car I didn't recognize: black and shiny and sporty.

If what Tamara Wahl had said was true, which I still couldn't wrap my brain around because it was utterly-completely-*totally* insane, but if I allowed myself even to consider that I'd really lost five whole years of my life, then more than just who drove what had changed.

I know Austin's mom believed what she said, and she definitely had some evidence to back up her story. Austin was off at college, or so she'd told me—living the life we'd always planned, attending his last year at Central Washington University in Ellensburg. And Tyler—pipsqueak Tyler, who used to follow us around the house, intruding on conversations and telling the same annoying jokes that we used to tell when we were his age—was now a junior at Burlington Edison High, the same school Austin and Cat and I had once gone to. I couldn't deny that part, that he'd changed—I'd seen it with my own two eyes.

And, obviously, my mom and dad had moved.

All those things made it hard to argue with her. But that didn't change the part where everything inside of me said she was wrong.

I wanted to cry and scream at the same time, and I was so ridiculously confused, I could hardly think straight.

Five years was a lifetime. An eternity.

I was surprised, then, when my mom stopped her sleek black car, not in front of Austin's house, but in front of our old house. Habit, I supposed. It was the first place I'd gone too.

I watched as she emerged from her new car. Her hair

was more highlighted than I remembered and shorter, skimming her shoulders rather than falling to the middle of her back.

I wondered if I looked different too. I'd tried to wash up and had examined myself in the mirror. I didn't feel changed, and I couldn't see anything that said five years had gone by, right down to the farmer's tan where my uniform sleeves hit, from spending hour after hour practicing in those last days of softball season. I even had the same bruise on my right shin from where I'd banged it against our coffee table when Cat and I had been wrestling over the remote last weekend.

Well, last weekend plus five years.

But how was any of that possible? How could I have the same bruise and suntan? How could I still be wearing my uniform and the ribbons threaded through my hair, and smell like sweat and softball field if five years had passed?

Those were the things that made me hesitate, no matter how logical Tamara Wahl's explanations might seem. No matter how much Tyler had grown.

Outside, my mom faltered for a moment, looking up at the blue-gray house I'd tried to barge into before she made her way across the street toward Austin's house.

Toward me.

My stomach fluttered nervously.

"This must be so weird for you." Tyler's voice came from behind me. It was the first time I'd heard him say anything in his new, deep voice since that moment I'd collapsed in his arms in the kitchen. Vaguely, I could make out the shape of

26

him, still too tall to reconcile with the Tyler I remembered, in the reflection of the glass. But all my focus, all my energy was directed on her . . . on my mom.

I nodded and then slipped away from the window to meet her at the front door. She didn't go around back like I had.

I opened it before she could knock, startling her.

Seeing her there, her face looking drawn the way it did, her lips pinched and her eyes strained, I could almost believe that everything I'd been told was true. It truly had been five years since I'd last seen her.

Tyler looked five years older. My mother looked five years wearier.

Tamara had said that, after a few years of private investigators and police, my parents finally had to go on with their lives and had left it at that, even when I'd tried to probe to find out what exactly "go on with their lives" meant.

I guess I was about to find out.

"Kyra?" My mom's voice was more like a question. A terrified, hopeful, incredulous question. And suddenly she was just my mom. The same mom I'd had breakfast with yesterday. The same mom who shared dorky memes on Facebook and who laughed at my dad's lame jokes and who'd continued making me Mickey Mouse pancakes on Sunday mornings long after I'd told her I didn't care if my pancakes were shaped like cartoon characters.

"Mom . . ." Just saying the word made it real, and I started to cry, but really only because she was crying, while at the same time she did the mom-thing and wrapped me in her arms and started whispering nonsense words that tumbled over one another. Words like how she never thought she'd see me again and how I hadn't changed a bit and how she was never letting me out of her sight again.

I stayed inside the circle of her embrace, listening to it all. She made promises and we cried, and she hugged me and I hugged her until my arms ached and hers probably did too. When her grip loosened, I finally found the words to ask "Where's Dad? Is he coming too?"

I thought she might have stiffened, but I couldn't say so for sure. I didn't have the chance to decide, because we were interrupted by that man, the one from across the street. The one who'd chased me out of his house earlier.

His actions made sense now, I guess, since I was a complete stranger who'd been trying to shove her way into *his* home; but it didn't make me bristle any less when he appeared at my mother's back.

Or when his hand fell on her shoulder.

Like he knew her.

Knew her, knew her.

Her brow crumpled when she turned to face him. "Grant." She spoke to him in such a familiar way, in a way that made my stomach drop. The same way she spoke to my father. "I haven't had a chance to tell her yet." When she looked back to me, her expression was apologetic. "Kyra."

"I'm so sorry," the man said. "I should've recognized you. From your pictures."

I looked up at him, really looked at him. Tall and dark eyed, and, even now, holding the little blond boy in his arms. She didn't explain *who* he was. She didn't have to. The toddler reaching for my mother said it all when he squealed, "Mommy!"

She took the little boy, and he clutched her, looking more like a monkey than a child the way he clung to her. He dropped his head on her shoulder and sighed contentedly, and I briefly wondered if I'd done that, too, when I was his age.

I looked at the boy, and then my mom, and then the man again, at the way his hand stayed on her shoulder.

Five years . . .

My parents had gone on with their lives. . . .

But not with each other.

This was her new family. This was her son. And her husband. Her *new* husband . . . shiny and sleek and new, like the car parked in front of the house.

"I didn't want you to find out this way," she told me, reaching for me with her free hand. She squeezed my arm, trying to pull me to her, to make me part of the embrace with her and the little boy in her arms.

Maybe she didn't get it, how much this was for me. That this was happening too suddenly, and it was too, too, *too* much. Or maybe she did, because then she said, in a voice that was almost too hopeful, making me wonder if she was talking to me or to the little boy in her arms, "This is Logan. Your brother."

I tried to look at him—this replacement child—but I couldn't. He might be my brother, but I'd never asked for him. I didn't want him. I wanted my old family. The one I'd had yesterday. "Where's Dad?" I finally asked, turning to look at my feet, the only place that felt safe.

"He's coming, Kyr. He's on his way." She was trying to sound sympathetic; I knew she was.

"Good. I'll be inside. Let me know when he gets here."

"What else do I need to know?" I asked when Tyler appeared in the doorway to Austin's bedroom, the only place that seemed semifamiliar and nontoxic at the moment.

Tyler smiled at me from where he leaned against the doorjamb, and I realized why I'd mistaken him for his brother when I'd first seen him. His hair was slightly darker and longer and more mussed, and his skin was lighter than Austin's, as if he spent more time indoors than out, but there was that same confidence about him. Those same green eyes that crinkled when he grinned his sideways grin.

Tyler shrugged. "Flying cars, for one."

"Shut up," I scoffed from where I was sprawled on my back on the bed. "I'm not in the mood."

"Well, not so much flying as hovering, but we've almost got the technology down."

I lifted my head, unwilling to allow myself to smile. My eyes glanced over to the clock on the wall, and I wondered how much longer it would be till my father would get there.

"Oh, and mind reading." His teasing half grin grew to a

full-blown smile, dazzling me because it was so reminiscent of his brother's.

A pang of longing threatened to do me in.

I threw a pillow at him, and he dodged it. "Can I call him?"

I didn't have to explain who "him" was, and Tyler came inside, joining me as he sat on the end of the bed. It was strange to be here with him. In one sense I'd known Tyler his whole life. I'd been to all of his birthday parties, teased him when he had a lisp because he lost his front teeth, walked him to school on his first day, pushed him on the swing set until he cried mercy because it was too high, and built snowmen with him on snow days.

In another sense he was a virtual stranger, someone I barely knew.

But at this very moment he felt like the only link I had to Austin.

"I'm not sure that's a good idea. Mom called and left a message, letting him know you were back. I'm sure he'll try to get in touch with you." Even his voice was too similar. It was so freaky uncanny.

I pulled out my phone, suddenly understanding why I didn't have service. Life went on, cell phone contracts didn't. "I don't have a phone."

Tyler thought about it for a second and then handed me his.

"What'll you use?"

"I already told you . . . mind reading. No phones

necessary." He shrugged when I raised my eyebrows at him. "I'll get a burner. Besides, your mom'll probably get you a new one in a couple'a days."

Now it was my turn to shrug. "Or my dad." He didn't say anything to that, so I ran my thumb over the screen of his fancy phone, rubbing away the fingerprints he'd left there. "How long have they been divorced, anyway?"

He shifted on the bed, and I figured I'd made him uncomfortable. He rubbed the back of his neck and leaned forward, balancing his elbows on his knees. "I don't know about the divorce, but your dad moved out about a year after you . . . you know. . . ." His words trailed away. "I don't know if I should even say this, but it got weird. After a while there were accusations. I don't know who started them, but people started saying it was him, your dad. That he was the one responsible for . . . well, for you going missing—"

"No," I interrupted. "No! No way. Not my dad. We were fighting, yeah—arguing over college and Austin. Stupid stuff, really. I got mad and decided to walk. But my dad would *never* hurt me." *I shouldn't even have to say that,* I thought, defending the man who would've thrown himself in front of a bus for me.

Tyler made an apologetic face. "That's what my parents always said too. They said rumors are dangerous, and people talk when they have nothing better to do. My dad said no one believed it, at least no one that mattered."

I nodded, relieved, that his parents had known that my father was innocent. Austin's dad was a cop, and I felt better knowing that the police, even if he was the only one, hadn't suspected my dad of anything shady.

Then Tyler's eyes met mine, and he asked me the question I'd been asking myself over and over again. "So where were you then? This whole time you've been gone, where were you?"

If I had an answer I would have given it to him. Surely I wasn't asleep behind the Dumpster for the entire five years—the Rip van Winkle of the Gas 'n' Sip. The same went for wandering along Chuckanut Drive after my fight with my dad. I had no memory of anything past getting out of his car that night.

Just the flash of light. And then nothing.

Five years gone in a blink.

I glanced again at the clock, but its hands hadn't moved since the first time I'd looked, perpetually frozen at 3:34. "I don't know. I honestly don't remember anything at all. For me it's like it was yesterday." I shook my head, as baffled as everyone else by the question. "They looked for me?"

"Of course," he offered, his green eyes earnest as they sought mine. "Everyone. Not just your parents or mine, but the entire school. The whole city, maybe the entire state. There were fliers and alerts, and private investigators. You were like one of those milk carton kids."

"And Austin?"

His head bobbed. "Austin too. And Cat. They searched with everyone else."

Cat. I hadn't even thought of her, and my eyes stung all

over again. My face crumpled as I clutched Tyler's phone even tighter in my fist. I'd have to call her tonight. She'd want to know I was back. Of course she'd want to know.

He studied me, silent for a long, tense moment. "Can I tell you something strange?"

I half choked on a sob. "Stranger than me reappearing after all this time with no memory at all of the last five years?"

The corners of his mouth slid up the tiniest bit, and he cocked his head. "Yeah, sort of. It's just that . . ." His eyes slid over every part of my face. "You don't look any different." His brow fell as he tried to explain. "What I mean is, Austin looks older. He *looks* twenty-two. But you . . . you still look . . . sixteen."

My dad had always been dorky. And by dorky I guess I mean cheesy but sweet.

He was the hands-on kind of dad. When I was little, he was the dad who volunteered to go on class field trips, and coach my softball and basketball teams when all the other dads were too busy working. He worked, too, but his job as a computer programmer gave him the flexibility to telecommute, which meant he'd collected coach's trophies until I went into middle school and his role was usurped by coaches who collected *real* paychecks for what they did.

But he'd never missed a single game or recital or parent-teacher conference.

He was *that* dad.

So seeing him now, five years—and one missing daughter—later was like a punch to the gut.

It wasn't just me he'd been missing all these years later . . . it was him.

He was no longer the same man I remembered from our fight over which college scholarship I should pursue. This man, this dad, was a bedraggled version of that one.

His eyes were what I noticed first. Where my mom's had been tense and drawn, his were red rimmed and vacant. Hopeless.

Unlike with my mom, however, there was no awkward hesitation. He was running toward the house the moment he stumbled from the beat-up van he'd parked haphazardly at the curb, the door still dangling wide open. I met him on the lawn, barely registering the fact that I was pushing my way past my mother and her new son and husband, past Tyler and his mom and his father, who was planning to follow us to the hospital—something my mother was insisting on, that I be checked out.

Gary Wahl—Austin and Tyler's dad—would take my official statement there. I was pretty sure that because I was twenty-one, and no longer a minor, I could make some of these decisions on my own, but I still had to answer questions about where I'd been, or at least about what I could recall . . . which was pretty much less than nothing.

But none of those things mattered now. I didn't care that we had an audience or that my dad smelled of whiskey or gin or some noxious combination of the two and that he probably shouldn't have been driving in the first place. He was here, and that was all that mattered.

"I'm sorry . . . I'm sorry . . . I'm sorry . . . I'm sorry . . . ," I mumbled at the same time he did.

His shirt smelled stale and warm—like him, but not. He was fatter and softer than I remembered, and my arms had to reach farther to find their way around him. The scruff of his chin against my forehead had gone past grizzled and grown softer, like a beard, even though it was patchy and, from what I'd seen of it before he'd grabbed me and clutched me to him, grayer than I thought he should be.

I felt a hand on the small of my back, an unwelcome interruption. "We should get going," my mother said softly. "We can take my car."

I glanced up at my dad, feeling like this might be too weird for him but not sure which of us I was more worried about, him or me. He just shrugged, as if he didn't care about her or who drove, but his grip on me remained the same. Firm. Secure. Like an anchor.

We followed her, and I didn't look back to see if her new family followed us.

The inside of her car was cramped. Or maybe it was just me, sitting in the passenger seat feeling all awkward with my parents, who were now eyeing each other warily, like they were complete strangers.

My mom sat beside me, fumbling with the ignition and her seat belt, and then some more with the seat belt, pretty much anything to avoid looking in the backseat, where my dad was straining to lean forward, trying to be as close as he could to me.

Finally, when we were away from Austin's house and from the new husband and the house I'd grown up in, away from everything and everyone that should have been comforting and ordinary but made me feel as out of place as I did sitting here trapped between my parents, my mom broke the silence. "Can you remember anything, Kyra? Even the tiniest detail so we can try to figure this out?"

But it was my dad who answered as he slumped forward, his elbows on the center console and his fingers slipping through his greasy hair. "It was the light. How many times do I have to tell you? It was the goddamn light that took her."

They argued the entire drive, and I just sat there, listening mostly, because I didn't have anything to offer.

"Do you remember the light?" my dad kept asking.

I'd already answered his question. Of course I remembered it. How could I not? It was bright, blinding, brilliant.

There was the light . . . then . . . nothing. Not a single memory.

"How many times do we have to go over this? How many times?!" My mom's voice bordered on hysteria as she clutched the wheel, and I knew why. He was repeating himself—maybe he had been for years. Maybe this was the same argument she'd been hearing from him since the night I'd vanished.

I knew what she was thinking: how could he possibly

blame *a light* for my disappearance? It was . . . well, it was insane to say the least.

But my dad didn't see it that way. He was convinced. And not just convinced, but the way he talked about that light—all reverential and crazy eyed—reminded me of those guys who made tinfoil hats or pulled out all their fillings so the government couldn't read their thoughts through radio frequencies.

That kind of convinced.

He didn't actually *say* the word *aliens*, or even *abduction*. Instead, he talked about internet message boards and government cover-ups, and he'd even mentioned crop circles at one point, so it wasn't exactly like he was being subtle either.

Aliens. My dad thought I'd been abducted by aliens. Awesome.

I guess it sort of explained the nonshowery look he had about him and the stench of booze he wore like cologne. And I was starting to also maybe-sort-of see why my mom had kicked him out.

But from where I sat, he was still my dad, and the sense of guilt that this was all somehow my fault was overwhelming. If only I hadn't argued with him. If only I hadn't forced him to stop the car. If only I hadn't gotten out in the middle of Chuckanut Drive.

If only . . .

It was a terrible game to play. One he'd probably played a million times over.

I twisted around in my seat, and put my hand on his.

It was like a role reversal of all the times he'd squeezed my hand, silently reassuring me with his touch that everything would be okay. I wanted to convey that too. To let him know I was here now. That I wasn't leaving again.

His bloodshot eyes found mine and stabbed my heart. "They work like that, you know? They just *take* people."

I tried to shake my head, to deny his words. I might not have my memory to rely on, but I was certain it hadn't been little green men who'd come down in their flying saucer and whisked me away to probe me for five years, only to bring me back and deposit me behind a Dumpster at the Gas 'n' Sip.

"Ben," my mom said when I didn't seem to be able to come up with anything useful to add. "Maybe you should go home and get some sleep. You'll feel better in the morning."

My dad shook his head violently, vehemently. "Nuh-uh. No way. I'm staying with Kyra." His hand flipped over and squeezed mine. "No way I'm letting you outta my sight again," he vowed.

The emergency room is never the kind of place you want to hang out. The last time I was here the whole team had shown up to check on our shortstop, Carrie Dreyer. She'd come barreling into second and hit the base weird. When she went down screaming and everyone gathered around her, we realized that her bone was sticking clean through her skin. It had been a compound fracture, and she'd needed two surgeries and a titanium rod, and couldn't come back that season.

And now, because I'd disappeared, I had no idea if Carrie had ever played again.

The ER was slow when my mom and dad walked me inside, so we didn't have to wait long. It was strange to fill out my own admission forms, or any forms for that matter, since I'd never done that before. But now that I was an adult—which was even stranger—my parents were no longer allowed to sign for me. They also weren't allowed to make decisions on my behalf. The staff made a point of speaking to me instead of to them, and I had to give permission for them even to be in the room while I was examined.

It was as if I'd suddenly been emancipated, something I'd heard other kids at school talk about before, about how cool it would be to make their own decisions and not have to answer to their parents anymore.

Yet now that I was here, faced with that exact thing, I was terrified. I felt more and more like a stranger trapped inside my own body. Like a little girl playing dress-up in my mom's high heels, waiting for someone to come along and send me back to the playground with the other kids.

I was glad when they stuck me in a private room, since it was hard enough to talk about all this with the people who were there to support me. I couldn't imagine having to explain it in front of complete strangers. The big sliding glass door that led to the hallway outside made a whooshing sound whenever someone came in or out, and I jumped every time it opened.

Austin's dad had been right behind us, so after a nurse had taken my vitals—my blood pressure, temperature, pulse—and noted them on my paper-thin chart, he tapped on the door. The glass whooshed as it slid open. "Mind if I come in?"

I waved him inside, while the nurse told me the doctor would be coming to check on me shortly.

Gary Wahl didn't seem any different than he had the last time I'd seen him—a little grayer maybe, if I was looking for it, but other than that the same as he always had.

He eased onto the stool next to the bed; his eyes, so similar to Austin's, found me. "I know you already said most of this, but we gotta make it official." He tapped his pen on a notebook he was holding. "I'll make it quick," he added, smiling in a way that made me think of Austin, and my stomach lurched. But I swear, everything made me think of Austin right about then, and I couldn't wait for all this to be over with so I could be alone to call him. I just wanted to hear his voice again.

"You said you don't remember where you've been all this time, the entire five years. Is that right, Kyra?" His voice was so serious, so *not*-Austin's-dad's voice, that I almost— even though it wasn't even kinda funny—giggled. In all the years I'd known him, I'd never heard him use his cop voice before.

I took a breath and bit the inside of my lip, nodding solemnly instead. "Yeah. Uh, yes, that's right."

He scribbled my response. "So why don't we start at the

beginning. Tell me where you were and what the last thing you remember was?"

The game, I thought. I remembered the championship game. I opened my mouth to tell him that. About how Austin had been there, and how he was going to meet us at the Pizza Palace. But my dad answered first. "The light. Tell him about the light."

"Oh, Jesus H. Christ," my mom snapped, pinching her eyes between her finger and thumb. And then she dropped her hand with a sigh and glared at my father. "Are you kidding me with this? You're not really starting this now, are you?"

"The light?" Gary looked at each of them and then at me.

Just then I heard the whooshing sound of the door and I jerked; my attention landed on a woman in the doorway wearing blue scrubs under her white lab coat—the doctor.

But behind her, in the hallway beyond the door, I saw Tyler and realized that Gary hadn't come alone. Tyler had come with him, and he was watching me through the glass, looking at me the way Austin should have been if he had been here the way he was supposed to be.

Like he was worried about me.

Things quieted down once I kicked my parents out of my room, something I could do now that I was a legitimate grown-up.

Before, I would've gotten crazy satisfaction from the ability to do things like that.

My parents went grudgingly, giving the doctor a chance to do her examination, which was pretty limited. She was nice, but there wasn't much for her to do since I didn't think there was anything wrong with me.

"Does this hurt?" Her small hands probed my belly as her eyes, which were sympathetic, met mine.

"Uh-uh."

"What about this?" She poked harder, around my hips and into my lower abdomen.

"No." I shook my head to emphasize my point. So far there was nothing unusual.

She looked back to where Gary was making some notes and pretending he couldn't see or hear us, even though there was no way he couldn't. I'd asked him to stay, not really wanting to be alone but not wanting my parents arguing over the top of me either.

"What about sexual assault?" She asked the questions as casually as if she were asking whether I preferred vanilla or strawberry ice cream. "Would you like me to examine you for signs you were assaulted?"

I wanted to crawl beneath the exam table and never come out. I didn't bother to see if Gary was looking. I just shook my head again. "I'm fine."

She nodded and made a quick note on my chart and then gave me her hand to help me sit up. "Well, I don't see anything that jumps out at me. I'll order up some blood work and send that off to the lab, but I don't see any reason you can't go home. Do you have any questions?"

A million. But again I shook my head. She offered to send in my parents, but I told her to wait. I wanted just a few more minutes of peace.

I hated this new version of my parents. I hated that they seemed to hate each other and that they couldn't be in the same room for five minutes without freaking out on each other. I hated the blame I could feel oozing from my mom, and the weird stuff my dad was fixated on, and the way the air between them was overflowing with bitterness. But I hated even more the guilt inside me, simmering just below the surface like it was ready to boil over at any moment. Like this was all somehow *my* fault.

I clenched my fingers into fists and hid them beneath my legs, where no one could see them, all the while screaming silently inside my own head, where no one could hear my inner tantrum. I bet I could implode, disintegrate into ash on this very spot where I was perched in my hospital gown on the edge of the bed, and no one would even notice.

I was still answering, or rather not answering, Gary's questions when a man came in carrying what looked like a blue tackle box filled with test tubes and gauze and white tape and needles.

"Kyra Agnew?" he asked, as if he had a habit of wandering into the wrong room. He gave Gary a strange look, and I wondered if everyone knew why I was here.

"Uh-huh."

"Just need to get a little blood for the lab before you go." He grinned and set his box down while he pulled on a pair of latex gloves. He checked the ID bracelet on my wrist against the name on my chart and started getting the tubes and a needle ready.

Gary pointed to the hallway. "We're all done here. I'm just gonna have a word with your parents, and then we'll see you back at the ranch." He leaned down then, not a cop thing but an Austin's–dad thing, and kissed me on the cheek. "It's good to have you back, Kyr. Let us know if you need anything. Anything at all."

My eyes stung. I didn't want to cry, but I kinda was anyway. Even though I hadn't had the chance to miss anyone, it was nice to know they'd missed me. "Thanks," I croaked.

When we were alone, the lab guy examined the crook of my arm. "This'll only take a second. Anyone ever told you you have great veins?"

I shrugged because I'd heard that before.

He seemed pretty young, but I had no idea how to judge that. By the tattoos that covered the parts of his arms I could see? The piercing in his eyebrow that he tried to cover up with one of those little round Band-Aids but was obvious anyway?

"How old are you?"

He grinned down at me. "Why? You worried I don't know what I'm doing? I'm twenty-four, but I been doin' this for two years at least. I'm the best around; you won't feel a thing," he bragged.

Twenty-four. Just three years older than I was now, and two years older than Austin and Cat.

My eyes roved over him as he wrapped a strip of rubber around my upper arm and tapped one of the blue vessels that bulged. "Don't make a fist," he told me when I started to curl my fingers. "It's not necessary."

He said some things that were probably meant to be distracting, but all I could think was that we could be friends if we wanted to, we were that close in age. He caught me staring, and I dropped my eyes to the needle as it plunged into my arm.

I'd never been squeamish—not even when it came to watching my own blood being drawn—so it was strange when I felt the prickling, the tingling around the needle.

"Is it supposed to feel like that?"

"Like what? Are you feeling a little light-headed or anything?"

I shook my head. "Just . . . it's kinda . . . tingly."

He popped the second vacuum-sealed vial into the syringe, and it rapidly began filling with blood. He glanced at me and then back to his task, releasing the rubber strip from my upper arm with a snap. "I'm sure it's fine. And we're . . . just . . . about . . . done. . . ." With those last words he set the vial back in his box of tricks and reached for a cotton swab, setting it on top of the needle in my arm as he tugged to pull it free.

But it didn't budge.

He pulled again, harder this time, and still the needle stayed where it was, buried in my arm—deep in the vein.

The tingling sensation persisted, and now I felt a pressure too.

The guy frowned at it and then at me.

"Is something wrong?" I asked.

"No . . . it's, uh . . . fine. . . ."

We both knew that wasn't true. The needle should have slid out easily. I'd had this done before, and I'd never seen a needle get *stuck* before, not ever.

Beneath the surface of my skin, my vein swelled, bulging outward. The lab guy's eyes widened. He pulled one more time, this time yanking the thing like he was pulling on a nail stuck in a wall instead of a needle in the soft tissue of my arm.

I yelped, but more because he scared the crap out of me than because it hurt, although it did kind of hurt too. He staggered backward, a full step away from me, but he had the needle in his hand when he stood upright. He held it in his fist like he was declaring victory or something.

"Oh, shit!" he cursed when he looked down and noticed the blood that spurted from the wound on my arm. It was only a little bit, but his moment of triumph was over, and he attacked the red smear with the cotton ball. "Sorry about that. Not sure what happened." He secured the cotton ball with a strip of tape. "It should stop bleeding in about fifteen minutes, and you might have a little bruise for a few days. Nothing to be alarmed about, pretty routine stuff."

He had me confirm that my name was correct on my vials of blood and then cleaned and packed up his gear, and the doors whooshed closed behind him.

By the time I gave my parents the signal that they were out of "time-out" and could come back inside my room, the nurse had returned with my discharge orders. And just like my sketchy memory, there was nothing conclusive about my visit to the hospital. Even the discharge orders were vague. They included scheduling a follow-up appointment with my family doctor to discuss any unusual lab results that might come back, making an appointment with the dentist to have my chipped tooth looked at, a list of phone numbers for local counselors and support groups—in case I wanted to discuss *things*, which right now sounded like the worst idea ever since I didn't even know what "things" I would discuss— and getting plenty of rest. That last recommendation was the only idea I could really get behind.

I had a moment of panic, though, when we were getting ready to go and I was changing back into my filthy uniform—the same one I'd vanished in—and I suddenly realized I had no place to go. That I belonged nowhere.

I didn't have a home anymore, not really, because the place I remembered wasn't really mine anymore; it was just the house I'd grown up in. My home—the house I'd lived in just yesterday, in my mind—was gone now. My parents were no longer together—they'd moved on—and there was a new family living in that house: my mom and her husband and their son.

I was a stranger to that life.

The sensation of being unwelcome overwhelmed me even as my dad's hand closed over mine, and the decision was made for me. "I'll stay at your mom's tonight, with you." And before she could argue or say anything to the contrary, he faced her with his bloodshot eyes. "I'll sleep in the guest room."

"Ben," my mom interjected, sounding a million times softer than she had when he'd mentioned *the light*. "Kyra'll be in the guest room."

I guess my bedroom had been part of that whole "getting on with their lives" thing, like getting rid of my dad.

"Fine," my dad insisted, his grip tightening. "I'll sleep on the couch. I already told you; I'm not letting her out of my sight again." He looked down at me, and for a moment my hurt feelings evaporated. "I'm so, so, *so* glad you're back, Supernova," he told me on his boozy breath.

CHAPTER THREE

IT WAS OFFICIAL. I WAS A GUEST IN MY OWN BED-
room.

It was still my bed and my chest of drawers and probably
even my same pillows, but those were the only things that
hadn't changed in the five years I'd been gone. The bedding
was new and still had that stiff, fresh-from-the-bag feel as
if it'd never really been used and hadn't yet gone through a
single wash cycle.

It had been just as weird as I thought it would be, crossing the threshold of the house for the second time that day,
only this time understanding that everything really had

changed. That this was no longer the home I'd remembered.

The differences I thought I'd noticed before finally made sense to my confused brain: the new furniture, no longer the floral-patterned, overstuffed sofas that had once crowded our living room. Now there was a sleek, cool, gray microfiber sectional with a leather ottoman parked in front of it. The big entertainment center that had once housed our giant TV and had been cluttered with books and family photos and handmade ceramic bowls and ashtrays and framed drawings I'd done as a little girl was now gone altogether. There were new photos on the walls, a different family than the one who had lived here before with only one common denominator: my mom.

I'd wiped my feet on an unfamiliar rug inside the door and saw that my mom removed her shoes and placed them in a basket by the entrance—something we'd never done before. I'd followed suit, while my dad came in behind us, ignoring the new rule entirely.

The kitchen table was the only thing in the house I recognized.

I didn't bother asking what they'd done with all my personal belongings. My clothes and my comforter—the one that I'd had since I was eight and was probably too girlie and even a little threadbare but was so pliable it was like soft, warm dough blanketing me whenever I'd climbed into bed. And there were all the pictures of Cat and me that had been plastered on my corkboard, which was also missing, and my posters and ribbons and trophies and stuffed animals.

A lifetime of memories, all vanished. Erased. As if I'd never existed at all.

There was a soft rap at the door, and my mom eased inside.

"I got your dad all set up on the couch for the night, and I brought you these. The pants are probably too short, but you should feel better after you get a shower and put on some clean clothes." She handed me a pile of clothing, letting me borrow hers since all I had to my name was the uniform I was still wearing.

I smiled wanly, wishing a hot shower really could fix everything. "Thanks." I tugged at my grubby shirt. "This thing *is* pretty foul. I think I preferred the superflattering hospital gown with my butt hanging out for the whole world to see."

Her brow puckered. "Are you sure you're okay? I can call someone from the list the hospital gave us. We can probably get you in with someone tomorrow if you want to talk about . . . anything." I wondered what the "anything" might be.

"I'm fine, Mom. All I want right now is that shower."

She tilted her head to the side and smiled, and I thought she might be vacillating, trying to decide whether to leave it at that—just light, polite, meaningless conversation. Nothing heavy or real. And then she hesitated. "You can tell me, you know," she blurted at last, almost as if she hadn't meant to say it at all. "About what happened that night. About where you've been all this time." She frowned, her face a study

52

in gravity as she came back to the bed where I was sitting cross-legged, my fingers tracing the geometric pattern on the coarse comforter. "I know what your dad thinks, what he claims, but you can tell me what really happened to you."

I hadn't taken the time to consider the endless possibilities that existed, or all the speculations that might have been made over the years about my whereabouts. I knew what Tyler said, about the suspicions about my dad, but I wondered how many nights my mother had lain awake trying to guess where I was, torturing herself with her own version of what-ifs.

I could see them now, etched all over her worn face.

Suddenly the truth seemed inadequate, even though it was all I had. "I honestly don't remember. If I did I would tell you."

I watched her sag and wondered if she believed me or not. If she thought that, for whatever reason, I was covering up my absence.

So I asked her instead, "What do you think happened?"

Her eyes shot up to mine, her narrow, tweezed brows finding their way to the bridge of her nose. She contemplated me for several long seconds before answering. "You ran away. You and your dad had a fight over colleges—he told me you did—and you ran away."

I thought about *not* denying her version, because for all I knew she was right. I couldn't remember what happened, and her version sounded more right than the theory that I'd been abducted by aliens.

But there was no way I'd have done that. I would never have left my parents, and I surely wouldn't have left Austin.

"It doesn't make sense," I said, pulling up my pant leg to reveal the bruise I couldn't stop thinking about. "Besides, how do you explain the fact that I still have this, five years later?"

She looked at it, but there was a skeptical edge to her expression, as if she didn't see it the way I had. "A bruise? Kyra." She said my name the way she'd said my dad's earlier. Like I was grasping at straws.

"It's exactly the same as it was. In exactly the same place. You don't think that's weird? And what about my phone?" I pulled it out, the one with the NO SERVICE message flashing on the screen. "Why isn't it dead? If it's really been five years, shouldn't it be dead by now? But look . . ." I held it out to her so she could see what I did. "It still has half its charge."

She closed her eyes for a long moment as she shook her head wearily. "I'm not saying I have all the answers. Obviously this is all very . . . confusing." She reached over and patted my knee. It was self-conscious, the gesture, and felt more like something a casual acquaintance might do. Not really the kind of thing a mom does when she hasn't seen her one-and-only daughter in five long, tormented years.

Steel fingers clutched my chest, making it hard to breathe and making me aware of how unwelcome I felt here, in a place that should have been steeped in memories and warmth and understanding.

"And what about Dad? How come you . . ." I shrugged,

slipping my knee from beneath her hand. "Why is every-thing so *different* now?"

She sighed, and I knew this was all hard for her too. Hard to explain. Maybe even hard to have me back. "You saw him, Kyra. He's been like that ever since . . ." She frowned over her own explanation. "Ever since you've been gone. He couldn't get over it—you disappearing. He stopped going to work. At first we all did; we were all so focused on finding you. But eventually, when everything led us to dead ends and there were no real clues to follow and no signs you were ever coming home . . . eventually we had to get back to living again. It was hard, almost impossible, but we had to. Your dad, he couldn't do it. He started hanging out online all day, trying to find evidence, explanations, anything to figure out where you'd gone, even if they weren't logical." She sighed. "When he lost his job, I told myself to give him time, that he just needed time." Tears welled in her eyes, and she shook her head. "But time just made it—*him*—worse. He started drinking. Eventually . . ." Her voice wavered. "Eventually, I asked him to leave. I just couldn't do it anymore. I'm sorry," she told me, reaching over and trying again, this time squeezing my knee. "Things'll be okay. We'll be okay," she offered pensively. The attempt wasn't great, but it was better. She got up then, the bed shifting the way it used to when she was finished reading to me after she'd tucked me in at night.

My tongue glided over the chiseled plane of my tooth as I watched her go, back to her other family. When the door was closed, I reached beneath the pillow to where I'd stashed the phone Tyler had given me.

I longed so badly to hear Austin's voice. Maybe then I'd stop feeling so adrift. So . . . alone.

I opened Tyler's contacts list and found Austin's name right below someone named Ashley. I figured now was as good a time as any—it was barely after ten o'clock, early still.

Yet five years too late.

My stomach knotted as I pressed the button and waited.

I didn't wait long. "Hey, Ty-Ty," The girl who picked up on the other end was most definitely not Austin, but I knew her voice almost as well as I knew my own.

"Ty?" she tried again.

I was suddenly less certain than ever, and I thought about hanging up and pretending I'd never placed this call in the first place. Maybe even set the phone on fire.

"Tyler . . . ? Are you there?"

I swallowed, trying not to vomit on my own incredulity as I opened my mouth to speak. "Cat? Is that you?"

My words were followed by the longest pause in history. Longer even than the time I dared Cat to call Nathan Higgins, her eighth-grade crush, and she'd accidentally professed her love to his dad in way-too-explicit terms.

As I waited, I thought maybe we'd gotten disconnected, or that she'd had the same thought I had and decided to toss her phone in the trash and direct a flamethrower at it.

And then I heard her. "Oh my god, Kyra, is it really you?" It wasn't really a question, even though it technically was, and I knew right away that she'd already heard from someone that I was back. "I—I—" she started, but she choked on her own words.

On my end, I couldn't say anything. I wasn't sure what I felt. I didn't know whether I was relieved she'd recognized my voice or curious about why she was answering Austin's phone . . .

. . . or angry because I wasn't really confused at all.

It all made perfect sense.

They were together . . . at CWU. Living the life Austin and I had always dreamed of.

She cleared her throat, and then I heard her again, her voice all watery and wobbly. The way I felt inside. "Kyra, oh my god, I never thought I'd see you again, and then we— I—heard you were back, and I couldn't . . . I can't . . . I . . ." She fell apart again, and I could hear her hiccupping as she tried to gather herself so she could start rambling once more.

But I didn't want to listen to her ramble. Heat crept up my neck, and my jaw tensed. "What're you doing there, Cat?" I asked, not wanting to sound like the jilted girlfriend but feeling it all the same.

She sniffled. "Kyr . . . come on. . . ." It wasn't an explanation, or even an apology. But I understood all the same.

"So that's it then? You and Austin?" My voice cracked. "Really? My best friend and my boyfriend?" It was the oldest and lamest story in history. Betrayed by the two people you trusted most in this world.

There was another record-breaking pause. I had no idea if she was alone or if Austin was there with her, and they were communicating silently while I sat on my end like a fool.

"Kyr," Cat tried again. "I swear to you, we never did anything before . . . well before . . . you went missing. . . ." She fumbled over her words, and my humiliation deepened. "We searched so hard for you, with everyone else. And we waited forever for you to come back. We just . . . we thought you were . . . dead."

I wanted to slink beneath the too-stiff covers in my fake bedroom and hide away forever. Instead, I hung up the phone.

Some habits died hard. And sneaking out to Austin's house in the middle of the night came to me as naturally as riding a bike or tying my shoes or adding extra butter to my popcorn at the movies. I get how that sounds, but mostly when I'd snuck into Austin's room at night, we really just slept. We'd been doing that since our parents had put a ban on our boy-girl sleepovers, deciding they were inappropriate the older we got. We thought the late-in-the-game rule change was unfair of them, especially after we'd grown accustomed to our overnight playdates.

Still, they weren't really wrong to ban the sleepovers, because somewhere along the way, sometime during middle school, Austin and I had crossed that line between just friends to something more. Something experimental and unknown to us. Something far more interesting and exciting.

We'd started by holding hands in a different way, not like little kids anymore. Our fingers would intertwine, moving in and around and over, exploring and testing. My stomach would flutter and lurch as I learned the feel of each of his fingertips. I remember taking his hand in mine as an excuse to touch him, and I would trace the lines of his palms, pretending to read his future in an ominous voice.

Eventually, holding hands wasn't enough, and, on a late-summer day while we were at the river, we'd kissed. We'd crossed a line and never went back. After that we'd begun whispering whenever grown-ups were around, our conversations no longer as innocent as they'd once been as we navigated into uncharted waters.

And then one night I'd snuck into his bedroom and fallen asleep there.

That was it. A ritual had been born, and no one—not my parents or his, maybe because they all worked or maybe because they were too trusting to check on us—had ever realized what we'd been up to.

Or maybe they'd known all along and never said a word.

Only it wasn't Austin I was looking for tonight.

But since Tyler wasn't accustomed to me coming over at all hours, his window wasn't unlocked when I got there. Not that I would've just climbed in the way I would have with Austin. That was different; Austin and I had been different.

It was disquieting all over again to see Tyler appear at his window, a slightly darker-haired version of his older brother. And one who, apparently, didn't wear a shirt when he slept.

I tried not to look at how defined his bare chest was. Tried to keep my gaze from moving lower and noticing his muscled stomach and his navel, which was surrounded by a tuft of dark hair.

Hell, I chastised myself, reminding myself that I was still four years older than him. *He was still Austin's brother!*

Forcing my gaze upward, I caught him smiling at me, but not in the I-caught-you-being-all-lascivious way, and I knew I'd made the right decision, coming here. His window slid open on old aluminum tracks that scraped a little too loudly for my liking, since they hadn't been oiled the way Austin's had in order to keep them from broadcasting my arrival.

"Hey," he whispered down at me, sounding more alert than he should, considering it was approaching midnight. Unlike me, he had school tomorrow. At least according to the calendar I'd consulted no less than a dozen times when I'd finally given up trying to sleep. I just couldn't wrap my brain around the time leap I'd taken.

Crazy, considering I'd missed so many milestones that should make me feel like an adult: getting my driver's license, graduating high school, starting college, voting. Going to a bar.

"What are you doing here?" Tyler rubbed his hand over his face, something Austin used to do to wake himself up.

I bit the side of my lip. "Couldn't sleep. It's just so . . . *weird* over there."

He balanced his arms on the window ledge. "I bet.

You're all my parents talked about all night." Leaning to the side, he offered, "Wanna come in?"

I grimaced. Suddenly it was weird over here too. Looking at him, with his too-much-like-Austin looks. "Nah. I just wanted to give you this." I held out the cell phone. I didn't need it anymore, so there was no point keeping it. The only two people I thought I'd wanted to talk to were now the enemy, camped out together and colluding against me. Despite Cat's tearful pleas, I couldn't help picturing them together, having a good laugh over the way I'd called up and thought we'd pick up right where things left off.

Tyler winced as he looked at the phone, and I assumed he understood why I was returning it. He must've known. I mean, of course he knew about his brother and Cat, and now he knew that I knew too. He at least had the good grace to look sheepish, and I hoped he meant it. "Sorry" was all he said.

"Yeah," I answered, looking down at my borrowed yoga pants and wishing my mom were a few inches taller so they didn't skate over the tops of my ankles. "Me too."

I left Tyler's house—it was still strange to think of it like that, Tyler's house and not Austin's—and felt lost for a minute. I figured I might as well go home, but suddenly I wasn't sure where *home* was exactly.

The word felt foreign, even in the space of my own thoughts. Home should be the place you were most at ease. Most comfortable. Most secure.

I felt none of those things in my mother's house, at least not anymore. I was a houseguest in a home she'd made with a new family.

Instead of crossing the street, a straight shot to the home-that-wasn't-home, I wandered down the sidewalk, heading nowhere in particular. There was a breeze, and I was again aware of how exposed my ankles were as the wind whorled around them, tickling my skin. Despite the supersweet high waters I was sporting, it had been really nice to wear something that didn't reek of softball diamond or day-old sweat.

I'd expected to have to shave through five years' worth of leg hair with my mom's Lady Bic, maybe go through one or two of her disposable razors in the process, but when I'd run my hands over my legs, I'd realized they were still smooth. As if I'd just shaved them the day before, right before the championship game.

The idea that someone might have shaved them for me while I was out cold gave me the heebie-jeebies. If that were the case, I wasn't sure I ever wanted my memory back.

After showering, I'd tentatively reached out to touch the steamed mirror, whisking away the condensation so I could see better, looking at that other me through the damp halo. The me staring back was the same me I'd seen every day for as long as I could remember. There'd never been anything remarkable about me, unless you counted my eyes, which I'd always thought were crazy big for my face, and the freckles that splashed across my nose, making me look younger than I was. Something no teen ever wanted.

I'd never been like Cat, with her shockingly blond hair that grew that way straight from her head rather than coming from a bottle, and her exotic-shaped eyes that she accented with jet-black eyeliner, and a pointed chin that she always held high, giving her a badass vibe. The kind of vibe I'd always wanted but could never pull off because grandmothers wanted to pinch my cheeks and give me a quarter for being *so adorable*.

I'd spent forever staring in the mirror, studying myself for evidence of changes or nonchanges. It was harder than I'd expected, to dissect myself like that, and that same woozy sense of déjà vu hovered over me, like I was having some sort of freaky out-of-body experience.

I stopped walking when I found myself in front of our neighborhood park. Like me, it looked the same as it always had. Standard-issue park stuff, really: slides, swings, sandbox, grass.

The lights all around me were off for the night since it was way past curfew, yet I could see everything I needed to see. I knew this place like the back of my hand. It was the perfect place to be alone, and I hopped the short fence, wondering who it was possibly meant to keep out since I was practically tall enough to *step* over it, and then realized it probably wasn't meant to keep anyone *out* at all. It was designed to keep small children inside. It was like a kid corral.

The swings were near the tree line, and beneath them there was sand so that if you fell, you'd land in the soft powder instead of scrape a knee, or crush a skull.

Mostly, I think neighborhood cats liked to pee in it, though.

Austin and I used to swing as high, and as fast, as we could and then jump, measuring to see which of us had landed the farthest. That was, of course, before all the kissing had started.

From that point on the park had become an after-dark hideaway where we'd curled up among the turrets of the jungle gym or in the tunnels as we'd practiced and practiced and practiced on each other. Making sure we got that whole kissing thing just right.

I sat in one of the swings, suffocated by memories as I wrapped my fingers around the chain and kicked my legs. Maybe the park hadn't been such a great idea after all.

Moving back and forth, I tried to let my mind go blank. I pushed higher and higher in the air, leaning my head back and watching as the stars blurred together.

"You're a supernova, Kyra. Someday you'll burn so bright none of us will even be able to look at you." My dad always used to say things like that with a chuckle, right before he said something like "No pain, no gain" while reminding me to keep practicing or telling me that I needed to straighten out my pitch. Or sometimes he'd just reach over and brush away a stray hair and tell me how beautiful I was.

Dads say things like that sometimes.

Said, I thought, squeezing my eyes shut and sitting upright once more. *Sometimes they* said *things like that.* I wasn't sure what kinds of things *my* dad said anymore.

Behind me, I heard a sound, a shifting or rustling in the trees that bordered the park. The place where Cat and I always imagined creepy pervs hung out in their raincoats, watching the little kiddies play on the teeter-totters.

I turned sharply in the swing, the chains twisting together as I strained to see into the craggy shadows that filled the space between the trunks and shrubs and thick layer of ferns that choked the ground.

I waited, holding my breath as I listened. The back of my neck prickled as I scanned, unable to stop searching, unable to let go of that strange feeling of being watched.

I should leave, I finally decided when my heart refused to slow, even when I couldn't pinpoint anything to be afraid of, other than my overactive imagination. Five years hadn't changed the fact that I could still freak myself out in the dark.

As I got up, the swing jerked against the backs of my legs, rotating first one way and then the other as the chains worked to right themselves once more. Suddenly I didn't feel safe out here, in the park in the middle of the night, all by myself, and I wondered what I'd been thinking coming here.

I was just about to go, pivoting in the soft sand beneath my feet, when I saw him standing there, near the entrance to the park.

"What are you doing here?"

"Sorry," Tyler offered, taking an uncertain step back.

"I didn't mean to scare you. It's just that I saw you take off this way and thought that maybe you shouldn't be out here alone. I don't want to intrude or anything, but . . ." He cocked his head to the side as a slow smile slid over his face. "I can't in good conscience leave you out here by yourself."

I glanced around at the deserted playground. "You afraid some bully might push me down or something?" I grinned, and it felt like the first time I'd really smiled since I'd been back. I sat down again on the swing, keeping my eyes on Tyler, disappointed that he'd decided to wear a shirt this time.

He came closer, his feet sinking in the soft sand. "Or something." He took the swing next to mine.

We stayed like that, moving back and forth on the swings, not in a hurry, not racing or trying to swing higher or matching each other's rhythm, just swaying as I tried not to look at him too much or too often. It was hard, though. My gaze kept shifting in his direction, and I didn't want to stare, but I did want to at the same time.

He was of course older now than I remembered, but different too. More so than anyone else.

"What do you remember? About me, I mean?"

I grinned again when he asked the question, because it was so close to what I'd just been thinking. "I remember you liked chalk. That you always did these cool chalk drawings all over the sidewalks," I said, twisting in my swing to face him.

He made a face. "Ouch. Really? That's what you think

of when you think of me? Chalk?"

"That's not bad, is it?" I laughed at his reaction, pushing off again and letting the swing drift. "Why? What do you remember about me?"

He stopped moving, stopped swinging as he inhaled, his eyes—those green eyes—following mine. "I remember thinking Austin was the luckiest guy I knew."

My breath caught in the back of my throat, and my feet hit the ground, stopping me.

"What?" Tyler insisted, swinging sideways until his shoulder nudged me. "Don't pretend you didn't know I had the hugest crush on you, Kyra. It wasn't my fault I was only in the seventh grade and you barely noticed me."

He was right; I'd barely noticed him back then. Most of my memories of Tyler were fragments, held together by Austin.

"See how you went and made things all awkward?" I accused, getting up from my swing and dusting off the back of my borrowed yoga pants.

Undeterred, Tyler fell into step beside me as we made our way toward the park entrance. "Awkward or not, you should know I'm glad you're back." He flashed me a shy smile as he added, "And now that I'm older, I'll try to be a little more memorable."

CHAPTER FOUR
Day Two

I BARELY SLEPT, IF AT ALL; MY BRAIN JUST KEPT tripping over facts and nonfacts, memories and illusions, trying to sort through what was and wasn't and might have been. Considering I didn't remember sleeping, I felt fine by the time the sun started coming up and the smell of coffee brewing found its way down the hall to my fake bedroom.

I'd almost forgotten about The Husband—which is what I'd silently dubbed Grant, since it made me physically ill to even *think* his name—but he was the one I stumbled into in the kitchen. He was already dressed in a suit and on his way out the door, thank God, because, like I'd mentioned, that whole stomach-wrenching, physically ill thing.

I checked the clock over the microwave—it was 7:42.

The Husband poked his head back inside a minute later—I knew because my eyes automatically flicked to check. "You might want to see this."

I was still in my mom's clothes from the night before, and I grudgingly trailed after him, keeping enough distance so he didn't get the wrong impression or anything. No matter what he had to show me, there was no way this was a truce.

I stopped dead in my tracks when I saw what it was he'd come back in to share with me. And then I smiled, because how could I not?

The illustrations were detailed and elaborate. And even though they were created with chalk, they were vibrant and lifelike.

Tyler had drawn a cobblestone pathway that stretched all the way from one side of our street to the other, bridging our two houses, practically from my front door to his. And running across the top of the pathway was a saying, written in beautiful, scrawling script. It said:

I'll remember you always.

It took my breath away. I couldn't believe he'd gone to all this trouble for me. He must've stayed up half the night to finish it.

I glanced over to his house, but he was probably already at school.

The Husband made a whistling sound. "Pretty impressive."

I'd almost forgotten he was there, and I wiped the smile from my face, not wanting him to get the tiniest glimpse into what I might be thinking, and then I stalked back inside. Once I'd locked the door and leaned against it and was sure The Husband could no longer see me, the grin slipped back to my lips.

My mom was at the coffeemaker, pouring herself a cup just as my dad shuffled into the kitchen.

"Yes, please," he told her, nodding at the pot in her hand as he sat down at the table, taking the same spot he'd always sat in when we'd all lived there together.

She rolled her eyes at him but reached for another mug anyway. She didn't ask if he wanted cream or sugar, even though he always did; she just handed his coffee to him black.

He grumbled, but he got up and went to the fridge. After a minute he peered around the door at my mom. "Don't you have anything that *isn't* soy? Something that comes from, oh, I don't know, a cow? I'll even take goat."

"Sorry." She shrugged, not at all apologetically, plucking the carton of soy milk from his hands and settling down at the table.

I sat down, too, taking my old seat. The familiarity of it should have been comfortable, but it so wasn't. My dad sitting across from me, my mom between us, like we were still a family.

But we weren't.

"Pretty cool, what that Tyler kid did," my dad said, breaking the tense silence.

I cringed. "You . . . saw that?"

"Saw him do it. Right after you snuck back in." He raised his bushy eyebrows at me, folding his arms across the belly he'd never had before.

"You *snuck out?*" my mom demanded, glowering at me and then turning her glare on my dad, probably for not cluing her in sooner. "How could you . . . do you have any idea . . ." She stammered, unable to come up with the right argument. And then seemed to deflate all at once. "Kyra, you can't do that. We . . . just got you back."

And that was it. That was the right one, and even though I was technically an adult, her words were like a knife through my heart.

"Sorry," my sixteen-year-old self mumbled, feeling properly scolded.

"She was fine." My dad assured, reaching over and patting my hand, maybe because he couldn't pat hers anymore. "They went to the park and came right back. They were gone less than half an hour."

My eyes widened. "You knew? The whole time?"

He lifted his still-black coffee to his lips, and his mouth turned downward evasively. "I might'a followed you, might'a didn't." He winked then, and I shook my head, thinking of the way I'd heard something in the trees. Had he seriously been spying on us?

"That's weird. *You're weird.*" But it felt better, joking with him like that, like nothing had changed. Well, not as much at least.

My mom cut in. "I think we should get you some clothes today." She eyed my outfit skeptically, and I was tempted to remind her it was hers. "And maybe a new cell phone."

A loud wail erupted from down the hall, and I felt myself blanch as she jumped up from the table. I'd practically erased the kid from my memory, almost as effectively as I'd forgotten the past five years. If only.

With my mom gone, my dad leaned in, and I could smell his breath. I wondered if he wasn't still a little drunk from the day before. "I'm not much of a shopper. I think I'll leave you all to it. I should probably get home and see how Nancy's holding up."

Nancy. I let this new name sink in, even as my world tilted sideways once more. Suddenly there was a Nancy too. What was that all about? Now I had two new parents to deal with?

I no longer had a bedroom, or parents who could stand each other, or even a real home of my own.

My vision blurred, and when I couldn't stand to look at him for another second, I let my eyes slip to the digital clock on the microwave. It was 8:31.

After a moment he got up from the table, his chair scraping along the tile floor. He kissed me on the top of my head, his beard catching strands of my hair as he did. "I'll come back later, kiddo. We can talk more then." My mom came back into the kitchen carrying her new kid, and my dad smiled, but it never really reached his eyes. "Maybe I'll even bring Nancy so you can meet her."

Shopping with my mom and the new kid was less like shopping and more like wrangling an errant steer. The kid had to be herded and restrained at every turn. But I kept my mouth shut because I didn't want to hear my mom call him "my brother" again.

She kept saying that. "*Your brother* holds a spoon just fine, Kyra. He's only two." "Can you hold *your brother*'s hand while we cross the street?" "*Your brother* has a name; it's Logan."

It was as though, if she said it enough, she'd somehow force some nonexistent bond between us. Make me feel something for him.

Fine, whatever. He might be my brother by blood, but that didn't change the fact that he was a virtual stranger.

Worse, he was the brat who'd stolen my mom.

By the time we reached Target, which was only our second stop after the cell phone store, my mom managed to secure the mangy little beast into a shopping cart with a strap that was surely meant to contain monkeys. She got him to shut up for five whole minutes by buying him a bag of popcorn that he threw around like it was confetti and the New Year's Eve ball was dropping in Times Square. He was the most embarrassing thing ever, and I couldn't believe she thought I'd ever lay claim to him.

He didn't start screaming until he realized he couldn't

wiggle out of the shoulder harness he was strapped into.

After about fifteen minutes of that I covered my ears. "Forget it." I glanced at what was in the cart: a couple of T-shirts and one pair of jeans I'd already picked out. "I don't wanna do this anymore." I glanced meaningfully at the kid writhing in the seat and held out my hand for the keys. "I'm going to the car. Pay for this stuff, or don't. I couldn't care less."

I stayed in my fake bedroom the rest of the afternoon; at least there it was quiet. And away from the kid.

My mom tried to come talk to me, but everything was so different now—even with her. It was like chatting with a stranger.

When The Husband came home, which was earlier than I expected, she asked if I wanted to try again with the whole shopping thing. I refused, deciding I'd rather have my fingernails ripped off one by one than suffer through more of her painful attempts at small talk. I worried that letting her go by herself to "bring me back some things" would mean my closet would soon be overflowing with mom jeans and cardigans in every color of the rainbow. I'd be the youngest forty-year-old on the block. But it was worth it since all I wanted to do was scream at her for not being my old mom, the one who could talk to me about anything, and everything, and nothing at all.

I remembered one time, when I was thirteen and I'd first gotten my period, that my mom and I had stayed up well after midnight watching chick flicks and eating ice cream straight out of the carton while she'd explained to me all the important girl-stuff, like tampons and condoms, and boys and kissing.

She told me about her first date with my dad, when he'd forgotten his wallet and she'd had to pay for everything. And their second date, when he forgot it again and how he'd had to beg her to give him a third chance, promising that he'd show her his cash when he picked her up, because he didn't want her to think he was a total loser and was just trying to get free meals out of her.

She'd wrapped her arms around me then and told me all about the night I was born, and the way my dad cried harder than anyone in the room, including me.

And here we were, strangers in a strange house with nothing to say to each other.

The knocking at my window startled me, and I practically leaped off my bed. I looked at my open curtains and saw Tyler glancing at me from over the edge of my windowsill.

Smiling and shaking my head, I loped toward the window, my socks whispering across the floor as I came to a skidding stop. I slid my window open and leaned out a little, looking toward the front, and then the back, of the house to see if anyone else was around. "Why didn't you come to the door like a normal person?"

Tyler grinned back at me. "I thought this was our thing." When I stared at him blankly, he raised his eyebrows. "You know, you came to my window; I come to yours." He shrugged and pushed his hands into the pockets of his zip-up hoodie.

Letting out a small laugh, I balanced against my elbows. "I'm not sure we have a thing, but okay." I didn't tell him that using the windows had been mine and Austin's thing, because it didn't matter anymore. Austin and Cat had new things now. Things that had nothing at all to do with me.

"So, how was it? Your first day back and all?"

The fact that he was here, standing outside my window and asking me how my day was, almost made me cry. No one else had bothered to ask how I was. He was the first person who wasn't pulling me at both ends, like I was a rope in a tug-of-war. "You really don't want to know," I answered. "This whole returning thing isn't all it's cracked up to be."

"Yeah? What was it supposed to be like?"

I considered that for a moment, leaning forward against the windowsill as I chewed the side of my lip. "Good question. I feel like people should be showering me with gifts and cakes and shooting confetti cannons in my honor. And maybe someone should carry me on their shoulders. A little less with the crazy dads and the bickering parents and . . ." I stopped short of saying how boyfriends should still be boyfriends and not be hooking up with my best friend the first chance they get.

Ex-*best friend*, I corrected silently.

"Or making chalk masterpieces for you?" Tyler asked, grinning mischievously as he bit his bottom lip.

"Yeah." My voice dropped, and I shrugged, trying to

act like it was no big deal even though it was a huge deal. I leaned farther out the window so I could get a glimpse of his handiwork. "Like that."

Tyler was studying me, his green eyes, just a shade darker than Austin's, never leaving mine. I could've sworn his cheeks flushed just a little, but he managed to change the subject effortlessly. "People are talking about you. At school."

"Talking good or talking bad?" Not that I cared, really, but I couldn't help being curious about the kind of gossip my reappearance had stirred up. I guess towns like Burlington were that way; news always spread fast.

"Wrong, mostly. A lot of stupid speculation about where you've been all this time. Abducted, runaway, sold into white slavery, that kind of shit." He smiled, and his teeth flashed white and straight, and I wondered if he'd had braces when I was gone or if they were always that perfect. I tore my eyes away from them.

"Hey, check it out." I left the window and came back with a shiny new phone. Before showing him, I pressed the button to check the time on it. "Look what my mom got me today."

He leaned back on his heels, that flawless grin lighting up his entire face. A groove etched its way into his cheek, producing a dimple, something I had no business noticing. "Told you she'd get you a new one. Here." He held out his hand, and I let him take it from me. His fingers moved expertly over the phone's slick, flat screen, waking it up

77

and pulling up the contacts list. I knew exactly what he was doing. He didn't mention the fact that his would be the only name in the list, and I didn't mention the tiny flutter that erupted in the base of my stomach because I was now in possession of his number.

I watched as he dialed himself then, and the phone in his pocket vibrated. "Now I have your number too." He handed it back to me and we stood there for a moment, our eyes locked. It was too long, and we both knew it, but neither of us looked away, and then it was way, *way* too long. I'm not sure if it meant something, or nothing, and I hated how badly I wished I could see inside his head, to read his thoughts. But eventually my cheeks got hot, and I blinked first.

"So, I have this thing . . ." he started, pointing in a general way toward his house or his car but making it clear he had to go.

"Oh yeah. Sure. Go ahead." I was stammering, and I hated that he was making me stammer at all. "I'll see you lat—"

"You wanna come?" Our words overlapped, and I stopped talking so I could process what he'd said, to make sure I'd heard him correctly. He stood there rubbing the back of his neck sheepishly and waiting for me to answer.

I lifted my shoulders. "I mean, sure. I guess. It's not like I have a whole lot goin' on around here." I glanced behind me at a room that was sterile and practically begging me to make a break for it. When I turned back, I wrinkled my nose. "Do I have to change?"

He stood on his toes so he could check me out. I was wearing the jeans and one of the T-shirts my mom had gone ahead and paid for during our shopping trip from hell. "Nah. You look good in clothes that fit," he told me, his eyes sparkling.

"What?" I gasped, feigning surprise. "Are you sure? Because I'm pretty sure I nailed it with my mom's highwater yoga pants. Are you saying they're *not* in style, because they totally were five years ago?"

His expression became a little too serious, making me catch my breath. "I'm pretty sure you could pull off just about any look you wanted to."

"Good." I laughed, hoping he couldn't hear the shakiness in my voice. "'Cause I seriously don't have anything else, and I really don't want to put my softball uniform back on again, like ever."

I checked the time again, and it was still just before six o'clock, same as it had been a couple of minutes ago. I lifted my foot to the window ledge and held out my hand to him. I thought about leaving a note or something for my mom to let her know where I'd be, but then I figured she had my number—because she was the only one, aside from Tyler, who did—and she could call if she was worried.

Tyler's fingers closed around mine. Austin's hands had always been dry, sometimes cracked even. He'd spent years applying special creams and moisturizers to protect against all the chlorine and sun damage, but they always had this rough quality about them, like fine-grit sandpaper. He'd spent half his life in the pool, the other half in every available lake, river, and stream. He was one of those people who probably wouldn't have minded if he'd been born with webbed toes.

Tyler's hands were soft. Not like a girl's or anything, but not calloused like mine—which still made absolutely no sense since, according to *everyone*, I hadn't picked up a bat in five years.

But now that I stopped to think about it, there were *so many* things about Tyler that were different from his brother, it was hard to imagine I'd ever mistaken the two of them in the first place. His hands, and his eyes, which were green but were mossier colored than Austin's. And the dimple that appeared once more when I bumped against him as I hopped down, making him look somewhere between gorgeous and stunning.

I blinked hard, trying to snap some sense into myself. *Where the holy hell did that come from?* I balked at the idea of Tyler as anything but Austin's younger brother, because no matter what, that's what he was—*Austin's brother*—and I struck a silent deal with myself to never, *ever* think about him as anything other than a friend, because that is all he could ever be.

CHAPTER FIVE

"*OKAAAY*, I GIVE UP. WHAT ARE WE DOING HERE?"
I asked, surveying the less-than-savory alley where Tyler had
parked. "Shouldn't we be someplace a little less . . ." I raised
my eyebrows. "Stabby?"

Tyler shoved open his car door in a way that made it clear
his car door was the kind that needed a good shove in order
to open. "Relax," he assured me. "It's perfectly safe."

He smiled, and that made me feel a little happier, if not at
all safer, as he got out and came around to my side, opening
my door and waiting for me. No one had ever opened my
car door like that, not even Austin.

I blushed and ducked my head as I eased past him, trying not to notice how tall he was or the way he smelled, which wasn't at all like back-alley garbage. He locked the car and went to a door that was dented and painted black. He didn't knock or anything but let himself inside. He held the door long enough for me to realize I was supposed to follow, so I trailed after him and found myself in a storage room of some sort crowded with metal shelves and stacks of cardboard boxes and plastic crates that filled every possible space. There seemed to be no order to the chaos. Mostly, it looked like books and catalogs, but there were also stacks of rolled posters and piles of photographs, and magazines and comic books.

Tyler didn't stop, though. He slipped right past the hoarder's haven not giving it a second glance, leading me without a single word into an even more cluttered bookstore beyond.

This wasn't one of those chain bookstores, though, the ones where everything is perfectly aligned and tidy, and where there were tables strategically positioned to highlight this week's hottest sellers. There was no soft jazz playing in the background or a café with easy chairs so patrons could kick back with a pastry and hang out to browse their selections. This was more like a thrift store for books, which made sense, I supposed, when I spied the bold neon sign on the other side of the plate glass window that read USED BOOKS.

It had that smell too. That musty, old-book smell. The smell you notice when you got your assigned reading in

English class. The smell that wafted up from the pages of a book that's been passed down year after year, the one with the dog-eared pages and highlighted passages, and rips and a tattered cover. And if you were really, really lucky, some kid with nothing better to do, because he for sure wasn't going to *read* the book, drew pictures of ladies' boobs at the front of each chapter.

That was how I'd forever remember *Of Mice and Men*— as amateur pencil porn.

The guy behind the counter was wearing a checkered shirt and black horn-rimmed glasses, and was hunched forward on his elbow as he worked on a crossword puzzle from the newspaper. He lifted his eyes disinterestedly as we approached—a halfhearted attempt at customer service— but when he caught sight of Tyler, he dropped his pencil and hopped up from his stool.

"Hey! I was waitin' for ya." His grin spread wide and made his scruffy, unshaved face look more welcoming than his what-the-hell-do-you-want glance had. It was clear that when he chose to, like now, he had an infectious quality about him, as his eyes crinkled with enthusiasm.

"Okay . . ." The guy went behind the desk excitedly and reached beneath the counter. "This came in, and I immediately thought of you."

Tyler took a step closer, and I tried to see around him. Whatever it was—and from where I stood it looked like a magazine, a really old magazine—it had Tyler's full attention now.

Tyler leaned forward, pursing his lips. "Can you take it out?" Tyler asked, his voice low and filled with what was unmistakably awe.

"Dude, of course I can take it out. But trust me, I've already checked it from cover to cover. It's practically mint. It's exactly what you've been looking for." The clerk slipped it from the plastic sleeve that protected it, and Tyler's eyes went wide as his fingers cautiously, gingerly, reached down.

When he brushed the cover, I saw him suck in his breath and hold it.

This thing was seriously important to him.

All I could see was faded print and creased pages, and a chunk missing from the bottom-right edge of the cover.

There was clearly a discrepancy in our interpretations of "practically mint."

But after inspecting it, neither of them even haggled over the price; Tyler just laid down several bills, way more than I thought anyone should ever pay for a relic like that.

Tyler put his *prize* back in its plastic covering, and the guy behind the counter double-bagged it for him, making it more than obvious that you should never be too careful when it comes to protecting your secondhand junk.

I cleared my throat, and Tyler glanced my way self-consciously, as if he'd only just remembered I'd been standing there the whole time. "Oh yeah. Hey. This is Kyra," he told the clerk, who had also suddenly noticed me now that their transaction was coming to a close. At first the guy gave me a quick once-over, like he wasn't all that interested. And then he did a double take, and his gray eyes scoured me with laser intensity. I squirmed beneath his examination.

He frowned then. "I know you," he told me as if it were irrefutable. "From somewhere . . ." I could see the cogs in his head turning as he tried to nail it down. "Did you go to Emerson?"

Did? he'd asked, and I shook my head, studying him right back and wondering if I'd ever seen him at the rival high school. "No. I went to Burlington."

He nodded as if that made sense, but he was still scowling, still trying to decipher where he knew me from. I was sure he didn't look familiar to me, so I couldn't help him out. I was almost positive we'd never crossed paths before.

And then he snapped his fingers. "I got it! *I got it!* You're that girl! The one who went missing. I knew I recognized you. Man, your face was everywhere. Everyone knew who you were." He grinned his infectious grin, only this time I couldn't return his smile. "Heard you were back. What the hell happened to you anyway? Where you been all this time?"

Suddenly my legs felt wobbly, and my stomach rolled uneasily. I hadn't considered that people might actually *recognize* me after all the efforts that had been made to find me five years ago. And that when they did they might ask questions I wasn't prepared to answer—*couldn't possibly* answer. I turned to Tyler. "I—I think I'll wait outside." I staggered away from the counter, suddenly anxious to get out from between the disordered stacks of decaying books and magazines that felt like they were closing in on me. I didn't wait to see if Tyler was coming or not because I didn't care.

In my rush, I crashed into someone before I could make it to the back room. I murmured an apologetic "I'm sorry." I glanced up only briefly as I went to brush past him.

"No worries," the dark-skinned boy mumbled as I shoved past him. I hesitated as I caught his eyes, which were unusually copper colored, but then I kept going, through the storeroom and out into the alley behind the shop. That was when I realized I didn't have the keys, and I was locked out of the car. It didn't matter, though. I didn't mind the garbagey stench of the alley, because it was better than the suffocating scrutiny of too many one-sided questions.

The back door of the bookstore opened, and I glanced up to find Tyler standing in the doorway, watching me with a concerned expression contorting his features.

"I'm okay," I said before he had the chance to ask.

"I'm sorry," he told me, his voice low and rumbly near my ear as he leaned over my shoulder to unlock the passenger side door. My heart rate tripled at having him there, at my back, so close I could smell the crisp scent of his soap.

But I didn't want him to apologize, because none of this was his fault.

"Please. Don't worry about it," I begged. "It is what it is, right?" When the door opened, I collapsed into the seat. Melted into it, more like. My bones felt like liquid butter, and even shrugging was a major undertaking. "I better get used to people asking me things like that, or I'm gonna be

86

spending *a lot* of time holed up in my bedroom. It just took me off guard is all. No big." I flashed a quick smile up at him, the kind meant to reassure him, because I really wanted him to believe what I'd said. I wanted to believe it too. And then I changed the subject. "I don't get it." I nodded toward the Fort Knox of all bags he clutched in his hands. "All that fuss over, what, a comic book?" I bit back a teasing smile.

He rolled his eyes. "Okay, one, this is *so* not a comic book," he began tolerantly, as if this wasn't the first time he'd had to explain his hobby.

"Looks like a comic book to me."

"This," he said, plucking his plastic-encased treasure from the safety of its double bags. He held it up delicately so I could get a better look. On the cover was an old-fashioned red airplane with several other, smaller planes in the background. I couldn't tell if they were chasing the red one or if it was one big, happy airplane family. The title on the cover read: *Bill Barnes Air Adventurer. 10 cents.* "*This* is a pulp magazine. A July 1934 *Air Adventurer* with a Frank Tinsley cover, to be exact." He was grinning so proudly that he nearly convinced me that was something to be proud of.

"So, it's a . . . *magazine?*" I prodded, intentionally needling him because I could see he was serious about this.

"Yeah. I mean, no. Not really." Scowling over his inability to make his point, he sighed and closed the door before stomping around to the driver's side. Inwardly I was grinning, because I'd gotten exactly the reaction I was hoping for. When he got in the car, he tried again. "It's a pulp novel.

They're books. Some of them used to be published in serialized form, like this. A lot of the best writers wrote pulp novels in their time: Isaac Asimov, H. G. Wells, Ray Bradbury, Jack London. Even Mark Twain. I've been looking for this one for a long time. That's why Jackson called me when it came in." He frowned and then shrugged as if it wasn't worth explaining.

He was right; I'd probably never understand his level of intensity. I wasn't a huge reader, and for that matter, I couldn't recall seeing Austin read any of the required books for school. But it was downright adorable that Tyler was so passionate about this crappy, moldering old magazine that he treated like a rare and delicate treasure.

It made me wonder how he'd treat a girl. You know, if he cherished her the way he cherished that book.

I twisted in my seat so I could get a better look at him. "So, what you're telling me is that you're a total nerd. Is that it?"

The dimple reappeared, digging so deep into his cheek I thought it might make a permanent groove. My heart nearly stopped.

Austin had outgrown his dimples when he hit puberty. I thought I'd been glad because he looked older without them. But now . . .

Tyler started the car and pretended he was ignoring me, concentrating instead on backing out of the alley, but I caught his sideways glances, and the dimple never really disappeared entirely. "That's *exactly* what I'm saying."

Before long I turned to stare at the town I'd lived in my entire life as we drove. I was surprised how many changes there were, but since I hadn't been here, the new shops, and the closed ones, were glaring and out of place. If I'd been here the whole time, I probably wouldn't even have noticed them. The evolution of industry.

Just then we passed the high school, and a boulder settled over my chest.

But it wasn't the school that caught my eye; it was the fields, with their big box lights shining down on them. Even from the car I could make out the chalked outlines of the infield.

The boulder threatened to crush me.

"Hey." My hand shot out to Tyler, and I gripped his arm. I couldn't tear my eyes away from the grass and the dirt, the stands and dugouts. "Pull over, will ya?"

Without asking why or making a big deal about it, Tyler pulled to the side of the road and cut the engine. I stumbled out of the car, and I didn't look back to see if he was behind me.

I was captivated. Enthralled. Terrified.

My vision tunneled as I approached, so that all I could see were the fields where I'd spent so much of my life.

When I reached the chain-link fencing, I curled my fingers through it, feeling light-headed and unsteady.

I would've been a senior if I hadn't vanished. I should've had one more year—one more season—on these very fields with the rest of my team.

I hadn't heard Tyler get out of his car, but I knew he was right behind me when I heard his voice. "It has a name now." His breath tickled my neck. And then, before I could say anything, or breathe even, his hand was covering mine where my fingers curled through the fence. My stomach plunged.

Oh my god, what is wrong with me? Didn't I have enough to worry about without letting myself get all gooey over a boy who was far too young for me?

And Austin's brother no less?

All at once I realized Tyler was saying something to me, and I hadn't heard a single word of it. I felt like an idiot. I wondered what it was about him that turned me into such a girl—the kind of girl who daydreamed about things like dimples. I spun around to face him. But he was too close—*we* were too close. I realized that fact too late as I found myself lodged between him and the fence. I swallowed. "Wait, what did you say?"

He shook his head, and his lips were so beautiful, so full and tempting, that I swore my eyes were glued to them, and I found myself tracking them like a cat following a play toy. I blinked, hard, when I realized what I was doing, and I prayed to God he had no idea why I was so distracted.

"I was saying that the field has a name now." He reached out and brushed a piece of hair from my forehead. "Agnew Field. They named it after you."

I jerked back, away from his touch and away from his words.

Suddenly I knew—*knew*—it was wrong.

This.

All of it. Me and Tyler. Being here at the school. The fact that they'd named the field I'd once played on after me. In memorium . . . like I was dead.

And I had been dead in a way. For five long years everyone had mourned me. They'd let me go and "moved on," and everything had changed.

And now I was back. A corpse with a second chance.

I slipped out from beneath his arm, from where I suddenly felt trapped, cornered by his presence. "I have to go," I insisted, pulling out my phone and checking the time. "I need you to take me home. Now."

There were four messages waiting for me on my bed when I got back, all written on multicolored sticky notes that were stuck together so precisely they formed a perfect neon-rainbow fan. I assumed they were also in chronological order.

Flipping through them, I noted my mom's handwriting and was grateful she'd decided to take phone messages rather than to give out my new cell number. It wasn't even nine o'clock when Tyler dropped me off, but my mom and her new family were already tucked away in their bedrooms for the night, so I had the house to myself.

In the kitchen there was a plate covered with plastic wrap. Through the film I could see she'd made me my favorite: spaghetti with Grandma Thelma's homemade meatballs. I felt a stab of guilt for not being there for dinner, but the very idea of sitting through a meal with them and pretending we were an actual family made me nauseous.

Maybe if I tried harder, though, maybe if *I* made more of an effort to talk to my mom, she would finally say something real to me.

Taking the calendar off the wall, I carried it, along with the plate of spaghetti, to the table. I looked at the time on my phone and double-checked it against the time on the microwave. It bothered me that the two weren't exactly in sync—they were a minute apart—and I watched until the microwave's clock caught up to the time on my phone before turning to the calendar.

I flipped to May and put my finger on today's date, and the moment I did, the panic in my chest subsided. I knew why. It had become like an obsession with me, keeping tabs on the time. The constant reassurance that I hadn't lost another day. Or another hour or minute or second. That I was still here, and time was moving at the exact right speed it should.

I didn't reheat the spaghetti because I'd always liked it better cold anyway. I peeled back the plastic wrap and thrust my fork into the center, thinking I should be starving. I hadn't eaten anything since I'd stolen a handful of popcorn from "my brother" while on our shopping trip. I twirled the fork, mesmerized by the way the pasta swirled and whorled around it, gathering it into a bulging wad, and then I lifted the entire mass and plunged it into my mouth.

My mom had always complained that watching me eat

spaghetti was like watching the animals feeding at the zoo and that I might as well lift the plate up to my mouth and shovel it directly in. She wasn't entirely wrong; I did love my spaghetti.

Clamping my teeth down on the first bite of the soft pasta, I closed my eyes, preparing to savor it, letting it roll over my tongue. But I knew immediately that something wasn't quite right with it. Maybe it was the recipe. Maybe my mom had tweaked it over the years. Or maybe there was something wrong with the ingredients she'd used. Regardless of the reason, it definitely wasn't the same spaghetti I'd remembered.

I chewed anyway, forcing it down. I tried the meatball. My grandmother's recipe had been handed down from her mother and then passed to my mom, and would eventually be passed down to me. My dad used to say I'd cut my teeth on these meatballs.

But it was just like the spaghetti. The meatballs were the same, but not. Like everything else since I'd returned. They were . . . *off*.

I continued eating, but less enthusiastically, and halfway through my meal I finally gave up and washed the rest of it down the garbage disposal. It was the first time in my life I got no real joy out of my mom's spaghetti, and I couldn't help wondering if it was me or if she'd done something to sabotage it, although I couldn't for the life of me imagine why.

Tucking the calendar beneath my arm, I went back to

my room and threw myself on my bed to read through the messages my mom had taken. Three of them made my pulse rise all over again—the three from Cat.

Cat, and not Austin.

Cat, who'd called at 4:15, 4:53, and again at 6:36. Her cell number, which was the same as it had been five years ago, was also written down on each note, as if it wasn't permanently etched in my brain.

I crumpled up all of the messages and tossed them into one of the shopping bags my mom had left piled in my room, filled with the clothes she'd brought back with her from Old Navy, Macy's, and American Eagle—none of which I'd bothered looking through yet.

The fourth message was from my dad, letting me know he hadn't been able to make it back tonight but that he would definitely be here first thing in the morning to take me to breakfast.

Probably better that we'd be going out. Maybe without my mom around I could talk to him—really talk to him. And maybe he'd stop bringing up the whole light thing or his whacked-out theories about UFOs.

Maybe he'd go back to being my dad again.

When my phone buzzed, it scared the crap out of me.

I bolted upright and checked the time on the digital clock that I'd set so it was synchronized precisely with my phone, which I assumed was set to some sort of world standard. I hadn't been sleeping, but I'd been trying to, or at least pretending I was trying to, as I'd stretched out and stared at the ceiling, waiting for that drowsy-floaty feeling of sleep to claim me. If only I could shut off my mind for a few seconds.

I slipped my hand beneath my pillow and pulled out my phone, checking to see who was calling at this hour.

It wasn't a call, though; it was a text. From Tyler.

Your lights are on, it read.

I was suddenly glad I'd handed him my phone earlier, and completely embarrassed that I'd freaked out on him back at the school. We'd driven home in the kind of charged silence that had made it feel like we'd had a fight even though he hadn't done anything wrong. It was all me, really, being weird and jumpy about the fact that I was some kind of aberration who had no memory of what had happened to me for five whole years.

Very observant, I texted back, unable to stop myself from smiling now.

His response was immediate. *I left you something. Look out your window.*

I hoped that "something" was him.

But as quickly as the thought sprang to my head, I stamped it out. *Stop it. He's just a friend. Just a friend . . .* Unfortunately, that mantra wasn't working very well.

Still, I was a little disappointed when he wasn't standing there on the other side of my window. I frowned, opening the window and leaning out.

On the ground was a bag—the same smooth brown paper his comic book had been bagged in from the bookstore.

Like a seasoned veteran, I was out the window and back in my room in a blink. I peeled back the paper and peeked inside.

Immediately, I texted him back. *A book?*

After only a slight pause he answered: *One of the best in my collection.*

I looked again, to see what it was: *Fahrenheit 451* by Ray Bradbury. I'd heard of it but never read it. It was old, like the other one, and he had it in plastic even though this one was a regular paperback.

I don't want to ruin it, I responded.

I trust you. And that simple, three-word statement made me grin so wide my cheeks ached. A second text said, *I thought it might help you sleep.*

My mischievous side kicked in. *So you're saying it's boring?*

This time the wait was a little longer, and just when I thought maybe my teasing hadn't translated over text message and he wasn't going to answer, my phone buzzed again. *I'm saying I want to share one of my very favorite things in the world with you, Kyra.*

CHAPTER SIX
Day Three

I FINISHED THE BOOK AT 4:25 IN THE MORNING, exactly four hours and thirteen minutes after I'd started it. Since it was 238 pages, that was just under a page a minute, so I knew I wouldn't be winning any speed-reading contests or anything.

I knew now why it was one of Tyler's favorite things. I loved it. Not in the sense that I felt all warm and fuzzy after reading it or anything, but I couldn't stop thinking about it. About Montag, the main character who'd spent his life burning books, and his technology-addicted wife, and the free-thinking girl next door who was "different" from everyone else, never fitting into her strange, emotionless society.

I was different, I couldn't help thinking. Like Clarisse had been.

I continued to be haunted by the book long after I'd slipped it back into its synthetic sleeve and placed it on my nightstand. I was downright giddy at the prospect of seeing Tyler again, and maybe I'd talk about the book with him if it meant drawing out our time together, because I was so not above going there.

I glanced up when my bedroom door started to open, but then it stopped and there was a brisk knock.

"Yeah," I called, keeping my voice down since it was only . . . I checked: 7:47.

It opened the rest of the way, and The Husband was there, filling the doorway and studying me. We hadn't spent much, or any, really, time together. I'd avoided him as much as possible, staying in parts of the house where he wasn't— my room namely—and venturing out only when necessary. Just seeing him now made my stomach do nervous flips.

I couldn't help it; I still had that bitter taste in my mouth over our first encounter. Deep down, I knew none of this was his fault, but it didn't change the fact that I blamed him, at least in some part, for the way things were. For my parents' divorce, for that new kid in the nursery down the hall, for the guest room I was living in.

He made an attempt to smile. "Hey, kiddo," he offered, and inside I grimaced. My dad called me "kiddo," not him.

"Your dad's here. He's waiting for you in the kitchen."

I didn't say anything, just stared woodenly at him until he finally got the point and retreated with a shrug.

Since I hadn't really slept, I'd never bothered putting on pajamas, so I quickly stripped out of what I'd worn yesterday and snagged the first pair of jeans and a vintage-style T-shirt I could find in the bags my mom had delivered—glad she'd gotten my sizes right. She'd even bought me a pair of simple black-and-white Chuck Taylors, which, as far as I was concerned, went with everything. They were a little stiff for my liking, but I figured they'd be broken in soon enough.

My dad was alone and sitting at his same spot at the kitchen table when I came in. He looked up at me earnestly.

Without meaning to, I caught myself giving him the once-over. Evaluating his clothes, his state of cleanliness, his posture, right down to trying to decide how red his eyes were.

He'd showered and changed clothes since yesterday, and if I wasn't mistaken, I thought he might have gotten a haircut. He hadn't shaved, but his beard looked . . . trimmed . . . less scruffy. Even his eyes were clearer as they caught mine.

"Sorry I didn't make it back here last night; I got tied up." He shook his head and glanced away from me.

I sat down at the table across from him like always, so we were facing each other. I was nervous—he was making me nervous. He looked like he had something to say, and I was worried it wasn't something I wanted to hear. He probably would have tried to reach for my hands if I hadn't had them buried in my lap and balled tightly. "Anyway, I just wanted to tell you I shouldn't have said all that stuff yesterday. . . ."

He didn't finish, but I knew he was done talking when he winced and waited for me. I guess I was supposed to say something then.

I wanted to; I just wasn't sure what that something was. It was so weird to be tongue-tied around my own parents, so I shrugged because I couldn't think of anything else. I checked the microwave, thinking that only three minutes had passed even though it felt like forever.

More than anything, though, I wished he'd fill this awkward silence with one of his stupid expressions. I wished he'd say something like "An apology is a good way to have the last word." Or "It's easier to apologize than to ask for permission"—not that that one would have made sense in this situation, but I would have welcomed anything to break the tension right now.

And then he snorted. "Man, that kid across the street sure likes you, doesn't he?"

My eyes flew open, and I stared at him. "Who? Tyler? What's that supposed to mean?"

He wiggled his eyebrows at me, something that was *so* my old dad that I almost laughed at him. "The new art out front. He's got it pretty bad, is all I'm saying."

"Dad!" I jumped up, not wanting to admit that what he told me meant a million times more than it should. That it was killing me not to bolt to the front door so I could see if Tyler really had drawn something new for me. "You have no idea what you're even talking about." I tried to sound like it was nothing when, really, at that very moment, it was everything. "He's Austin's brother," I tried again, and this time I could hear it, the fact that I was so not convincing. There was no way my dad hadn't heard it too. But I was already making my way out of the kitchen toward the front of the house.

I heard my dad laughing at me from the table. "See for yourself, and then tell me it's nothing," he called after me.

When I stepped outside and saw what he meant, I knew. . . .

He wasn't wrong.

The old drawing—the path—and the writing—"I'll remember you always"—were gone. Erased. And in their place was a new "masterpiece," and it was infinitely more beautiful and more meaningful.

It was the birdcage in the center of the road that caught my attention first: chalk drawn and intricate, with its delicate bowed, golden bars. Its door was hanging open wide, and a small blue bird was just taking flight, with small chalk wisps depicting it gathering momentum as it broke free from its confines.

And below the bird, tracing the path of its trajectory, were the words Tyler had chosen . . . just for me.

The script was so different from the morning before, yet just as elegant and lovingly crafted, each letter carefully placed and delicately drawn. But it was the meaning of them, those words, all together that made me pause as I stepped closer, taking them all in at once:

The best things in life are worth the risk.

I inhaled sharply, telling myself I shouldn't be grinning but unable to stop myself. I thought of the way he'd taken my hand when I'd jumped from my window yesterday, or the way his dimple carved into his cheek whenever he smiled at me. I doubted *those* were the "best things" he meant, but my mind went there anyway, because clearly I was beyond redemption.

"Come on, *Juliet*," my dad said, slapping his hand on my shoulder. "Let me buy you some coffee with *real* cream. Maybe we'll even get eggs from a chicken instead'a that Egg Beaters crap your mom buys."

It wasn't half bad, hanging out with my dad. He wasn't the same or anything, but he was trying way harder than my mom was. Or maybe he was trying *differently*. It was like he wanted to be his old self, but he'd forgotten who that was exactly.

Five years is a long time.

He didn't push me, though. I think he wanted to, especially when I hadn't touched more than a bite of my Rooty Tooty Fresh 'N Fruity, the pancakes smothered in strawberries and whipped cream that had always been my favorite. From the worried looks he shot my way, you'd've thought I'd kicked a puppy or something.

"It's no big deal," I told him, shoving the plate away from me. "I guess I just don't like it anymore is all."

He lifted his hand to wave our server over, but I stopped him. "It's okay. I wasn't really hungry anyway." He dropped his hand, looking more satisfied by that answer than he had by the idea that my tastes might have grown up over the past five years. "Sure. Okay." He reached for his coffee and dumped in a disgusting amount of cream, until it was more tan than brown.

He didn't mention this Nancy person, and I didn't ask, even though I probably should have because it seemed like the polite thing to do. But I didn't feel like being polite. Nancy could wait.

I'd have to deal with her and The Husband and "my brother" and probably a whole lot of other people soon enough. For now I was still figuring out where I fit into my new bizarro life.

After we left IHOP, my dad took me straight back to my mom's place. The edges of the chalk drawing had been somewhat blurred from being driven over, but the birdcage—and the words beneath the bird—were just as captivating the second time around. I was glad my dad didn't call me on the fact that I'd stood on the sidewalk way too long, taking it all in once more.

Since The Husband had taken "my brother" to day care, or wherever they kept him when they went to work during the day, it was just the three of us at the house: my mom, my dad, and me. It was exactly as awkward as it sounded, so my dad pretty much excused himself right away.

"How was breakfast?" my mom asked, watching from the front window as the van pulled away.

My shoulders tensed. I didn't want to start this whole small-talk thing with her again. "Good. Fine."

She nodded and went to the microfiber sofa that I hadn't even bothered sitting on yet. I knew she wanted me to do what she did, make myself at home, but I stayed where I was, standing stiffly in the doorway.

"Have you thought about what you'll do now . . . ," she started. "Now that you're back?" I wasn't sure what she was getting at, and I frowned. She kept going. "You know, school? We should probably figure out a way for you to finish high school, and maybe get you started in college." She ran her hand along the arm of the sofa.

School. I hadn't thought about that. The idea of sitting in a classroom with a bunch of high school kids, even if they looked remotely like Tyler, was absolutely out of the question. I'd be a total outcast, even if I wasn't twenty-one. I'd seen the way that Jackson guy from the bookstore had gawked at me like I was an oddity—the girl who'd up and vanished.

"No thanks," I rebuffed her idea. "Maybe we can find an online school or something. Or I can get my GED and go to Skagit Valley." The community college was a far cry from the kinds of scholarship schools my dad had once tried to shove down my throat. But it was close to here, and it would give me a chance to sort out what I wanted to do next.

"I suppose that'd be okay. As long as you're not sitting around here all day, watching *Judge Judy* and hanging out with your dad."

My heart stuttered, and I blinked at my mom in disbelief. "Seriously? You didn't just say that, did you?"

"What?" she asked, getting up from her place and giving me a look that said she had no idea why I was so bent. "What did I say?"

I threw my arms wide and let out a noisy breath. "Did you not even hear yourself? Can't you say anything nice about him? He's still my dad."

Pinching her lips, she turned to gaze out the window. I heard her sigh exasperatedly. I started to tell her I didn't want to hear her talk about my dad anymore—not another word—but then she whirled around once more, only this time she looked ashen. Her face was masked in the kind of worry only a mom could manage. She finally looked exactly like she should. "Shit, Kyra," she said. "Austin's here."

I wasn't even sure I registered her words right away. I mean, I knew what she'd said—I understood her and all— but it didn't sink in right away.

Austin, she'd said. *He was here. Now.*

I was suddenly more nervous than I'd been since I'd been back, maybe than I'd ever been in my entire life. This was all I'd wanted: to see him, and for him to want to see me. And now that he'd come . . . I don't know . . . I wasn't as sure.

Four days ago Austin and I had been destined to spend the rest of our lives together. I'd been willing to turn my back on scholarships and softball and everything in order to make that happen.

Then I woke up behind a Dumpster and found out that he and my best friend, the girl I'd grown up with and told all my secrets to, were living the life I'd always dreamed of living.

Was it really so strange I might be having second thoughts about facing him now?

When the doorbell rang, it reverberated through my entire body. My mom leaned over and whispered to me ninja-quiet, "Do you want me to tell him you're not here?"

I let out a nervous laugh, but even that sounded too shrill, and I had to remind myself to breathe. "No. I can do this," I assured her, totally sounding calmer than I felt inside.

Bracing myself, I went to the door. My lungs ached, and I was definitely light-headed, but there was no going back now. No matter what happened, I needed this. I tried to think of one of my dad's inspirational quotes, but all I could come up with was something about "opportunity knocking," which was totally inappropriate because it wasn't opportunity at all—it was Austin, and he was standing on my porch ringing the doorbell.

When I opened it, my mouth went completely dry. Tyler had been right about Austin; he did look older.

His eyes were the same green as always, just shades lighter than his brother's; but beyond that he was completely different from what he had been that night after my championship game, when I'd kissed him by the softball diamond, promising to meet up later at the Pizza Palace.

His hair, which had always been sun bleached and chlorine damaged from spending so much time in the water, was darker now, and his face was leaner than I remembered. Not sharp, but more defined, as if age had chiseled in the angles.

A part of me had hoped his new life with Cat would have turned him fat and soft and, yes, maybe too hideous even to look upon, like some fairy-tale troll. But he was none of those things. He was older and more matured, but he was also still Austin.

"Oh my god. It's really you," he breathed, drinking me in. "I thought . . . we all thought you were gone for good."

He touched my face, and I flinched. "Can we . . . ?" He shifted nervously, and I was relieved he was at least sort of uncomfortable facing me in person. He looked past me to where my mom was standing at my back like some sort of Mafia enforcer, and his voice rose. "Can we talk someplace private?"

Silently I was grateful to my mom for giving me that— the whole solidarity thing—but I still needed to do this on my own, so I closed the door on her, giving Austin and me some space.

I stepped away from the door and led him down the steps so she couldn't eavesdrop either, because I wouldn't put it past her, not if she was anything like my old mom. That mom would have no qualms about putting her ear to the door so she could listen to what we were saying.

We had to cross the street to reach his car, which meant walking over the top of the chalk birdcage, and I tried not to stare, but my eyes kept straying downward, taking in the bird and its feathers, and marveling over every tiny detail Tyler had put into it. Self-consciously, I wondered if Austin knew that his brother had drawn the birdcage or that it was meant for me. I seriously hoped not.

We stood there, each studying the other for what was probably only a few seconds but for what felt like hours. Austin rubbed the thick shadow of whiskers along his jaw that used to be the finest of stubble, and I crossed my arms, mostly to hide the fact that my hands wouldn't stop shaking. I kept looking away to avoid his eyes and his face, pretty much all of him, because looking at him gave me that itchy déjà vu sensation all over again.

"Cat misses you," Austin said at last, clearing his throat loudly.

And with that, any nerves or worry that *I* might not say or do the right thing evaporated. Maybe it was hearing his voice again, because at least *that* hadn't changed all that much, or maybe it was the fact that he'd said something so incredibly insensitive to start off our very first conversation, but suddenly I couldn't see him as anything but plain old Austin anymore. Older, yes, but still just a stupid boy who said stupid things when he opened his mouth. "*Cat?* Really? You drove all this way to talk about Cat?"

Had I forgotten that about him, the way he sometimes

bulldozed right over my feelings, not because he didn't care, but because he was so totally oblivious?

"I mean, no. Of course I didn't." He shifted some more, almost like he was doing some sort of dance, and I winced because it was so . . . strangely pathetic. God, he couldn't even talk to me; he could barely look me in the eye at all. "It's just that she wanted to come, too . . . to see you, but we . . . I mean, *I* . . . I thought it was a bad idea. I thought I should see you first."

Inside, in a place where Austin couldn't see, where he'd never know what this meeting was doing to me, my heart felt like it was shattering into a million little fragments. It wasn't like I didn't know this already, that we were really-truly-*completely* over, Austin and me, but to see him now and hear him stammering for something to say to me . . . I guess it finally hit home.

But that didn't change the fact that I was pissed at him for giving up on me in the first place, or for choosing to go on with his life with Cat, of all people! I didn't realize I was crying until I heard myself yelling at him. "Why couldn't you wait, goddammit? Why did you"—I choked on a sob—"have to give up on me?" And then, before I knew what I was doing, I hit him, but it wasn't a real hit, and we both knew it. My fist struck him square in the chest while I yelled again, tears streaking down both sides of my face. "Why'd you have to do all the things we were supposed to do with *her*?"

I felt his arms go around me, and even *that* wasn't the same anymore. I should've loved that he was finally touching me, hugging me. Except he wasn't hugging me, not really. He was comforting me, and that isn't the same thing at all. I felt like a little kid who'd skinned her knee, and Austin was just trying to make it all better.

Thing was, I didn't want to be comforted. Not by him. I writhed inside the circle of his arms, but instead of realizing I meant it, that I wanted him to let me go for real, his grip tightened. Understandable, I guess, since in the old days I would've wanted him to keep hold of me. To wait out my stubbornness.

But not now.

I shoved harder. "Get. Off," I demanded, making sure he understood I meant it this time.

When he released me, my faced felt flushed, but not in an attractive, you-just-made-me-blush kind of way. I knew it was blotchy and gross, but I didn't care. I wiped my nose on the back of my hand.

Just then Tyler's car pulled to a stop behind Austin's. Austin barely seemed to notice his younger brother, but Tyler was all I noticed now. I hadn't realized how close I'd been standing to Austin until Tyler got out of his car and his dark eyes moved from me to Austin and back to me again.

I swallowed hard as I took a step back, wishing more than anything I'd never come out here in the first place.

But Tyler didn't skip a beat. He nodded at me like we were old buddies rather than the kind of people you stay up half the night drawing chalk masterpieces for as he jerked his backpack from his backseat.

When he approached Austin on the sidewalk, he didn't step around him like a normal person would have. Instead, he bumped into him with his shoulder, shoving his older brother out of his way.

"What's your problem?" was all Austin said as Tyler passed him, which wasn't much of a greeting from one brother to another, but I guess neither was the shoulder-bump thing.

After Tyler had slammed the front door behind him, leaving us all alone again, Austin turned his attention back to me and beneath his breath muttered, "Jesus, Kyra, this is really hard for me."

"Hard for *you*?" I managed when I finally stopped glancing up to their house to see if Tyler was in there, watching us.

Austin exhaled, running his hand through his hair. I knew the gesture. He thought I was overreacting. "Yeah. I thought my girlfriend was dead, and now here you are. I'm confused, but I want us to be . . . friends."

I didn't know what to say. Nothing, I guess. We weren't friends, not anymore. We hadn't been for a really, *really* long time.

Shrugging and shaking my head, because what else could I do, I turned on my heel and left him standing there.

CHAPTER SEVEN
Day Four

I SAT IN DR. DUNN'S EMPTY WAITING ROOM, MY tongue running over the chipped tooth I was here to have fixed while I continued to rehash my confrontation with Austin yesterday. I'd been replaying it in my head over and over all night, but worse was the fact that I also couldn't stop thinking about Tyler, and the look on his face when he'd come home from school to find the two of us standing there together.

None of it should matter to me, mostly because it really *didn't* matter. I was nothing to Austin, and now that I'd seen him again, it was clear Austin wasn't anything to me either. We were *so* over.

Besides, on top of everything else, Tyler was still just Austin's little brother. Too young to be anything more than a friend.

So why had my already-fractured heart shattered a little more when I'd stepped outside this morning to leave for the dentist only to discover there was no new chalk drawing for me, only the birdcage from the day before—a little more smudged and worn?

Because if I stopped lying to myself for even a second, then maybe there was a part of me where Tyler mattered more than he should.

I watched as my mom's son ate a corner from a page of the *Highlights* magazine he'd been maniacally flipping through, pretending he knew how to read. I thought about asking my mom if there was something lacking in his diet that made him crave paper pulp as he chewed off a second piece, but I'd already offended her and The Husband that morning when I'd implied that, perhaps, he needed more practice with a spoon as more of the oatmeal had fallen off it than made it to his mouth.

To be fair, my exact words were something along the lines of a suggestion that they put him into physical therapy.

Considering that The Husband had given my mom a terse look, I decided it probably wasn't worth the effort to bring up her son's nutritional deficiencies too.

As if reading my mind, the kid looked up and grinned at me, his teeth all pulped out with mushy bits of newsprint. *Disgusting.*

"Kyra." A woman in faded pink scrubs read my name

from the file in her hands, as if the waiting room was teeming with patients all clamoring to get in to see the dentist on this busy Wednesday morning. I made a point of glancing at all the empty seats. Nope, still just me.

I got up and followed her. Behind me, I heard the door from the parking lot open and a voice I recognized said, "Sorry I'm late. I—uh—I overslept."

I turned to see my dad standing in the doorway. He had the same unshowered look he'd had the first day I saw him, like he'd just rolled out of bed.

"I told you, you didn't have to come. It's just a dentist appointment. I can handle this." My mom's voice was pinched and high-pitched, the same way it had been when she'd reminded me that "my brother" had a name. I just kept walking and ignored all of them.

I couldn't remember Dr. Dunn not being my dentist, but now, like everyone else—well, everyone but me, it seemed—he looked older. Fatter, too, like my dad, but cleaner, something I only just now realized that I appreciated in a dentist.

I watched him out of the corner of my eye as he washed his hands. He was whistling off-key to the music that played overhead. I remembered that about him, the way he whistled and sang beneath his breath like no one could hear him.

"So your mom says you chipped your tooth." He straddled the small swivel stool next to the examination chair I was reclined on, and he ducked in close. He nodded once, my signal to open wide. I did, and he asked, "What happened?"

His fingers were already in my mouth, probing over my molars, so I tried to talk around them. "A hee o' hang-ee" were the sounds that came out of me, nothing like "A piece of candy" should have sounded. I might as well have been a two-year-old with a mouthful of mashed-up magazine.

"Candy, huh? That'll do it," he answered cheerfully, his latex glove finding the broken spot on my tooth. His glasses had special magnified lenses on them that made him look like he was wearing miniature binoculars. He sat back and told the lady in the pink scrubs, "Let's get a quick set of X-rays to make sure everything's A-OK." He turned to me and winked with one of his giant eyes. "Then we'll get you all fixed up. Sound good?"

I shrugged. *Okay.*

She took the X-rays, and he came back in to check them, holding them up to the wall-mounted white box. I watched him disinterestedly as he scrutinized them and then asked his assistant to get my old X-rays, the ones I'd had done just last week. Or, rather, the last week I remembered.

He looked at those, too, and now I was more interested in what he was doing because *he* was more interested. I could tell because it wasn't a casual glance; it was a long, drawn-out perusal, the kind that you give to something curious or strange, something requiring a second or third look. He kept his back to me, so I couldn't see his face, but I imagined him squinting behind those giant-eyed lenses. Squinting and biting his lip and concentrating.

Then he left the room, both sets of X-rays in hand.

I waited a long time in the reclining chair before he finally came back.

"What was it?" I asked.

He dismissed my concern with a wave. A flourish, really. "Nothing," he answered, glazing over my question and moving on with the adept skill of someone used to dodging the prying questions of children. "Good news. Tooth is chipped but not cracked, so we don't need to do a filling or a crown. I can smooth the edge down so it doesn't bother your tongue."

He was lying, of course. All that *concentrating* over a chip that needed polishing? But I could tell he wasn't planning to give me any more than that, so I opened my mouth wide when he told me to and let him buff the chip into submission.

And on my way out, like I was still seven, he let me choose a prize from the treasure box the receptionist kept hidden behind the counter. It was overflowing with plastic rings and beads and spinning tops and toy soldiers with flimsy parachutes stuck to their backs.

I reached for a paddle with a rubber ball attached to a string, and when I did, I saw the way "my brother's" eyes lit up with desperate longing. He wanted my third-rate paddle-ball; I *knew* he wanted it.

I pretended not to notice, but inside I was grinning a pretty self-satisfied grin at my not-too-dignified jab at the toddler as I tucked it into my pocket, thinking I'd rather throw the stupid piece of junk in the trash than give it to him. And then I turned to my mom, who was looking at me like she knew exactly what had just transpired, and I told her, "I'm riding with Dad."

"So what was all that about? With Dr. Dunn? I know he saw something on my X-rays." I had to say it fast so I could get the words out in one breath, doing my best not to breathe inside my dad's pigpen of a van. The smell of stale fast food alone was enough to make me gag, but, like yesterday, it was the other smell, the faint odor of something . . . mildewy . . . or musty—I didn't know exactly what it was, but it was disgusting.

"Nothing, really." But my dad didn't gloss over things as well as Dr. Dunn had, and his "nothing" sounded more like an admission of guilt.

I kicked a crumpled paper bag at my feet and wondered just how often he got his meals at greasy drive-throughs. From the state of his van, I'd guess every one. "You can tell me. Actually," I said, sitting up taller, "I think you *have* to tell me. I'm an adult now. I have a right to know." It was so strange to say that out loud, especially since I didn't feel any older.

My dad reached up and rubbed his jaw, his fingers distorting the skin of his face. "Really, I can't tell you. Your mom—"

"She doesn't have to know you told me. What's the point in keeping secrets? It's just the friggin' dentist. How bad could it be? I have gum disease? I need a root canal? Come on."

My dad veered suddenly to the right, the van lurching along as he maneuvered us toward the side of the road. My stomach dropped. It reminded me too much of the night he pulled his car over, when I'd insisted I was getting out to walk.

"What are you doing?" My voice sounded hollow, weak.

He pulled out his phone. A flip phone that had been outdated even five years ago, and he dialed while I waited. "I'm taking her to my place," he said into the low-tech receiver. He flashed a knowing grin at me. "Yeah, she wants to meet Nancy."

The first thing Nancy did was lick me. It was the grossest greeting I'd ever gotten, but I forgave her right away because, after licking me, her tail was wagging so hard she could hardly stand still. It was as if someone had wound up her butt, and she no longer had control over her own actions.

Nancy was a mutt. And not just any mutt, but the muttiest-looking mutt I'd ever laid eyes on. She had to be at least part sheepdog, and maybe part wolf, but there was definitely part something else in there too. Something mangy. She was bushy to the point that she was in danger of being considered some kind of mongrel prehistoric ram or a mutant woolly mammoth rather than just a regular old dog.

But when she stared at me with her enormous, liquid-brown eyes, I could see why my dad had fallen in love with her in the first place. And also why he put up with her unholy stink. It was exactly that smell that I'd noticed in his van: the Nancy smell.

"So, what'd'ya think of my fancy Nancy?"

She had her chin perched on my knee and was staring at me all longingly and doe-eyed, as if she had no intention of letting me get away. Ever. "Not that fancy, I gotta say." I reached out and ruffled the top of her head, her ears flopping in two different directions when I did. "But she's not so bad."

I glanced around uneasily, less comfortable with my next question. "Dad, what are you doing here? What *is* this place?"

My dad followed my gaze. "I know it's probably not what you expected, but it's my home. This is where I live now. Ever since . . . well, since . . ." He lowered his head, rubbing his whiskery chin again. He went to the small kitchen, not really a separate space in the cramped trailer, and he turned on one of the gas burners. He kept his back to me as he filled a kettle. "It's not so bad," he finally finished, using the same words I'd used about his dog before facing me once more.

I winced. *Not so bad.* I didn't really agree. It was worse.

There were stacks of newspapers and magazines and bills and notebooks on every surface that wasn't covered with dirty dishes or laundry or bags filled with who knew what. There wasn't a TV that I could see, but there was a giant telescope standing in the center of what I assumed was supposed to be the living room but was really more of a glorified walkway, complete with a two-seater couch that was also littered with clothes and newspapers. I didn't see the booze bottles or empty beer cans, but that didn't mean they weren't here somewhere.

My dad, who had once been the epitome of neat-freakness, brushed aside a place for my mug at his wobbly kitchen table, where I was sitting with Nancy's head in my lap. "Really? 'Cause it looks that bad to me. I'm not staying here, just so you know."

He shrugged again. "You can if you want, but I won't make you. Besides, I'm not sure your mom would let you anyway."

I bristled at his words, and almost decided to stay just because he'd said that. I wondered if that was *why* he'd said it, because he knew how much I hated to be told what I could, and couldn't, do. "She doesn't have any say in the matter. I'm an adult, remember?"

At the stove, my dad cleared his throat nervously, and the gesture made me hyperaware that he, that all of them—my mom, my dad, and the dentist—were keeping something from me.

"What? Why are you acting so weird? I mean, besides rooming with a dog and looking all"—I waved my hand at him, indicating his disheveled appearance—"hobo chic?"

He pulled the whistling kettle off the burner and filled my mug, handing me a tea bag. I'd never really liked tea, never really had it before, so it seemed strange that my dad was offering it to me. I unpeeled the worn paper wrapper and plopped the tea bag into the steaming water. Before I could ask if he had any sugar, he was handing me a bowl of clumpy-looking sugar crystals.

Everything in this place was sketchy, right down to the sugar.

He cleared his own spot at the table, shoving a stack of papers and news clippings out of his way so he could set his own tea down in front of him. "The reason I'm acting weird*er* than usual . . ." His emphasis on the *er* almost made me smile, like even he realized he wasn't exactly the dad I'd known. He raised an eyebrow at me as he scooped several spoonfuls of the sugar into his mug and concentrated on stirring. "Is something the dentist—Dr. Dunn—noticed on your X-rays."

I raised my eyebrows back at him. *Got that,* I relayed with my impatient look.

"So he showed us the ones he took the week before you disappeared, when you'd been in to see him for your checkup, and he compared them to the ones he took today." He spoke slowly, deliberately. It was painful the way he drew out each syllable and emphasized words like *before you disappeared* and *compared* and *today,* as if there was some significance to them that I should understand. I didn't, and I just wanted him to get to the point already.

And then he did. "They're the same. Five years later, they're exactly the same."

I didn't understand. He was looking at me as if this was a big deal, something monumental, but I didn't know why. *"O-kaaaay . . ."*

"Five years," he repeated, still doing that drawing-out thing that was driving me crazy. "Five years is a long time, Kyr. Five years and not a thing, not one single thing, has changed on your X-rays."

I lifted my shoulders. What was I supposed to say to that?

"It's not possible," he finally said, making his big, bombshell statement.

I still didn't get it. "What do you mean, 'not possible'? Of course it's possible. You just said that's what he saw."

He shook his head. "No, I mean, it's not *possible*." He said it differently now, the word *possible*, like he was saying something magical. "He explained it to your mom and me in the waiting room. In five years, things change, especially in a teenager. Teeth erode from wear, nerves shift, cavities change—you had a cavity, did you know that? You had a little bit of decay between two of your teeth that your mom and him had decided to wait and watch, to see if the next time you came in it had changed, grown, and would need to be filled. Well, guess what? Five years later, and it's exactly the same as it was. *Exactly.* Not bigger, not smaller. Just . . . the same."

I stopped scratching Nancy's scruffy woolen head, and she yawned against my knees but stayed where she was.

"So . . . I'm just different than most people. . . ." I wasn't sure if I was trying to convince him or me, or if I was asking a question or making a statement.

My dad just shook his head and repeated, "Not possible."

"But it is. . . ."

He scowled at me like *I* was the one who wasn't making sense. And then he glanced toward the telescope, and I swore I finally understood what he was getting at.

I shot up from the table. Tea spilled, and Nancy yelped as her chin banged on the wooden chair I'd been sitting in. "Uh-uh. No way. *That's* what's not possible. Dad, please, stop it. You're scaring me. You don't really believe . . ." I couldn't say it; it was so hard because it meant I was admitting just how crazy he was. "There are no such things as aliens."

"Kyra . . ." He sounded so reasonable when he said my name that I almost didn't notice the crazy mountain-man beard or the stains on his flannel shirt—the same shirt he'd been wearing when he'd come to see me that first day. "You don't know what I do. You haven't been living with this, gathering information for the past five years, trying to find out what happened to you. If you'd just stop to think about it, it makes perfect sense, really. And it explains what the dentist told us today, if you'll only listen to me. Please, just . . . just try to have an open mind." He stood now, too, and my chest constricted as his hand reached toward mine. His fingers, though . . . his touch when his fingers closed over mine was so comfortingly familiar that my legs nearly buckled. "For me," he whispered as his eyes locked on mine.

It was that—those two words—that were my undoing. He was still in there, my dad. My number one fan. Begging to be heard. For me to take him seriously.

I didn't know if I could, but I owed it to him—didn't I?—to at least try.

"So you're trying to say that I'm . . . I'm still sixteen?" Just saying the words sounded beyond insane, and I hated that I felt like I was indulging his delusions. "That I've been . . . what . . . stuck in some alien spacecraft for the past five years . . . and they just . . . put me back here? Why, Dad? Why would they do that? Why would they keep me all that time and then just . . . send me home?"

Something about my questions, or maybe about the fact that I wasn't running the other way, set my dad in motion then. Like *snap!* and he was pulling me toward the back of the trailer. Nancy followed us, not nearly as leery as I was about my dad's sanity. I wished I could be as trusting as her, maybe then my heart wouldn't be trying to beat its way out of my chest at that very moment. Maybe my eyes wouldn't be stinging with frustration and fear that my old man had cracked.

When he flipped the switch inside the only bedroom, the one I'd assumed he slept in, I realized I'd assumed entirely wrong. There was no *sleeping* going on in that room.

It was full-on crazy-town in there. Like the *X-Files* had thrown up in there.

"Look, I don't know why they do the things they do," he was saying, but all I could think was *What the holy hell is going on here?* Was my dad part of some alien conspiracy cult? Because I was looking at four walls that were plastered in what could only be described as star charts and maps, and photos of blips in the night sky that I assumed were supposed to be alien spacecrafts, and drawings of beings with skinny bodies and oversize heads and eyes, and more photos and drawings; and across them were pieces of string connecting one thing to another in a way that seemed to make no real sense at all. And in one far corner, just above a desk that was as cluttered as the walls, with books and more maps and a computer that had newspaper clippings taped to it, was a series of missing-person fliers and milk carton cutouts.

There was one, in the very center of them all, that I recognized all too well: my own.

They'd used my sophomore class picture, the one where I was wearing Cat's silver sweater and was quasi-hung over because Cat had decided that we should try shots of tequila the night before, when her parents had gone to the symphony. After watching her throw back three of them, I'd finally let her convince me to try one, and I'd nearly thrown it up before finally gagging it down.

Yet somehow she'd managed to talk me into four more. Cat had always been like that—persuasive.

None of that showed in the black-and-white image that stared back at me now. "You have *got* to be kidding me," I finally managed.

My dad cleared his throat, and I was glad he had the grace at least to be a little uncomfortable about bringing me to his cracked-out shrine to martians. "Please, try to have an open mind about this."

I shrugged a "Fine, go ahead" shrug. But inside I was thinking, *He'd better make his point soon, because he is losing me. Fast.*

No one could ever accuse my dad of doing anything half-assed, and that included this alien conspiracy thing. He'd definitely done his homework on the matter. He'd taken his ideas—his *theories*—and run with them. And apparently he wasn't alone. I'd sat in stunned silence while he'd pulled up website after website, showing me, basically trying to *prove to me*, that there were others out there in *our* situation. That was how he kept putting it, like calling it "our situation" somehow recruited me to his way of thinking.

There were blogs and support groups, and a lot of them posted under pseudonyms and code names.

My dad's was Supernova16.

He told me about people who had flashbacks and some, like me, who were missing chunks of time . . . and still others who'd seen the flashes of light themselves.

He quizzed me then, asking me questions interrogation style. Things like "Have you had any weird dreams or flashbacks since you've been back?" and "What do you think of when I say the word *spaceship*?" or my personal favorite "When the dentist was polishing your teeth, did you have any 'unusual' reactions to his drill?"

"No," I insisted to his last question, but I knew by the determined set of his jaw and the way his eyes narrowed that he wasn't buying it. Like he thought I might be holding something back. And I felt sick, because the more he dug in, the more I realized just how warped his thinking really was.

He held up a picture of some kind of creature with a freakishly large head and huge, pupil-less eyes and a short, squat body. He held up one after another, like they were flash cards, flipping through them almost too fast for me to process. Some looked kind of like insects, with long grass-hopperish arms, and others were gray skinned and sickly, with giant-brained heads. "Do any of these make you uncomfortable?"

I shook my head because *uncomfortable* definitely wasn't the word that came to mind. All they really made me was sad about what the heck my dad had been going through all these years that had led him to *this*.

I let him keep going because I'd promised him I would, and then he asked me the weirdest question of all. "Did you see them, Kyr? Did you see any fireflies that night?"

That one made me falter. "Fireflies?" I asked, wondering where he was going with this line of questioning. Aside from TV or movies, I wasn't sure I'd ever actually seen a firefly in real life at all. I mean, I knew they were bugs and that they glowed, like little insects with lanterns in their butts. But that was as far as my knowledge went. "No. Why would I? What do fireflies have to do with anything? Why are you even asking me that? All I saw was . . . *that light* . . . and then you were screaming, and then . . ."

Shit . . . nothing else. There was *nothing* after that.

A tear trickled down my cheek, only this time it wasn't

like when I'd been crying with Austin, and my dad didn't try to force his arms around me. Maybe he should have, but he didn't. He just stared at me.

We were at the exact same standstill we had been when we'd started. He believed and I didn't, and I was sad because of who he'd become, and sad because I almost wished I *could* confirm one of his whacked-out ideas—something—to make it seem a little less . . .

Sad.

I stood there, holding my breath, when his eyes found mine. After a long, *long* moment, he blinked hard, and a pained expression crossed his face, and I was sure I saw him there—my old dad, buried behind the beard and sad, puppy dog eyes. "You're right," he finally admitted with a shaky breath, and I felt my shoulders and breath loosening, because he *was* still there. There was still hope for him. For us.

And then he spoke again, and he ruined everything. "I knew it was too much," he said. "I knew I should've waited."

I felt my own heartbeat pulse in my ears, right before my heart stopped.

"Dad, no . . ." My voice was barely a whisper, but he heard me all the same. He hadn't given up on it at all. And it was then I knew the truth; he wasn't in there anymore, in that husk of a body, not *my* dad. This was some other dad. Some replacement dad.

I thought I'd stopped crying, but I tasted the tears when I opened my mouth to say, "Just take me home."

★ ★ ★

The minute I walked through the front door, my mom started questioning me, but she was the absolute last person I wanted to confide in. She was half the problem. If she hadn't pushed my dad away in the first place, there was no way he would've ended up in that crap-ass trailer overflowing with star charts and hidden booze bottles. But instead of facing her like a grown-up, I opted for the more mature choice of running to my fake bedroom and locking myself inside. And by locking I mean pushing my nightstand in front of the door.

She at least had the decency not to shove her way inside, which she totally could have since my nightstand weighed like ten pounds.

Instead, she stood out in the hallway and spoke to me through the door, which is how it felt like she'd been talking to me ever since I'd been back—through a barrier.

Listening to her attempts to coax me out was almost worse than listening to my dad tell me about his online forums and how everyone on there agreed with him, that I was certainly-surely-*most-definitely* a victim of alien abduction. I pinched my eyes in an effort to suppress the headache my dad had given me with all his crazy talk and did my best to stop thinking about my father and what he'd become. I wondered if he'd ever, *ever* come back to me the way I'd come back to him.

I stayed quiet until, eventually, my mom gave up and went away.

When my new phone buzzed in my pocket, I regretted

checking it almost the moment I did.

Can we please talk? the text from my dad read.

I'd never, in my entire life, ever avoided my dad before. I mean, yeah, maybe once or twice, when I didn't want to go to practice or that one time when I got detention for texting in class. Or the times when I didn't want to talk about which college I should go to.

But never like this. Never when I was afraid of hurting his feelings because I was sure he'd lost his freaking mind.

Suddenly I had a glimpse into what my mom must've gone through, and I hated it. I hated her for giving up on him, and hated myself for being on the brink of doing the same thing.

There was a first time for everything, I thought, ignoring his message. I knew I couldn't put him off forever, but I wasn't yet ready for another round of Kyra Meets E.T.

The worst part was, there were parts of his story that made sense. Maybe that would explain why I still had a bruise on my shin, or the reason I'd been wearing the same clothes when I woke up behind the Gas 'n' Sip, or how my phone was still charged.

Or maybe I was starting to sound as whacked out as he did.

Why on earth would aliens have a charger for a Motorola Razr?

Every explanation left me more confused. More lost.

And more alone.

When the text from Tyler came in, I almost didn't notice it because I'd been ignoring messages from my dad for hours.

But when I finally saw who it was, I let myself forget all about unchanged dental records and crazy dads and prying moms, and everything else that had turned my day to total crap.

After what had happened in front of his house yesterday, I'd worried he might not want to be my friend anymore. And Tyler was pretty much the only friend I had. I couldn't bear the idea of losing him before we even got a chance to really know each other.

I left you something. To make up for this morning, his text said.

This morning? I wondered. *What about this morning?*

But I remembered the last time he'd texted about leaving me something, and I was already leaping from my bed to find out what it was.

When I opened my window, I leaned all the way out, thinking that maybe he'd meant another chalk drawing on the road. But even as dusk fell I could see the road was the same as before.

And then I saw the small gift bag beneath my window.

Without going outside, I lowered myself far enough that my fingers brushed the top of it and snagged it before pulling myself back inside. When I closed the window, I sank to the floor and peeked into the bag.

It wasn't anything elaborate, the bag. There was no tissue paper or sparkly shreds or anything, just a single piece of paper, rolled up and secured by an ordinary rubber band.

Slipping the rubber band free, I uncurled the sheet of paper and gasped.

I leaned in closer, to get a better look as a wide smile slowly drew my lips apart. It was incredible.

I'd been wrong when I'd assumed it wasn't another chalk drawing, because it was. Only this one wasn't drawn on the road. This one was so much more personal, and meant solely for me.

It *was* me.

Me, the way I'd looked the day I'd come home, when I'd first stumbled across the street and fallen into Tyler's arms, still wearing my uniform, with the ribbons tangled through my hair.

He'd captured my image perfectly, with precision and depth and life. Somehow he'd made my eyes, which I'd always thought were too big, seem beautiful in a haunted kind of way; and I no longer questioned whether they fit my face. He managed to re-create the arch of my brows and the shape of my jaw and each and every freckle splattered across my nose.

Immediately, I texted him back: *I love it. Thank you.* Because what more could I possibly say?

CHAPTER EIGHT
Day Five

THIS WAS MY MOM'S FIRST DAY BACK AT WORK since I'd been home—probably the longest she'd been off work at one time since she'd squeezed out her new kid, so it hadn't been hard to convince her I'd be fine and that I could fend for myself for a whole eight hours.

It was Thursday, according to my obsession with the calendar, which meant Tyler, the only other person who might've kept me company, was at school too. I was completely on my own for the day.

By 8:01 I was pacing the house.

By 8:16 I'd taken a complete inventory of the refrigerator,

the kitchen cabinets, and the pantry, and noted the sad lack of nonnutritional, preservative-laden snack foods.

By 8:43 I was bored out of my frickin' skull.

I finally settled down on the couch and started flipping through the channels, most of which were morning talk shows aimed at the stay-at-home-mom crowd. I paused when one of those talk shows was interrupted by a local news segment. My throat felt tight and scratchy as I stared at the familiar face on the screen.

I knew him. It was the lab guy who'd taken my blood at the hospital the night I'd come home. And according to the news report I was watching, he was dead.

I tried to read the ticker that ran continuously across the bottom of the screen, but I could only catch bits and pieces of it:

. . . A phlebotomist from Skagit General Hospital . . . found dead in his apartment last night by his girlfriend . . . hemorrhaging from his mouth and eyes . . . autopsy will be performed to determine exact cause of death . . .

I switched to several other channels to see if there were any other details, but when I couldn't find anything, I gave up and decided to see if I could find anything online. Trouble was, the computer was password protected, and I would rather have been forced to wear my mom's high waters every day until the end of time than to break down and ask her, even via text, what her password was.

I tried a few semi-obvious combinations: *Password, Kyra,*

Logan (because it seemed logical), *Supernova* (which was far less likely), and my birthday. I would've tried "my brother's" birthday, but I had no idea what that was.

After a while I got bored with that, too, and gave up.

Eventually I took a shower and started sorting through the clothes my mom had picked out for me.

I had to admit, and this was coming from someone with zero idea of what was in style anymore, I didn't hate what she'd selected. I'm guessing she'd steered away from anything supertrendy, which was probably good since I doubted she had any better notion than I did what would rock the community college scene these days. But at least she'd remembered my size and that I liked vintage-style tees and jeans that felt broken in already.

I spent forty-three minutes unpacking and cutting off tags from T-shirts, underwear, pajamas, socks, tank tops, and jeans—everything a girl newly returned from a five-year hiatus could possibly need. I slipped into a pair of jeans and a worn-looking T-shirt with the Count from Sesame Street on the front and couldn't help smiling just a little that my mom remembered, too, how much I'd loved the number-obsessed vampire when I was a kid.

When the doorbell rang, I stopped what I was doing and checked the digital alarm clock against my phone to make sure the two were still in sync. 10:06.

I slipped my phone into my pocket and went to see who it was.

The man standing on the front step looked like any other man who wore stiffly starched suits and stiff, plain black ties: *Stiff.* I couldn't tell if he was a salesman or one of those church guys who goes around trying to convert people, but he definitely wasn't a deliveryman, not in that getup.

I would've discouraged him right off with an immediate "My parents aren't here," but the first rule drilled into every latchkey kid is: never tell a stranger you're home alone. So I waited to see what he wanted.

Shockingly, it wasn't my parents he was looking for.

"Kyra Agnew?" His voice came out just as stiff as his suit. It was sort of daunting, the way he said my name— and the fact that he *knew* my name—with authority, like a principal or a coach, and I found myself standing straighter because of it.

"Uh . . . I . . . yeah . . . ," I stammered, because sometimes when I was intimidated, I was smooth like that. My pulse sped up the tiniest bit.

He reached into his jacket and pulled out some sort of leather wallet thingie. It was black, too, like his suit, and when he flipped it open, there was a slick-looking badge inside. I focused on the golden beetle in the center of it while he said his name in that same no-nonsense manner that made me want to salute him. "Agent Truman. National Security Agency. May I come in?"

He tucked his wallet back inside his jacket and took a step forward. My mind reeled, but before his foot even hit the ground I was yanking the door closed. I didn't slam it on him, but I closed it enough so that I was wedged between the opening. It was the same move The Husband had pulled on me when I'd tried to barge in on him that first day. There was no way I was letting this guy into my house.

First of all, neither of my parents was here, something I obviously couldn't tell him without violating latchkey kid rule number one. Second, I had no way of knowing if that shiny badge was even real. I had a badge once too. I got it from my Cracker Jack box. So, yeah, no thanks on letting the potential serial killer inside.

"We can talk out here."

He raised his brows and considered me, a small smile tugging at the corners of his lips. "Whatever you prefer," he said in his authoritative voice.

I lifted my chin a notch. "What's this about? You said National Security Agency? What's that?"

"Miss Agnew, I have some questions for you," he answered, not really answering my question about his "agency." He pulled out a notepad and flipped open the cover, perusing whatever was written in there and then addressing me again. "We heard about your disappearance. What was that, five years ago?"

My pulse picked up, and the sound of blood rushing filled my head. I swallowed. "That's right."

"According to the police report, you were on your way home from a baseball game." He glanced up with just his steely eyes, the leathery skin around them crinkling as he trained his gaze on me.

"Softball," I corrected, reaching up to scratch my elbow.

"Softball," he amended, scribbling the note in his book.

"And you were in the car with your"—he consulted his notes—"father, on Chuckanut Drive, when you got out of the car."

This wasn't a question, but I nodded anyway, scratching harder.

"What happened next?" This time he wasn't looking at the notepad; his gaze was directed solely at me, and I had the feeling my answer was important.

I stopped scratching, my mouth suddenly too dry to answer. I lifted my shoulders, my eyes widening slightly and my mouth turning down in a frown.

He waited for something more, and then when it was obvious that was all the answer he was getting from me, he pried. "What does that mean, precisely? Are you saying you don't know what happened?"

I shrug-nodded and then tried my voice, because I thought I should be a little more decisive than a bobblehead doll. "I mean, I guess so."

"Nothing"—his eyes narrowed as he prompted me— "*unusual* or *out of place*?"

I thought of the light. The flash. And the importance my dad placed on in. I thought of my dad and the way he'd become obsessed with where I'd been, and my stomach clenched.

I didn't want to answer these questions.

"No, nothing. I'm sure you already know I had a fight with my dad, and I got out to walk. After that . . . I don't remember anything."

The man—this Agent Truman, he'd said his name was—sighed. His expression relaxed. The lines in his face that a moment ago made him look hard and a little threatening now reminded me of the way my grandpa had looked right before he'd died. Weary. I could almost imagine this man smiling. *Almost.* "Look. I get it. This is a tough subject. You've been through something difficult. You're confused. We're just trying to help. We want the same answers you do. We want to help sort this whole mess out." He did smile then. It wasn't exactly endearing or anything, but it was nice enough. "Are you sure I can't come inside?"

I bit the inside of my cheek. I was confused enough about who he was and why he was here without him playing both bad cop *and* good cop. "I don't think it's a good idea. . . ."

His hand was now on the door, gripping the wood as if I'd already given him permission. "We can talk about your father's version of events. See what he thinks happened to you."

My dad? Why was he talking about what my dad thought happened that night?

Or was he talking about that other thing, the one Tyler had mentioned where some of the people in town thought my dad might have had something to do with my disappearance in the first place?

He might as well have smacked me in the face with that enormous hand of his, the one that was still on my door, and I suddenly felt cornered, trapped. He was bigger than I was. And if his badge *was* real, then he actually had some authority and maybe could insist on coming inside. Maybe I had no right at all to keep him out.

Right now, though, none of that mattered. I lodged my foot against the bottom of the door to keep it from budging. "My father? He doesn't have anything to do with this." I didn't wait for his rebuttal, because I didn't care what he had to say. I leaned my shoulder and all of my weight against the door, surprised that Agent Truman was pushing from the other side in an effort to stop me. "I have to go," I insisted. "I don't have time to talk to you." I shoved harder to emphasize my point.

Through the opening, we faced each other, and Agent Truman didn't try to convince me again. After a moment, the longest split second of my life, he let the door close, and I locked it behind me.

Then I bolted it and sagged to the floor, my heart pounding in my chest.

I never saw Agent Truman leave, probably because I'd never seen his car in the first place, but after an hour or so of patrolling the windows—and after the third time I'd read *Goodnight Moon*—I was sure he was gone. I was also sick to death of being cooped up in the house and watching the clock. Check that, *clocks*.

Scrounging through the change jar my mom still kept in the kitchen, I took a pocketful of quarters, deciding to walk the mile to the Gas 'n' Sip. I almost changed my mind when I came outside and found Agent Truman's business card on my front porch, but instead, I glanced in every possible direction, and then I tore it into tiny bits and tossed it in the trash bin on my way out. There was no way I was talking to anyone from the National Security Agency about my dad.

No one could ever convince me he had anything do with my disappearance, no matter how unhinged he might be.

The Gas 'n' Sip had always been my favorite junk food dealer. When we were finally allowed to walk there on our own, Austin and I used to pool our allowance money and trek there during the summer for ice cream bars and Mountain Dews and packages of powdered doughnuts. When Austin got his license and started driving us to school, we'd stop there in the mornings for some of the strongest-brewed coffee in town. And sometimes for powdered doughnuts too.

I'd spent almost as much time at the Gas 'n' Sip as I had on the softball fields.

Being here now, though, I felt like a total loser. A loser with a pocketful of change.

I strolled the aisles in record time, picking up some Red Vines, a Dr Pepper, and obviously doughnuts, before dropping my mountain of change on the counter. The cashier glared at me for not paying with bills or a debit card, but I ignored her, making it her problem to count it out while I perused the trashy magazines displayed in front.

Not much had changed in the gossip magazine since I'd been gone; a lot of the same celebrities hooking up and breaking up or checking into rehab. One of the less-reputable newspapers had a headline that made me think fleetingly of my dad because of how far-fetched it was: "Bat Boy Spotted Living in Cave in Arkansas."

I glanced away guiltily when I realized just how far my opinion of my own father had fallen.

I noticed him then, the boy standing in the same aisle I'd been in just a moment earlier, rapt in concentration over the selection of Snickers and Milky Ways.

I might not have given him a second thought, or even a second glance, if it hadn't been for his eyes. Eyes that I'd seen before.

Eyes that were strikingly copper colored.

He was the same boy from the bookstore. Not the hipster cashier who'd sold Tyler his magazine thing, but the one I'd run into on my way out. The darker-skinned boy who'd made me pause because of his unusual eyes.

He wasn't looking at me now, though, and I tried to study his features without him noticing me. There wasn't much else distinguishable about him. His hair was cut short, almost to his scalp, and his skin was smooth. His mouth and nose were normal size, and he was average height.

He was just . . . *normal*.

"Need a bag?"

I turned back around to face the lady at the cash register. "I . . . yeah, sure." I took my change and the receipt, and after she bagged my loot I took that too.

And when I turned back around, the boy was gone.

As if my day couldn't get any worse, it totally did.

When I got back, my former best friend was sitting on the front porch of my mom's house, looking as if she belonged there and had been sitting there every day for the past five years without skipping a beat. If it hadn't been for her oversize shoulder bag, an accessory she used to insist was for women who'd given up on trying to be sexy, I might have overlooked how . . . *grown-up* she looked.

Except that I probably wouldn't have. Because she did. Look grown-up, I mean.

So, so much more than I did, standing there in my Sesame Street T-shirt and Chucks.

Her expression, though, that Cat expression of unbound exuberance that no one else in the whole wide world could emulate, hadn't changed a bit. And when she saw me wandering up the sidewalk, that liveliness that I'd always loved about her lit up her entire face.

"Kyra!" she gasped, jumping to her feet as she clutched her grown-up purse in front of her.

"Cat? What the hell?" I gripped my plastic bag in front of me as if it could somehow shield me. I wasn't sure what I was more indignant about, being blindsided by her visit or suddenly realizing just how different she was from the last time I'd seen her, and how *exactly the same* I was. "Shouldn't you be at school? Shouldn't you have called or something?"

She frowned. "I did. I called like a million times, Kyr. I left messages with your mom. Didn't she tell you?"

I thought of the sticky-note rainbow my mom had left on my bed.

I glanced at my feet, shoving down the deluge of feelings I couldn't sort through. I was more than just confused or hurt. Yes, she and Austin had betrayed me, but it was different seeing her in person now than it had been seeing Austin. It was harder, somehow, to ignore the years—the lifetime—that she'd just been Cat, my BFF. "You shouldn't be here." It was difficult to say, but I so wasn't ready for this.

In the fringe of my vision, I saw her take a step closer. "What did you think, that I was gonna stay away? You're my best friend, Kyra, and you've been gone for five whole years. I *had* to come."

"Were," I told her, looking up to find her watching me with those perfectly lined eyes. Even her shockingly blond hair looked less high school and more college. No longer ponytailed or braided with wild strands flying loose the way it had been when we'd been on the field. Now it fell in perfect waves that made it clear she'd made a skilled effort with it. "You *were* my best friend."

She stopped, and for a long—I mean a *really long*—time we were both quiet. I thought that was it, that I'd pushed her away, too, like my dad. But then she laughed. "Okay, well, just because *you* say we're not best friends anymore doesn't make it true."

I looked up, and I saw the person she was now. The person Austin went away to school with . . . and was probably living with. That he was definitely-positively-*for-sure* in love with, because how could he *not* love Cat. She was everything I wasn't, and just because I had no idea what was cool anymore, I knew that *this Cat* was the epitome of all things cool, right down to her knee-high, lace-up boots and her knotted batik scarf.

I loved her even while I hated her. "You might not want to be my friend," she declared vehemently. "But you will always, forever, be mine. So don't be stupid, of course I was planning to come here and see you."

Cat blurred out of focus. I wanted to ask her about how she could have ever hooked up with Austin in the first place and why she hadn't come the other day when he had, but pride made those questions impossible. I wanted to tell her how sorry I was that things had changed, and how pissed I was at her, and that I wished, more than anything, we could just go back. . . .

Back.

To five years ago.

And then, as if she'd read my thoughts, because, like any good best friend, Cat had always been able to do that, she reached into her bag. "I brought you something."

At first I didn't get it, the significance of what she held, and then she told me. "It's from that night. It's the game-winning ball." She stepped the rest of the way down from the steps and presented it to me. "We all signed it," she said, her words getting all watery. "Hoping we'd give it to you as a team when you came back." She ended on a strangled sob, until she was full-on crying.

I took the ball from her, concentrating on it so I didn't have to face the fact that mascara was streaking down her pink cheeks. The feel of the ball was so achingly familiar,

145

yet so foreign, that I almost dropped it as soon as it was in my hand.

I had always believed that, like any good pitcher, the ball was an extension of me. That I understood it in ways other people didn't. I'd spent hours memorizing each tiny stipple in the surface of the leather, and the pattern of the stitches and seams. I knew when a ball had gone bad or the difference between a men's and women's ball even before I'd wrapped my fingers around it.

This, though . . . this felt strange. Right, but not right.

Like Cat and me.

I swallowed, and then swallowed again because I didn't want to cry. I'd always been stubborn like that. I didn't wear my heart on my sleeve the way she did.

"I'm not saying we're not friends, Cat. I'm just saying I can't do this right now," I told her. And I took my ball and went up the steps.

As I opened the door to leave her behind, I faltered. Stuck between the door and the jamb was a brand-new, not-torn-up business card from Agent Truman.

Goose bumps peppered my skin as I drew it out. I would've looked for him, up and down the street, but I didn't want to risk facing Cat again, so I pocketed it instead.

But even as I went inside, the question followed me: how had he known I'd thrown away the other one?

CHAPTER NINE

I REMEMBER ONE TIME, DURING THE SUMMER between my fifth- and sixth-grade years, right before it was time for me to start middle school, when I cried a whole lot. I didn't know why I was crying so much at the time, because I cried over pretty much everything: TV commercials, melted ice cream, a grass stain on my favorite jeans. But now that I think back on it, it was probably because I was so afraid.

I was no longer going to be sitting in the same classroom day after day with the same teacher and the same kids for the entire school year. This year, and each year going forward, was going to be all about lockers and choosing electives and showering after gym class and school dances. It was about endless possibility.

I would be embarking on a year of change, where everything was new and unexpected and . . . terrifying.

That was how I felt now.

This house and this family . . . it was all new but not new. Predictable yet unexpected. And utterly, totally, wholly terrifying.

After Cat had gone I couldn't shake that feeling. Seeing her again left me feeling squirrelly in my own skin. The stuff with my dad and the stalkery NSA agent made me question *where* I'd been for the past five years, but it was Cat . . . Cat, who'd driven all the way from Ellensburg to inform me that, whether I liked it or not, she intended to stay my friend, who had me wondering *who* I was going to be from this point on.

It was strange to think that she and I no longer had a single thing in common. She had spent the last five years living life, hitting those milestones I'd missed, and maturing in ways I had yet to even comprehend.

I wasn't even sure what it was I was supposed to do now. The idea of finishing high school, even if it was only online, was nauseating, yet I knew it would have to be done if I ever planned to grow up—in either the literal *or* the figurative senses.

The worst part of the whole thing, though, was that Cat had said the one thing Austin hadn't. Sure, he said he'd hoped we could stay friends, but I knew the truth: he hadn't meant it. Not the way Cat had.

When I finally realized that there weren't enough Dr Peppers and doughnuts in the world to drown my sorrows, I gave up on them.

Frustrated, I stripped out of my juvenile T-shirt and pulled on a plain black one instead. And then, because I didn't have any necklaces or batik scarves to make me feel less . . . *sixteen*, I took out the only real jacket my mom had gotten me. It had a canvas-like feel and pockets that gave it an almost military look. Not dressy exactly, but not a hoodie either.

Nothing, though, could convince me to change my Chucks.

That was how I filled the time between when Cat left and when school got out, trying to convince myself that I wasn't watching the clock and silently counting down the minutes till Tyler should be home. Or that I wasn't hoping like mad he'd come see me before I had to fabricate some lame excuse to call him first, because I totally would have. So when his car pulled up in front of his house—not that I was watching from the window or anything—I felt a surge of giddiness. Maybe this day was salvageable after all.

I'd expected him to go inside first—check in with his mom, drop off his backpack, grab something to eat—all the things Austin used to do after school. So when he started toward my house instead, I got fidgety all over again. I wiped my palms over the front of my jeans, feeling stupid for being nervous all of a sudden. It was just Tyler, after all.

What did I expect was going to happen?

After consulting the mirror one more time and deciding I was as ready as I was ever going to be, I gripped the knob and warned myself to "be cool" as I stood in front of the door and forced myself to take a couple of deep breaths. I didn't want to scare him away with my eagerness.

But Tyler didn't come to the door. We had a thing now, and instead of knocking, I heard him tapping on my bedroom window.

I raced across the house to my bedroom and saw him waving at me from the other side of my window. Trying to tell myself it was no big deal that he was here, I opened it and shot him my best I-wasn't-expecting-you face.

"Let's get outta here," he announced without any preamble.

His invitation caught me by surprise, and my inner voice abandoned me altogether. I forgot all about playing it cool, and suddenly I wasn't sure I even understood what that phrase meant. "Totally," I breathed, before climbing over the windowsill and dropping onto the soft ground below.

As if he was worried I might fall, Tyler reached out to steady me. He caught me by the waist because he didn't know I'd done this a thousand times before. But I let him believe I needed his help. I let his fingers close around my hips and pretended I needed him to keep me balanced because I liked the way they felt. His hands. On me.

"Thanks." I took longer than necessary to stand upright, but eventually I had no other choice. I couldn't let him think

150

the leap—or his touch—had somehow crippled me.

I'd been so focused on Tyler, and when he'd be home, that I'd nearly forgotten all about Agent Truman and his reappearing business card. But now that I was standing outside, in the open, I found myself searching for the dogged agent, for some sign that he was out here. Following me.

Except then I saw Tyler, holding his car door open for me again, and I realized it really was just the two of us, that there was no one else. I sighed and suddenly we were the last two people on Earth—all thoughts of ex–best friends and superspies were obliterated from my mind.

"You look nice," Tyler told me, flashing his incredible smile at me when he got in.

"Thanks. Just letting my mom dress me up, like a Barbie doll." I grinned slyly. "It was this or the holiday-sparkle gown. It's pretty fancy. I think you'da liked it."

Laughing, he pulled his car away from the curb. "I think you made the right call. Not sure you'd fit in wearing a ball gown." Tyler grinned. "But I like the new you."

I wanted to laugh, too, but instead I smiled weakly. *The new me.* That was the thing. *I* was the same; it was everyone else who'd changed.

"Yeah? Where we going?" I asked. Surreptitiously, so he wouldn't notice, I pulled my phone out and noted the time. It was 3:11.

"I figured I'd get you out of the house before the neighbors start to think you're some kind of shut-in or something." He tapped his thumbs on the steering wheel while he drove, and I wasn't sure if it was a habit or if I made him nervous. I hoped it was that last thing, because I'd hate to think it only went one way.

"Shut-in? I've only been home for five days, and I've barely been there. Pretty sure I don't qualify as a shut-in."

He shrugged. "Then I guess I thought you might want to grab some coffee with me." Cocking his head, he shot me a look. "Did they even have coffee in your day? 'Cause we could go someplace else. Maybe split a root beer float or something."

I shoved him. "Okay, smart-ass. Coffee's good." I laughed and wondered if he'd watched the clock half as much as I had today.

The coffee shop he took me to was cute, not a Starbucks or Seattle's Best Coffee—the kinds of corporate places Cat and I had sworn off because Cat had convinced me they were "bastardizing" the coffee culture. Austin had gone along with our boycott because he liked making out with me, but I'm not sure why any of us thought getting our coffee from the Gas 'n' Sip was any more humanitarian. It was a gas station, after all.

After ordering, Tyler dragged me to a spot in the back where we found a table away from all the noise. It was quieter and less crowded than near the counter, where people were coming and going, and the espresso machine hissed, and there was the constant banging as the baristas replaced old grounds with fresh ones. Tyler leaned forward, over the top of his double-shot mocha, and studied me pensively.

"I'm sorry about the other day," he blurted out. "About how I acted when Austin came by."

My eyebrows squeezed together. My chest squeezed even tighter. I'd thought about it more times than I could count, but I guess I hadn't really expected him to apologize. "It's okay . . . ," I started, and then realized the thing about Tyler was that I could talk to him. I'd nearly forgotten how good it felt just to be near him. How he didn't act like my feelings didn't count, and that I shouldn't rock the boat. "It sucked, really. All this time I've been back, all I thought I wanted was to see him, and then when I did . . ." I shook my head. "It wasn't at all what I thought it'd be. He was . . . he was a jerk. He didn't really care about me or what I was going through; he just came over to . . . make himself feel better, I guess. He didn't even ask how I've been . . . or where I was the whole time I was gone." I looked across the table to Tyler, who was just sitting there, listening. *To me.* "And then you got home, and all I could think was how you would've asked me those things. But you looked so upset, and I felt like a jerk for not stopping you when you went inside." He didn't try to console me or interrupt me or tell me that I was wrong to have the feelings I had, the way Austin would have. He just let me unload on him, and it was so . . . freeing. I kept going. "And then today, I had such a shitty day, and instead of going home after school, you came right over." I stopped talking when I realized I'd just confessed to spying on him. My cheeks felt like they might burst into flames, and I bit my lip before I said anything more incriminating.

153

His expression shifted from wistful concern to amusement in a blink. He grinned at me, obviously not about to let my slip pass that easily. "You were watching me?"

I made a face at him. "Whatever. I noticed you were home, that's all. Not that strange, considering I live across the street, you know?"

"And you just happened to be looking out your window at the exact moment I got home. . . . That seems a little strange. C'mon, admit it. You were waiting for me."

"Uh, no," I insisted, perfectly fine with the fact that I was lying through my teeth. "I was looking out the window, and I happened to see you. The end. But it's awesome you think I have nothing better to do all day than to sit around thinking about you."

He leaned back in his chair, his smile so wide, and his dimple so deep, he looked positively full of himself. When had little Tyler grown into this guy who oozed such confidence? And how could I have ever thought of him as little? "Okay," he allowed, but there was nothing in his tone to suggest that he believed a single word I'd said. "If you say so."

I didn't think it was possible, but my cheeks got even hotter. Lifting my plain-old ordinary drip coffee to my lips, I took a sip, hiding behind the cup for as long as possible.

"It *was* hard . . . seeing Austin again. Seeing how much he's changed and knowing the things I know . . . about him and Cat." And then I set down my cup again and confessed, "But it was worse today. I saw Cat."

I didn't know if it was too weird, sharing all this with

him. Even though I felt something—whatever it was—for Tyler, I couldn't ignore the history I'd had with Austin. Austin might have walked away from our past years ago, but it didn't stop the weight that had settled deep in the pit of my stomach, that felt heavier each and every time I thought of what we'd once had together.

Tyler was great and all, but he was just a distraction. A really adorable distraction.

At least that's what I told myself.

"I know." He set his phone on the table between us as if he were confessing something with it. "She called after she saw you, to see if I was out of school yet. She was crying. I think she just wanted someone to talk to." He shrugged and leaned forward again. His voice was shades more thoughtful than it had been when he'd been teasing me about watching him.

It was what made me feel comfortable confiding in him—that serious way of his, that quiet maturity. "She said you hadn't changed a bit, and that she wanted everything to be the same as before. She . . ." He paused and frowned, and I wondered if he was recalling his conversation, filtering parts of it and deciding what he should and shouldn't tell me. Holding back. "She wishes she and Austin could undo what they did."

My heart lurched. I wished for that too. So badly it was probably written all over my face.

I looked at Tyler, sitting across from me with his messy hair and concerned expression. He watched me without judging me, or asking anything from me I wasn't capable of giving, or making me feel guilty for not acting a certain way or believing things I couldn't believe. He was just here to help me figure out who I was and how I fit into this new world I'd been dropped into.

I hated that I found it harder and harder to hold on to my feelings for Austin, not to let them be eclipsed by these new and uninvited feelings Tyler had stirred in me.

"But they can't, can they?" I admitted. Emptiness filled my chest.

He shook his head. "They're not bad people, Kyra. It wasn't an accident, them getting together, but it wasn't malicious either. I was there. I was young, but I was around when it happened. Austin was a wreck after you vanished."

Tears pricked my eyes, and I blinked to keep them at bay. Tyler's hand reached for mine, to where I clutched the warm coffee cup as if it were the only thing in the world keeping me tethered to the ground at the moment. He stopped himself, right before he touched me, his fingers hovering so close I had only to twitch them to close the gap between us.

And I wanted to. To feel his touch again. To let our fingers intertwine. To let him comfort me the way I longed to be comforted.

It wouldn't take much, and when I saw the way he was watching our hands, too, I could see him offering me all that and more. He wanted it as badly as I did.

I cleared my throat, inching my coffee just the slightest bit closer to me and creating a chasm between us that felt unbreachable. "So what happened then? How could they have just forgotten about me? How did they end up . . . where they are . . . together?"

His hands stayed where they were. "I can't say for sure, but if I had to guess I'd say it was all the time they spent together—searching for you, talking about you, waiting for you. You were the glue that held them together at first. You were what kept them from drifting apart. And later, when they realized—when everyone insisted—you weren't coming back, I think they stayed together because it was . . . easy." Regret washed over his face. "It might not have been love back then, but it is now."

His words sliced me, not because I hadn't known the truth. Of course I had. I'd known from the moment Cat had answered Austin's phone that night, when I'd realized they'd gone away to college together. But hearing him say it out loud, and maybe because I knew it wasn't any easier for him to say than it was for me to hear it, was more than I could stand right now.

I shook my head, blinking furiously, trying to tell him to stop without words because my voice was lodged deep in my throat. And he did. He fell silent as I struggled to gain some of the composure I'd lost.

That was when my gaze landed on the boy in the corner, the one sitting at the table with his back to the wall, facing us. I stopped shaking my head. Stopped moving and blinking and breathing.

It was *him* again. The boy from the gas station, and from the bookstore too.

Just like this morning at the Gas 'n' Sip, when I'd been

standing at the counter to pay, he wasn't looking at me or anything, and he didn't appear out of place in the quaint, brick-walled coffee shop. But he was there nonetheless, and I had the strangest sensation that it wasn't a coincidence that he'd been at all of those places, the only three public places I'd been without my parents since I'd been back.

This time it was me reaching for Tyler. I gripped his sleeve, tugging him closer so he was forced to meet me over the top of the small table. Under any other circumstances I would have noticed the coffee smell of his breath and the way my heart fluttered from having his mouth so close to mine.

But this wasn't that time.

"Do you know that guy?" I murmured, trying my best to keep my voice down. For the moment I'd forgotten all about Cat and Austin, and I couldn't tear my eyes away from the dark-skinned boy who seemed to be everywhere I was.

Tyler sneaked a glance out of the corner of his eye to see who I was talking about, and then when he'd gotten a good look, he shook his head. "Nah. Never seen him before. Why? Do *you* know him?"

Frowning, I told him, "I keep seeing him everywhere I go. I think he might be following me." It sounded way crazier outside of my head; I knew it the moment Tyler cringed. "Okay, maybe not *following* exactly," I amended, trying to do some damage control before this whole thing got out of hand and Tyler ranked me right up there alongside my dad. For all I knew, insanity was hereditary. "But it's definitely weird. He was at your friend's bookstore the night we were there. And then I saw him again this morning at the Gas 'n' Sip."

"So basically you've seen him twice, and now you're accusing him of stalking you?"

"This makes three." Again, my evidence wasn't exactly rock solid or anything. Especially since the guy hadn't looked my way once. Considering that *I* was the one talking about him, he could probably argue that I was the one being creepy.

"You do realize that nothing's really changed in the past five years, don't you? Burlington's still a small town. Getting some new shops didn't exactly transform us into a metropolis. People run into each other all the time."

He waited a minute for me to process what he'd said. He was right, of course. The whole point of coincidence was that it was purely accidental. Chance. Like two people being in the same place at the same time.

Or one person being in the wrong place at the wrong time.

I released his sleeve and sagged forward on my elbows. "Ugh. I'm sorry. You're right. I totally ruined our . . ." I stopped short. I'd come *this close* to saying "date," which would've been a million times more embarrassing than admitting I'd been watching him from my window. Besides, it wasn't a date. ". . . coffee," I said instead.

His smile, when it lit his face, was mesmerizing. "You didn't ruin anything," he assured me, cocking an eyebrow. "I thought it was the perfect *coffee*."

I blushed again and tried to think of something to deflect attention away from my verbal slipup. "Metropolis, huh? Nice word."

"You like that? I like to pull out the big guns when I'm trying to make an impression."

My eyes lifted. "Is that what you were trying to do, impress me?"

There was a beat, a moment in which our eyes met and my heart leaped, and then his voice dropped, feathering my skin and making me shiver. "Of course I am, Kyra. I was sort of hoping you understood that."

Flustered, I shot to my feet, probably too fast. Definitely too fast. If I hadn't drawn attention to myself before, there was no doubt I had now with my graceless dismount from my chair. "I—I . . . uh . . ." I stammered superarticulately.

Tyler got up too. He didn't look embarrassed or confused by my reaction. Instead, he grinned as he reached for my coffee before I spilled it everywhere. "Take your time, Kyra. I'm not going anywhere," he told me as he came around the table and pushed my chair in for me. "I'll wait till you figure things out."

My mouth was suddenly too dry to speak even if I had been able to form a coherent thought. I let him lead me out then, between the maze of tables and chairs. We passed the boy in the corner who hadn't even looked up when I'd jumped out of my seat. My chest was tight and tingly, and I couldn't decide if it was elation over Tyler's not-so-veiled revelation about liking me or if I was experiencing the first symptoms of a heart attack.

When we reached the door, I stopped and turned back, curiosity about the other boy finally getting the best of me.

Only this time he was looking right at me.

6:44.

I wasn't a neat freak, not the way my dad had been before . . . well, before everything had changed. But since I was pretty much limiting most of my time at home to my fake bedroom, I decided not to let it be a total pigpen. I was just throwing out the plastic bag filled with my garbage from the Gas 'n' Sip when I noticed something written on the receipt.

I fished it out of the bag and smoothed it flat so I could read what it said.

Kyra, call me. There was a phone number written on it, and it was signed by someone named Simon.

I threw the receipt on the floor, seriously creeped out by the idea that someone had somehow managed to slip a note into my bag—*on my receipt*, no less—without me noticing. Someone who knew my name.

I thought of Agent Truman, who clearly had boundary issues, and wondered if this was his way of forcing me to talk to him.

And then I thought of the other guy, from the bookstore, the coffee shop, and—what do you know?—the Gas 'n' Sip. Why would he be following me and leaving me cryptic messages? Why not just come up to me and say, "Hey, we should talk"?

I'd be a lot more likely to have a conversation with him if that had been the case. Now, after reading his "call me" message, I was pretty sure I never would.

I collapsed on my bed and glared up at my ceiling as I tried to imagine what was so important that he'd slipped a secret message in with my junk food.

My mind pored over a hundred different scenarios, ranging from completely innocent—like he was into me— to downright menacing—like he wanted to wear me as a skin suit. But no matter how hard I tried, there was no clear explanation.

And then there was that other thing I couldn't stop thinking about no matter how hard I tried. The thing where Tyler had all but confessed he was interested in me. Even though it was way less mysterious, it was no less overwhelming. And even when I tried to push him out of my head, he found his way back. His green eyes, his new deeper voice, the way he teased me, his disarming smile. I couldn't stop thinking about *him*.

He hadn't said much the entire ride home, but what went unsaid was palpable. Like a heartbeat pulsing between us so loudly it continued to reverberate inside my head long after we'd parted ways at the curb.

It hadn't helped that after he'd cut the engine, he'd leaned across me to unlatch my door, as if I were suddenly incapable of letting myself out. He'd taken his sweet time about it, too, lingering over me; and I knew full well what he was doing. It would have been impossible not to know.

The way he smiled teasingly, boldly, as if daring me not to react to his nearness.

With that smug grin he wore, I wouldn't have given him the satisfaction of a response even if my underwear had caught fire right then and there. Secretly, however, everything inside me strained to be closer to him, to stop pretending there was a chance I might still be Austin's girl and to undo my seat belt so there was nothing separating us.

A part of me longed to know the feel of his lips and his skin and his heart beating against mine.

I wanted to touch my fingertip to his dimple.

Just once.

I hated how easily he kept wriggling his way back into my thoughts.

My phone buzzed, and again I moved to hit IGNORE. Already I'd disregarded a call from my dad. I knew I wouldn't really avoid him forever; I wasn't capable of that kind of coldhearted detachment. No matter how far off the deep end he'd jumped, he was still my dad. I couldn't stop myself from loving him.

Still, I needed more time before I'd be ready to jump aboard his crazy train again.

When I checked my phone, though, it was a new number, one I hadn't programmed and definitely didn't recognize.

Gooseflesh prickled my arms when I saw the out-of-state area code—area code 310. It wasn't the number from the back of the receipt, but I was sure I'd seen it somewhere before.

Jumping off my bed, I scrambled for the top drawer of my dresser and began digging through the stacks of straight-out-of-the-package underwear and socks.

"Kyra?" My mom's knocking on the other side of my bedroom door distracted me, and I stopped what I was doing long enough to shout back, "I'm not hungry. Go ahead and eat without me."

I glanced at the digital numbers on my nightstand while my phone—set to vibrate—buzzed once more. It was 7:26.

Outside my room it was quiet, but I knew she was still there. I could hear "my brother's" unmistakable footsteps—his short, staccato stride and the way he ran, rather than walked, everywhere he went. He whimpered briefly, and I could picture him straining with his chubby arms raised high above his head, begging to be picked up. Then there was a brief shuffling, and my mother murmured something soft and reassuring, followed by her quieter, and more measured, footsteps leading toward the kitchen.

I shouldn't feel bad for not wanting to spend time with them, I told myself. This wasn't my fault. None of it. I hadn't asked for a new family.

When my fingers closed around Agent Truman's business card—the second one he'd left me—I inhaled. I'd chucked it in my drawer when I thought I'd never need it again.

I picked up my phone and cross-checked the number on the card with the one that had just called me.

The two were a match.

The hairs on the back of my neck stood on end. How

had Agent Truman gotten my cell phone number?

Just as I pressed the button on my phone to check the time, a message popped up on the screen.

A text.

From Agent Truman's number.

I want to show you something.

For a long time that was it. I waited for more. For another message, something along the lines of *Call me back* or *Let's schedule an appointment* or *Meet me at . . .*

I wasn't sure how that last one was supposed to end since I didn't think there was a local NSA office in a town the size of Burlington, but it didn't matter. If Agent Truman was trying to freak me out with his ominous message, he was doing a bang-up job. I was freaked, all right.

And if he thought I would message him back, he was out of his ever-loving mind. I had nothing to say to him. I'd already told him everything I knew: that my dad had nothing to do with my disappearance that night. I wasn't sure what more I could say to convince him.

And then a second text popped up. A picture, followed by a single question:

Do you recognize this man?

I covered my mouth because I did recognize him, but I had no idea why Agent Truman was asking me, or why it even mattered.

Giving in to the urge to defend myself, even if my response was a total lie, I typed in two letters: *No,* and threw my phone on the bed.

I got up and paced my room, suddenly edgy and itchy and more than a little agitated. My eyes fell on the ball Cat had left me. The one from our championship game. The ball I'd hurled from the pitcher's mound, striking out batter after batter.

The ball responsible for making the other team cry.

I picked it up and ran my thumb over the stitching as I looked at all the names scrawled on it in various shades of blue, black, purple, and red pen. My teammates who'd signed their names in hopes I'd be home soon and they could give me the ball as a gift. Tears gathered in the corners of my eyes. I wondered where they all were now. I wondered if they knew I was back.

I tossed the ball up in the air and caught it. I did it again, and again, and again.

And then I grabbed my hoodie and my phone, closing out of the picture of the lab tech who'd been found dead the night before in his apartment, and texted my mom, who was just down the hall, in the kitchen with her replacement family.

I'm going out. Back soon.

CHAPTER TEN

I'D WALKED BETWEEN MY HOUSE AND THE HIGH school only a handful of times, and only when it had been a last-resort situation. Like the time I'd overslept when Austin had been at an out-of-town swim meet and I'd missed the bus. Or when Cat and I had gotten into a yelling match in the middle of practice over whether the pitch I'd thrown had hit her on purpose. The argument had gotten heated— to the point that the coach had had to intervene—and I'd insisted on walking home, refusing to speak to Cat for two days afterward.

That had been one of the downsides of having an August

birthday. I was always younger than everyone else in my class, which meant that, during our sophomore year, while everyone around me had been turning sixteen and getting their driver's licenses, I'd been relegated to hitching rides and counting down the days till my Sweet Sixteen.

It wasn't *that* big a deal since Austin's birthday was in October and Cat's was in February, and I could go everywhere they went. What *was* a big deal was that when August finally rolled around, I chickened out.

Maybe too much time had passed and I'd built up the whole driver's-license thing too much in my head.

Or maybe, *just maybe*, I'd failed the driving test twice already—a secret I swore I'd take to my grave.

I'd been too embarrassed to try a third time, so instead I made up some lame excuse about not wanting my license anyway, which was total bull because every kid in the universe wanted one. Your license meant freedom and independence. It meant joining an elite club where people could drive cars and wave at one another on their way to car washes and drive-through espresso stands and parking lots, where they would hang out and compare shitty DMV photos.

And here I was, all these years later, still walking.

And still sixteen . . . or so I'd been told.

By the time I reached the field, I was sweating and I'd stripped off my jacket and tied the sleeves around my waist. I was still clutching the ball, and it felt good. Right.

Being at the field again was a whole other story. It skeeved me out that they'd named it after me. I didn't see a sign or anything, which would have felt like a gravestone of sorts, but it was still strange knowing what I knew.

I was relieved that the fields were deserted, since it was still softball and baseball season and there could have been a game or late practice. I stepped out onto the empty field, walking straight to the pitching mound, facing my ghosts head-on.

It was unsettling to stand there again. It was the same place I'd stood dozens, hundreds, thousands of times before. I pressed my fingers alongside the stitching on the ball and closed my eyes, letting memory and reality collide.

When I reopened them, I zeroed in on home plate and envisioned the ball's trajectory, the point at which I wanted it to leave my hand, the way it should arc—just so—and where it would cross the plate. I rolled my neck and my shoulders, loosening my muscles. And then, taking a breath, I drove off the mound, swinging my arm and rotating my shoulder, all the way around, and released my pitch.

It was so natural, the rhythm so familiar, that it was utterly impossible to believe that five years had passed since the last time I'd thrown a ball. And when I saw it—that very same championship ball—hurtling across its mark, faster maybe than I thought it should have gone, I knew . . . I believed at last what Dr. Dunn had told my parents: I was still sixteen years old. Because there was no way, no possible way on earth I was any older than I had been just six days ago. My body, my muscle memory, hadn't changed a single iota. My body remembered the same way I did.

"Holy shit." The voice behind me whispered in awe. "I knew you could play, I mean, I'd heard stories, but *damn*, that was impressive."

I whirled around to find Tyler standing right there, and I wondered how he'd managed to sneak up on me. I grinned in response because I knew what I'd just done *was* impressive, more so even than using words like *metropolis* or having a killer dimple. "You ever play?" I inquired over my shoulder as I left him standing there while I went to retrieve my ball.

I knew he was trailing after me when he spoke, his voice low and playful. "Softball? Nah. I tried out once, but they said the other girls felt uncomfortable with me in the locker room, so I didn't make the cut."

Bending at the waist, I reached for the ball where it had landed near the backstop. Gingerly, I brushed away the dirt as I stood again. "I meant baseball, or just sports in general, smart-ass. Aren't you ever serious?"

His hand shot out, covering the ball as if he meant to take it from me, but he didn't, and his hand curled over mine. I inhaled sharply. "I'm serious about plenty of things," he told me solemnly, his gaze intense. He took a step closer, and without thinking or meaning to, and because I suddenly couldn't breathe with him standing in my space like that, I took one tiny step back. I let go of the ball, and it dropped back to the ground with a solid thud. It was so much quieter than the pounding of my heart. He took another step. I tried to hold my ground, but my throat grew thick, and my body temperature had risen at least twenty degrees. "There are more important things in life than games, Kyra." His eyebrow lifted, and his mischievous gaze raked over me.

I couldn't tell if he was mocking me, or toying with me, or whatever this was that he was doing. I hated even more that it was his fault I couldn't catch my breath, and I felt suddenly unsteady.

I shoved his chest, trying to give myself some space. "Yeah, well, I'm sure you and your *books* will be very happy together." It didn't escape my notice, the way his muscles felt beneath my fingers, and the solidness of him made me out-and-out feverish.

He caught my hand again, but this time I wasn't holding the ball, so I couldn't kid myself that he had some other motivation for his actions. When his thumb moved over my palm, heat burst in the pit of my belly and spread outward, curling the tips of my toes. "I'm serious about other things too."

I wanted to swallow, but my tongue felt like baked asphalt. "Stop," I insisted.

"Stop what?"

"Saying things like that."

His half smile made him look all wolfish, and completely daring. "Like what? That I'm serious? That I like you?" He moved a quarter of an inch closer, and involuntarily my lips parted.

"Yes," I confirmed, scowling because it was easier and far less obvious than gaping at him. "That's exactly what I mean."

His thumb skated up to my wrist. I was sure he had to

know how he affected me, that the thrumming of my pulse would totally give me away. "Then *you* stop."

I blinked once and then again. *"Me?* What did I do?"

He let go of my wrist and lifted his hand to my face. When his thumb feathered over my lower lip, so lightly it could have easily been a figment of my imagination, I shivered.

I saw a show on Animal Planet once about these fainting goats whose muscles froze up when they were startled, and they passed out. Like, they literally fell over if you scared them.

That was me, right now.

I was terrified and exhilarated and frozen all at once.

If I passed out, too, I would surely die of embarrassment.

We stood like that for fifty-five straight heartbeats. Our eyes remained locked in a game of chicken. His palm cupped my chin, and his thumb stayed right on my lip while I tried to find my next breath.

And for fifty-five heartbeats everything inside me begged him to kiss me.

"Being stubborn," he said at last, and I had no idea what he was talking about, or when he'd even been talking at all. He shook his head, breaking the spell, or whatever it was I was under—we were both under. "You're so damned stubborn. If you'd just admit how you feel, then we could stop pretending there's nothing between us."

I jerked back, away from his thumb on my lip, and my head collided with the fence behind me, which I hadn't even realized I'd backed myself up against. "I'm not being stubborn," I stated firmly, while he smirked as if I'd just made his point for him. I wilted against the chain-link, my fingers weaving through it for support. "I never said there was nothing between us." It was hard for me to admit the truth, and it came out all shaky and timid sounding. I wasn't timid, though, at least I never had been before.

"I wouldn't believe you if you had," he told me, and this time there was nothing playful or taunting in his voice. Nothing to make me weak-kneed and girlie. But that didn't stop my lip from tingling where he'd touched it.

I turned away while he picked up the ball, and I started walking back to his car, following the chalk path that led to first base.

"You ever start that book I lent you?" The sudden change in subject was as jarring as it was welcome.

I shrugged, spinning to face him and catching the ball when he tossed it to me. "I finished it, actually."

"What?" he drawled, flashing me a dubious look. "You're lying! And here I thought you were all dumb jock and zero substance."

Even though I knew he was teasing, I glowered at him and chucked the ball back in his direction.

Except that what I'd meant as a playful gesture ended up virtually lethal in execution. The ball didn't just lob from my hand in a good-natured, we're-just-messing-around kind of throw. It flew toward him at Mach speed, as if I'd just launched a missile at his head. He was quick enough, or

173

lucky enough, to get out of the way in time.

When it hit the backstop, splinters sprayed outward in an explosion that made even me flinch from where I was standing.

If Tyler hadn't ducked in time . . .

I covered my mouth. "Oh my god," I breathed incredulously.

He stared at me and then whipped around to inspect the damage—the crater I'd left in the wooden backstop behind him.

"I—oh my god," I repeated. "I'm so sorry." And I *so* was. I had no idea what had gotten into me or where the hell that throw had even come from. He had every right to be pissed at me; I'd nearly decapitated him with my runaway pitch.

"Jesus Christ, Kyra," he breathed as his fingertips traced around the fragmented wooden edges. "Have you ever done that before?"

I'd seen plenty of scuffs and dents in the backstop, mostly from foul balls or from the bats themselves, but never anything like what he was looking at.

I shook my head even though he wasn't looking my way.

"That's like . . ." He turned to face me, and I could barely meet his eyes. ". . . Damn."

"Yeah," I agreed. And then my throat closed when my eyes shifted, focusing on the street beyond him and the backstop and fencing.

We were no longer alone.

Parked at the far end of the street, almost, but not quite, too far to see from where we were, was Agent Truman, watching us. *Watching me.*

He leaned against a polished black sedan, his ankles crossed in front of him. The only thing missing were his government-issued shades.

He didn't give any indication that he'd noticed us and looked completely out of place loitering on the fringes of a baseball diamond.

But I knew what he was doing there, and I could feel his eyes on me. Everything about him made me intensely, insanely, inscrutably uncomfortable. He'd seen what I'd just done, and for reasons I couldn't quite put my finger on, it mattered.

I had no idea what was happening to me. According to my dad, and Dr. Dunn, and the mother I could barely stand to be around, I'd lost five years of my life but I was still sixteen. And now I find out my fastball is lethal?

All I knew for certain was that I didn't want Agent Truman knowing any of it. This was my life. I'd just gotten it back and I was just figuring it out. I didn't want him—or anyone else—knowing about it, or me.

"Let's get outta here," I told Tyler, waiting for him to catch up to me.

He didn't argue, and he didn't notice Agent Truman, who I couldn't take my eyes off of and who never, for a single second, stopped staring at me.

I was so consumed by the NSA agent's daunting presence

that I almost didn't notice when the back of Tyler's hand grazed mine. Except it was all I noticed, because my breath caught, and I glanced sideways to see if Tyler had noticed it too.

He caught me looking at him, and my face flushed when he grinned back at me. And then his fingers captured mine, this time for real, not an accidental brush of skin against skin.

We were holding hands, and my heart was pounding so hard I thought it might splinter the way the backstop had, and suddenly we were all alone then, just the two of us.

Just like when I'd picked up the ball, the feel of his skin was so achingly, beautifully, disarmingly right. Righter than I could remember it ever being with Austin, which felt like a betrayal just to think.

It was almost painful that the moment only lasted a few short seconds, which was how long it took us to skirt the edge of the fencing and reach his car. When we stopped, I untangled my hand from his, not wanting him to be the one to end it first.

"There you go again, being all stubborn."

I ignored the jab as I slid inside the car while Tyler held my door for me. I ignored the slamming inside my chest, and the fact that I could barely contain my smile no matter how hard I tried to bite it back.

By 10:36 Tyler had texted me no less than eight times, saying nothing in particular but revealing so much with his absurd messages.

Planning to sleep tonight, or should I be worried that you're some sort of creature of the night, like a vampire or bat?

I meant bat like the animal. Not of the baseball variety.

Did you get my last text? Am I bothering you?

I can bring you another book if you need one.

And my favorite, but mostly because it was so lame: *I'll be dreaming of you.*

I'd responded with a lot of *yes*es, *got it*s, *no*s, and *thanks but no thanks*es. But I'd learned three very interesting things from his attempt to text the pants off me.

He'd been keeping track of my sleeping habits, which could either be viewed as disturbing or sweet.

His flirting skills sucked.

He'd definitely gotten under my skin.

When half an hour had passed since his last message and I was sure we were done for the night, I set the phone aside and left my room in search of leftovers. As usual, the house was quiet at this hour; and just like every night since I'd been back, my mom had left a plate for me, another of my old faves: meat loaf.

And just like each night the food tasted . . . not quite right. I picked at it for a few minutes, choked down a few bites, and ultimately tossed the rest. I threw it down the garbage disposal so my mom wouldn't notice that I couldn't seem to stomach her cooking anymore.

As I stood in front of the sink, I peeled the curtains apart and peered outside. I didn't really expect to see Agent Truman and his cop-mobile out there, but I couldn't rule it out either. Not after he'd shown up at the softball field the way he had.

He had definitely gotten under my skin, and not in a good way.

On my way back to my room, I paused in the hallway. The faint glow of a night-light spilled out from the open door to "my brother's" room. I took a wary step forward, curious about this kid who was supposed to mean something to me.

His room was the exact opposite of what it had been the last time I'd been in there, when it had been filled with IKEA office furniture, and filing cabinets stuffed with my mom's work files, and bookshelves jam-packed with my trophies and team pictures. I wasn't sure where any of those things were now, but it seemed likely they'd been banished to the same place my personal belongings had gone. That, or thrown away. Remnants from another life.

Now it was a nursery, complete with crib and rocking chair and colorful letters on the wall that spelled out LOGAN. Even the smell was different, somewhere between sweet and too-sweet, like a noxious combination of floral air fresheners and baby powder. Since I'd seen the kid wearing diapers—something that made me further question his development, because shouldn't a two-year-old be using the toilet by now?—I guessed that the air fresheners were meant to cover up the gross stink that went along with pooping in your pants.

I approached the crib as quietly as I could manage, not wanting to wake the kid.

As much as I hated to admit it, he *was* cuter, or rather less annoying, asleep than he was awake. He sucked his thumb, I noted, unable to stop myself from judging him even when no one was around.

But since no one could hear my inner thoughts, I supposed it was safe to confess there were good things about him too. That his skin was so smooth and unblemished, and his lashes so thick, that any girl in her right mind would envy him. And his expression was so peaceful and relaxed, and he slept so soundly, that *I* envied him. He had soft curls that peeked around from behind his neck, and my first thought was that I wanted to pet him. To run my fingers through those downy, feather-like curls and to pinch his plump cheeks.

I was such a cliché. I couldn't afford to watch him for another minute or pretty soon I'd be carrying snapshots of him in my wallet and asking total strangers if I could see pictures of their kids. That's what grown-ups did. They pretended to be interested in the photos of other people's kids just so they'd have an excuse to show off their own.

I knew, because my dad had been a master at that game. He once even had giant buttons of my fourth-grade picture made, and he wore his everywhere he went. I found my mom's in her glove box the day she explained that she didn't need to wear my face on display to carry me in her heart.

I wondered if Logan had taken up my share of that heart.

"We're all trying, you know?" The hushed voice startled me, and I spun around to find The Husband—Grant—leaning

179

casually against the door frame, his arms crossed over his chest. He had on a plain white tee and flannel pajama bottoms. "Your mom most of all."

I shrugged, not wanting to have this conversation. Not here, not with him. Maybe not ever.

I tried to brush past him, but his hand caught my arm. He wasn't rough, just firm. "Kyra. We all get how hard this must be for you. Everything's different now, but it wasn't like we did it on purpose. Things just . . . changed. We want you to be part of our family."

I closed my eyes. I knew he was trying to help, but his words—the way he said *we* and *our*, like I was just supposed to accept him and his son because that was the way things were now—made me want to puke.

"I'm trying too," I said, and jerked my arm out of his grip.

When I reached my room, I closed my door and leaned against it to bar myself inside.

When was this going to get easier? When would I feel like I belonged somewhere, that I was part of a home or a family, or that someone really understood the person I was now?

I searched my nightstand for my clock, desperate to know how much time had passed, and when I found it, my eyes drifted to the beat-up copy of *Fahrenheit 451* sitting beside it. My heart fluttered.

Someone did understand me. Someone who didn't question where I'd been or how old I was now that I was back.

I eased away from my door so I could text him, knowing full well he was sleeping and wouldn't get my message till morning. But there was already a message waiting for me.

Not from Tyler but from Agent Truman.

His message had been delivered at 12:01 a.m.: *Were there fireflies the day you disappeared?*

I dropped onto the edge of my bed, my breath coming in short gasps.

Fireflies. Why on earth would Agent Truman ask me about fireflies?

My dad had mentioned fireflies to me too. Surely it wasn't a coincidence.

I squeezed my eyes shut and searched my memory for that night, because suddenly it seemed a zillion times more important than it had before.

We'd been driving on Chuckanut Drive, and I was purposely avoiding my dad, stubbornly staring out the window. There were blurs of light every now and then, flickers in the distance. I suppose they could've been fireflies, but I couldn't say for sure since I'd never really seen one in real life before.

Then I'd yelled at my dad to stop the car, and when he did I fled, and there was a flash. . . .

I pounded my fists against my thighs. Why couldn't I remember more?

And why was Agent Truman so interested in whether there were stupid glowing bugs out that night?

What if my dad wasn't as crazy as I thought he was?

A weight settled over my chest as I made a decision. I had to figure out what happened that night, but I couldn't do it on my own, and I wasn't about to go to my dad until I knew for sure how this was gonna play out.

There was only one person I could count on right now.

I picked up my phone and punched in a message: *Any chance I can talk you into ditching school tomorrow?*

I started to hit SEND and stopped myself. Adding another line to the text: *I need an accomplice.*

CHAPTER ELEVEN
Day Six

I STAYED IN MY ROOM UNTIL MY MOM AND Grant had taken Logan and left for the day. I was proud of myself for giving The Husband and "my brother" their names back. It was a big gesture on my part, even if they had no clue I'd taken them away in the first place.

By the time they were gone, I'd already changed my outfit three times. I chewed the side of my nail as I triple- and quadruple-checked the time. It was only 7:43.

I don't know why I was so nervous all of a sudden. I'd made Tyler a generous offer, hadn't I? Giving him the chance to risk truancy, and possibly restriction, just to hang out with me for the day. Clearly, my selflessness knew no bounds.

The drumming at my window made me realize I'd been wrong to doubt whether he'd show, and I rushed to meet him.

"Hey," I exhaled, sounding way more relieved than seemed warranted.

"Hey yourself. So what do you have planned for us? Bank heist? Jailbreak?" The way he looked at me, with that grin and that glint in his eyes, made me smile. But it was his touch, when I let him help me out the window again that made me beam from the inside out. He deliberately pulled me into him, practically yanking me to make it seem as if I'd lost my balance. My cheek smashed into his chest, not that I was complaining exactly. It wasn't the worst place to be. "Or maybe you have something more . . . *interesting* in mind," he suggested, his voice all gravelly sounding as it rumbled against the side of my face.

Grudgingly, I shoved away from him. "Jeez! Don't you ever get tired of trying to seduce me with your sorry pickup lines?"

Undiscouraged, he smiled down at me. "Trust me, if I was trying to seduce you, there wouldn't be anything *sorry* about it." He reached for my hand, and his fingers linked through mine the way they had the night before as we started walking.

There was something so endearing about the way he held my hand, the way it felt like something we'd been doing forever while at the same time it felt shiny and new. My stomach quivered, and I liked it.

When we were in his car, he raised an eyebrow at me, and I realized I'd never told him where we were going. I loved that he was willing to go along with whatever I had in mind, no questions asked.

"Oh, uh . . . to Cedar Lake High School." I paused when an expression I didn't recognize passed over his face. "Do you know where that is?"

"Uh, yeah. In Bellingham. It's the school you were playing the night you vanished." He frowned. "Are you sure you want to go back there?"

I nodded, more sure than I'd ever been. "I need to retrace my steps. I want to see if I can remember anything."

"Why? What good'll it do? The past is the past. You're here now. Shouldn't you be moving forward? Forget about what happened all those years ago?"

I hesitated, wondering how much I should tell him about my dad and his crackpot theories, and about Agent Truman, and the way they'd both asked me about fireflies.

"I wish I could," I started as I smoothed my hand nervously over my jeans. "But there's more to it than just that. There are things . . . *people* who are making it hard to let the past stay buried in the past."

He winced, and I wondered if the pained expression meant he thought I was talking about his brother again. I reached across to where his fingers gripped the steering wheel, his knuckles white. But I stopped myself because I felt self-conscious all of a sudden.

"Tyler, I'm not talking about Austin," I explained, keeping my eyes trained on him. "When I came back, I thought . . . well, you know . . . I thought you were your brother. And I thought we would . . . be together still." It was so much easier saying it out loud than I thought it would be. "But things are over between him and me, I get that now." I took a breath and shrugged. "I know I don't remember where I was all that time, but now that I'm back I *feel* so different. I'm not sure what it is about you. You were just a kid. . . ." My voice trailed away as I frowned, trying to find a way to explain. "It's kind of like when Montag from *Fahrenheit 451* asks Clarisse why it feels like he's known her for so many years, and she says, 'Because I like you, and I don't want anything from you. And because we know each other.' It's the same way with you."

His fingers relaxed on the steering wheel. His green eyes—ones that had once reminded me of Austin's but were now so obviously *not* like Austin's that I couldn't imagine having mistaken the two of them—glanced my way. I knew when I looked at him there was no going back. Whatever I'd felt for Austin really was in the past.

Somehow, in less than a week, Tyler had managed to make me believe I belonged here, in this weird, unfamiliar world I'd been dropped into. He was the only person I could count on.

He was my here and now.

His voice was decisive when he spoke. "I'm glad Austin acted like an ass. I'm not saying he's a dick or anything, because he's still my brother. But it was a dick move." He leaned nearer, removing his hand from the wheel and slipping it behind my neck, drawing me so close I could smell the toothpaste on his breath. "You deserve better than that, Kyra." And just when I thought he was going to do it, finally kiss me, his lips parted and he said, "And you might not want anything from me, but don't for a single second think I don't want something from you."

He was wrong, though; I wanted everything from him. Probably more than I should.

When his mouth fell on my forehead, my eyes closed while I waited for the explosion of butterflies in my stomach to settle down, but it never happened. They kept thrashing, for as long as he stayed there, which was forever, his lips pressed against my skin, burning me, scorching me. When he finally drew back, I was convinced there would be a mark there, a brand in the shape of his mouth.

He grinned, and then winked at me, before starting his engine. "Are we done messing around here? Because I think it's time for you to start telling me everything. Like who the hell's been dredging up all this past crap, and why it's so important that you remember what happened."

I wanted to tell him no, that I'd way rather stay here and "mess around," but he was right. It was time to confide in someone. In him.

I waited a few minutes, until my breathing had returned to normal, or as normal as it was going to be while the feel of his lips still blistered my forehead. But I knew he was waiting, even though he didn't press me.

We took the highway. We'd drive the other way, the way my dad and I had gone—on Chuckanut Drive—on our way back. I wanted to retrace our steps to the T, and my dad had taken the long way home that night because of road construction on the southbound lanes of the interstate.

Tyler's car slid evenly, smoothly over the pavement, and I leaned back in my seat, studying him surreptitiously. "Remember the day I came back, when you said I didn't look any older?"

The corners of his mouth ticked up, but he kept his eyes on the road. "Yeah."

Now that I'd started, I wasn't sure exactly where I was going with this. I shifted and fidgeted with my seat belt, readjusting it over my chest. After a moment I tried again. "Didn't you think it was weird that I'm supposed to be twenty-one, but I still look the same?"

This time he turned his head to look at me. "What do you mean 'supposed to be'? If you're worried that I think you're too old for me or something, I'm not." He directed his gaze back to the road, but he was scowling now. "It's not a big deal, Kyra. Really." His lazy smile made a fleeting appearance. "I kinda like the whole cougar thing you've got goin' on."

Oh my god, even when I was trying to be serious, he was ridiculous. "Uh, no. That's not it at all. And I'm not." I was tired of dancing around it, and tired of pretending to be something I wasn't. This, all of it, would either be better or a thousand times worse if I just spit it out already. "I'm not twenty-one, Tyler. I'm still sixteen."

There, I thought, and even if I wanted to—which I totally and completely did—*I couldn't take it back now.*

Tyler sounded far more reasonable when he responded than I had when I'd blurted out my admission. "What are you talking about, Kyra? You're the same age as Austin."

My throat felt scratchy, and I tried to clear it. "I don't think so," I admitted. "At first I didn't believe it either. It was the dentist who saw it first, when I went in to get my tooth fixed. He looked at my X-rays and compared them to the ones I'd had done right before I disappeared—five years ago. He told my parents they were the same. Exactly the same."

"Kyr—"

But I kept going before he could stop me. I was going to do this or completely chicken out. Either way I was in too deep, and I'd come out looking like a lunatic. I planned to at least have my say before Tyler walked away and never looked back. "But it wasn't just that. There were other things too. Things no one else would have noticed but me. Things like the bruise I'd gotten on my leg . . ." I leaned over and pulled the hem of my jeans up, showing him the purple splotch on my shin. "I got this when Cat and I were messing around the night before our big game. We broke my dad's favorite coffee mug and never told him." Just mentioning my dad and the WORLD'S BEST DAD mug I'd gotten him for Father's Day when I was eleven made me sick to my stomach.

I wondered what kinds of mugs I'd get him now. WORLD'S

BEST ALIEN HUNTER. MY DAD'S CRAZIER THAN YOUR DAD. If only I could have the World's Best Dad back again.

Tyler looked my way, his eyes alternating between the bruise and the road and me. "You could've gotten that anywhere," he told me, his voice so much softer and less teasing than it had been just a minute ago.

I shook my head, but I'd lost some of my conviction. "But I didn't. And this." I tugged up the sleeves of my T-shirt. "It's the tan I had before I left. From my uniform. How could it still be there, in that exact same place?"

When he didn't say anything, I fell silent. It filled the air, and I let my sleeve fall back in place. In that moment I wanted to slink down and just disappear again. I stared out the side window instead.

After a few seconds Tyler's fingers closed over mine and squeezed. "I'm not saying I don't believe you, Kyra. I'm just saying, give me a minute or two to process it, okay?"

While Burlington Edison's fields—or rather Agnew Field—had looked almost exactly the same as they had the last time I'd stood on them, Cedar Lake's fields, where we'd played that championship game, were completely rundown. The distinction between the outfield and infield was blurred as dirt and grass bled into each other, and the chalk lines were indistinct and drawn lazily. The dirt was clumpy, and the grass was weedy.

It was like looking at the softball diamond version of my dad.

But none of that mattered, as I stood there in the last

place where everything had been normal. Where I'd been Kyra Agnew, superstar pitcher, only child, teammate, and unquestionably sixteen.

"Anything?" Tyler asked, coming to join me in the dugout where Coach had given us her pregame pep talk and her postgame victory speech.

I shook my head. I tried my best to find something, anything that might trigger some small, seemingly insignificant memory, but there was nothing. Nothing new anyway.

Just Cat wrapping her arms around me and screaming victory shouts until my eardrums felt like they'd rupture. And later, near the parking lot, Austin wrapping *his* arms around me and whispering softer words. Promises that would never be fulfilled.

"Let's go," I insisted, taking his hand and dragging him away from there. "Maybe the drive back'll shake something loose."

The place where we stopped was way less daunting than I'd made it out to be in my head. I'd built it up to be this desolate stretch of highway straight out of a horror movie, complete with tumbleweeds and its own menacing soundtrack.

In real life it was just an ordinary two-lane road surrounded on both sides by farmland. Not a single sound effect for miles.

I wasn't sure this was the exact right spot, but it was as close as I could recall. Tyler backed me up when he said he thought he remembered Austin and Cat dragging him here with them to drop off flowers and balloons, back when there'd still been one of those roadside shrines in my honor.

Since five years had gone by, it was hard to confirm, though. All we could find were bits of dried-up dandelions scattered throughout the gravel shoulder.

"Is it weird?" Tyler asked when I clutched my sides and stared out at the fields that went on for miles.

"No weirder than me telling you I'm still sixteen."

"Yeah, about that . . ." He reached for my hip and drew me around to face him. Gravel crunched beneath my feet. "If *you* believe it, *I* believe it."

My heart thudded riotously as I faced him that way, with his hand still settled easily, securely, and maybe a little possessively, on my hip. "Simple as that, huh?"

His dimple made a surprise appearance. "Simple as that," he repeated, and I believed him.

"There's more."

He leaned his head back and groaned to the sky, which was turning gloomy and gray, dense clouds amassing. "You are seriously testing the boundaries of my confidence in you, you know? There are limits to what I can accept." Yet even though his words made a mockery of my revelations, his fingers laced through my belt loops, ensuring that I was snared. When his chin dropped down again, he inhaled deeply, as if he was gathering his wits and preparing himself for whatever bombshell I had to drop next. "Fine." He let out a breath. "Go ahead. Do your worst."

I rolled my eyes. "Stop being so dramatic." But I giggled when I said it, ruining the whole chastising effect I was going for. "This guy came to my house yesterday," I said earnestly. "He said he was from the National Security Agency, and he was asking me questions about the night I disappeared."

I had Tyler's full attention now. He was no longer joking or tugging at my belt loops. He stared down at me with eyes that looked like they'd never been anything *but* serious. "The NSA? What kinds of questions?"

I shook my head. "That's the crazy thing. He asked about my dad, which makes sense, I guess. . . ." My words slowed down there, because that was where the whole thing got sticky for me, more so than the part where I told him I hadn't aged. I grimaced as I broached the subject of my dad. "I guess you know what my dad thinks happened to me." I had an overwhelming urge to check my phone, to confirm the time, but it was so inappropriate that I stuffed my hands into my pockets instead.

"Yeah. I know. Everyone sorta knows he went off the deep end with the outer space stuff." He didn't say it like I would have. Like it was a big, fat joke.

I swallowed, grimacing. "And that guy, Agent Truman, asked me some weird questions that made me nervous. I thought about how you said people thought my dad might have been involved in my disappearance, and at first I wondered if he maybe thought that, too, because he wanted to know what all I remembered—which is almost nothing." I wrinkled my nose when I said the next part. "But then he asked me about fireflies."

"*Fireflies?* Why? What about them?"

"I have no idea, but my dad asked me the same thing. They both wanted to know if I remembered seeing fireflies. . . ." I nodded toward the darkening horizon. "The night I was here."

"So did you?"

I closed my eyes and inhaled the tang of the rain-swollen air. I felt one tiny drop on my cheek and then another on my nose. "I don't know. I'm not sure I know what they look like, really." I opened my eyes and looked at him. "Do you?"

He frowned, concentrating. "I mean, sort of, I guess. Do we even have them around here?"

I shrugged as more raindrops fell on me.

"So what *do* you remember?"

"We were coming back from my game, and I got out of the car because my dad and I were fighting over college, and about Austin, and I was going to walk to prove a point. I tripped because I couldn't see where I was going, and my dad was yelling for me. But before I could answer him, something really weird happened."

"Fireflies?"

I smirked. "No. There was this intense flash of light. It was so bright that I couldn't see anything else." I shut my eyes, and for a moment I was transported back there again, and I could hear my dad's screams, and I was blinded by the light that was everywhere all at once. And I felt tingly. All over.

Tyler's touch brought me back to the present as he wiped

my cheek. I felt tingly again, but in an entirely different way. "I'm sorry."

"Don't be," I told him, letting him wipe away yet another tear that was mingled with the rain, and then another, as the tiny raindrops became a full-on deluge around us. Neither of us moved, or flinched even, as we were drenched, drowned by the sudden downpour. I blinked the rain away so I could keep looking at his perfect, beautiful face. "If I hadn't vanished that night, then I wouldn't have come back, and I wouldn't have had the chance to know you now. Not like this."

And like that his lips found me. They didn't find my forehead this time but captured my lips, and I couldn't breathe when they did. They were demanding and sweet all at the same time.

Fire flowed through me while rain drizzled down my face. Our tongues teased and touched and danced together, and he crushed me against him in a way that made me believe he'd never, ever let me go.

I'd never been so alive, and I knew this was why I'd come back. To be here, right now, in this moment, with Tyler.

I clung to his shirt. Everything was dripping—me and him, our clothes. Water splashed up off the ground as soon as it struck.

Tyler's hands were as impatient as mine as he made restless fists with my T-shirt. And then, slowly, painfully, he withdrew his lips from mine while his fingers moved up to clasp the back of my neck tenderly.

I blinked dazedly at him. An unhurried smile found my lips, which pulsed, throbbing to the beat of my pounding heart. "Damn," I whispered.

Like some sort of idiot, I couldn't stop grinning. I grinned almost the entire drive home. I grinned when Tyler pulled into my driveway to drop me off at my house—even though it was right across the street from his. I grinned more than I thought was possible when he kissed me again, and that kiss was even better than the first one, because it was slower and sweeter, and he lingered as he held my eyes with his. And then I went inside and grinned some more while I stripped out of my wet clothes and toweled my hair dry.

I was pretty sure my face was going to bust if I didn't stop all this stupid grinning. But I couldn't help it. How had I gone from completely displaced and struggling to find my way, to utter and unrestrained bliss in just six days flat?

Oh yeah, Tyler Wahl.

Damn. The boy was that good.

After I'd changed into dry clothes and tossed my wet ones in the washer, I came back to my room and checked my phone. There was a message on it from my mom:

Don't go anywhere. I'll be home soon.

Weird.

I wondered if Grant had said something to her about me being in Logan's room last night, and she'd taken it as a sign I was ready to become *one* with her perfect little family.

I sighed. I seriously hoped that wasn't the case. Sure, I was fine with taking a baby step toward getting to know them if it meant making things better—and by better I meant actually talking to my mom again. But I certainly wasn't ready to don matching Christmas sweaters or go on family picnics or anything.

Besides, what was the rush? Even if I was softening toward them, we had all the time in the world. It wasn't like I was planning to vanish again or anything.

I was just about to tell her as much, maybe something along the lines of *I'd rather poke my own eyes out with a fork than listen to you say "my brother" again* when a noise from out on the street drew my attention.

It wasn't even two o'clock yet. My mom had just texted saying she was on her way, so it couldn't be her, and Grant wasn't due home for several more hours. Stuffing my phone into my pocket, I went to the front window to take a peek. I was grinning again because I was totally hoping it was Tyler, back in my driveway to pick up where we'd left off.

I never got the chance to find out, though, because before I got to the window, I was grabbed from behind. I felt a hand go around my mouth. And I almost-sorta-*absolutely* forgot to breathe for several beats too long. I was sure it had to be a guy because his hand was big and his grip was firm. It was horrifying, because I somehow knew it wasn't a joke even before the guy started dragging me backward, which he did before I'd even remembered *how* to breathe again.

My eyes went wide as I was jerked away from the window

and lugged down the hallway, all the way to the back of the house. I'd never really been a tough girl, not in the fighting sense, but I had no intention of giving in without a fight. I kicked and thrashed like hell, flinging my legs as wide and as wildly as I could. I did my best to hook my feet through everything I could along the way, trying to stop him from dragging me. I knocked over a table in the living room, shattering a lamp when it hit the floor, and kicked over a chair once we reached the kitchen.

All I could think was that I didn't want to vanish again. *Not again . . . not again . . . not again . . .*

"*Stop it!*" a voice hissed against my ear. It was hushed and came from someone far younger than I'd imagined.

But it didn't stop me from struggling, even though I wavered for just a moment.

Then he spoke again. "If you scream, they'll know you're in trouble and come busting in after you. We only have a few minutes."

Yes, I thought. *They'll come in here and help me.* I had no idea who "they" were, but they had to be better than the guy who'd just assaulted me in my own home.

"You need to trust me, Kyra," he whispered against my ear. "I swear I'm here to help you."

This time I went still. Fainting-goat still.

We were in the kitchen now, and the moment I went limp in his arms, I questioned my own judgment. After I stopped struggling, he tentatively let go of my mouth, and when I didn't scream—not that I wasn't considering it still—he leaned over the top of me and revealed himself at last.

It was the coffee-shop boy with the strange-colored eyes.

Seeing him almost sent me over the edge again. How the hell did he, of all people, end up here in my house? And now, of all times?

His smirk was not at all reassuring. "I can see you have questions, but trust me, now isn't the time. There are a bunch of people out there coming to get you—" And as if he'd coordinated the timing to confirm his ominous prediction perfectly, there was a thunderous crashing from the front room. It sounded like someone had just set off a bomb at my front door.

And before I could ask him what the hell was happening, and who "they" were and what they wanted from me, he was hauling me to my feet. "If we don't get you out of here right now, they will take you."

We heard footsteps and voices, and then we disappeared through the already-open back door.

He kept giving me hand signals, like we were part of some covert ops mission, but I didn't understand any of them. Mostly we just snuck through the neighbors' backyards, keeping low and moving fast. When we were finally far enough from my house, hiding between the overgrown shrubs of the O'Flannerys' house, I stopped panting long enough to glare at him.

I was still shaking all over, barely able to contain myself.

"I have no idea who you are or what the hell's going on back there, but this better be the best explanation ever or I'm calling the cops myself."

He told me, "I'm Simon." And then he held his hand out to me like we were introducing ourselves at some sales convention.

I stood there looking at it like it was something strange and foreign. Was he kidding with this? He wanted to shake hands right now?

I shoved his hand away from me. "Is this some kind of joke or something? You're the guy who left the note on my receipt, and now you come into my house and kidnap me?" I knew I was being too loud, but I could barely restrain myself. This was too much.

But Simon didn't give me the chance to fall apart. "I get it. This is a shock. But let me show you something."

He drew me out from the cover of the bushes . . . not far, but far enough so I could see all the way down the street. He kept his hand on my shoulder, ready to reel me back at any moment.

The scene unfolding on my front lawn looked like something straight out of a sci-fi movie. Car doors slammed as more and more people arrived. Many were covered from head to toe in what I could only assume were hazmat or some sort of biohazard suits. Whatever they were wearing, they were intended to protect their occupants from something harmful—something dangerous.

They seemed to be everywhere, with more of them

arriving by the second. The street, for as far as I could see, was lined with polished black vehicles: cars, vans, SUVs, and something that resembled a small bus or an ambulance with doors in the back that were opened wide. Inside I could make out a stretcher and what appeared to be medical equipment.

Someone was unrolling a giant tarp, and someone else was assembling a metal frame that was surrounded on all sides by similar plastic sheeting. There was a table set up at the far end of the yard, near the road. And even from this distance, I could make out the faint crackling of radio static and saw several people talking into black handhelds.

Seriously, the only thing missing was a squadron of armed soldiers and a helicopter flying overhead.

Whatever they were collecting must be extremely hazardous.

That was when I saw him coming down the front steps of my house. Agent Truman.

He paused long enough to talk to someone in one of the hazmat suits, and then he pointed at my house and shook his head.

"Jesus," I whispered, pulling back again. I hadn't even realized I'd said it out loud. "What's *he* doing here?"

Simon caught my expression, or maybe he'd heard the fear in my voice. "So you two've met already?"

Dazedly, I shook my head and then nodded in answer to his question. "I . . . yeah . . ."

Shouting drew our attention again, and we both inched out of the shrubs in time to see Tyler running toward my house, calling my name. When he reached the sidewalk on my side of the street, he was stopped by two men who weren't in hazmat suits. I could hear him arguing with a third man who had come to stand in front of him: Agent Truman.

Instinctively, I lurched toward him, but Simon stopped me. "You can't. We have to get out of here. He'll be okay. It's not him they want." He nodded at me solemnly, and my stomach dropped. And as much as I wanted to deny what he was telling me with that silent nod, all those people in biohazard gear said otherwise.

According to Simon, it was me they were after.

"Stay close, Kyra, and when I give you the signal . . . run."

He raised his eyebrows as if to ask *Got it?*

I glared back at him: *I have no idea what you mean.*

Turns out Simon's "signal" involved waving three fingers in front of his face and then pointing toward a car—a red one with tinted windows that stood out like a sore thumb on a street that was now teeming with black government vehicles. It was parked directly across the street from us.

Then he took off running without me. What about the whole no-man-left-behind thing?

Fortunately, years on the field had trained me to think fast.

Thankfully the red car's doors were unlocked, and when we reached it we climbed inside the vehicle before I could question whether we were making a huge mistake.

"They'll hear us," I insisted in a shaky breath. "They'll see us leaving and come after us."

But Simon gave a brisk shake of his head and then nodded toward my house, which was a ways down from where we were now. Several neighbors who were home during the day had made their way out to the sidewalk, wanting to see what all the fuss was about, and Tyler was still arguing with Agent Truman. "They're way too occupied to notice us. But we have to go. Now." And somehow, before I had the chance to second-guess him, the engine rumbled to life.

I stayed low, crouched in the passenger seat, and didn't dare to peek above the dash to see if anyone had spotted us . . . or was running our way. My head was pounding and my chest ached and my breathing was coming in uneven gasps.

I don't know how we made it out of there without anyone noticing us, but the next thing I knew we were driving. Above me, through the windows, I saw houses and trees, and eventually signs from businesses zipping past us. When I was sure I wasn't going to pass out, I sat up and started checking behind us to see if anyone was following us.

But there was no one. Somehow, someway, Simon had pulled it off. He'd gotten me out of there.

I didn't know how Agent Truman and his biohazard team expected to explain what they'd done when my mom and Grant got home to find their front door broken to smithereens, but that wasn't really my problem.

To calm my beating heart, I dug my phone from my

front pocket and checked the time. It was barely three in the afternoon, which meant that the schools were just letting out and most grown-ups were counting down the last hours of their workweek before the weekend.

Me, I was on the run from the NSA.

Simon's eyes widened as he saw what I was doing. "You brought your phone? Jesus, Kyra. Have you used it? Did you call or text anyone since we left?"

Frowning, I shook my head. "No. I was just seeing what time it was." But even as I said it, I realized what the problem was. Of course the NSA would be able to track my cell phone, the same way Agent Truman had been able to track down my phone number. Obviously, privacy wasn't an issue for them. "Can they find us if I didn't use it?"

Simon ran his hand over the top of his close-cropped hair. "They can do a lot of things." He jerked the steering wheel hard to the right and slammed on the brakes, and then he held his hand out for it. "We can't take the chance. We need to ditch it," he demanded, but I was already ahead of him.

I'd taken a marker from his center console and was copying down on my hand the only two numbers—of the three in my contacts list—I didn't have memorized. My mom's number, which was new since I'd returned, and Tyler's. My dad's was the same as it had always been.

When I was finished, I handed him the phone. He opened his door and set it on the concrete, and then smashed it beneath the heel of his boot.

Simon pulled back onto the road and concentrated on driving, while I kept glancing behind us.

"Here," Simon said, pulling onto a side road that looked a little like the alley Tyler had taken me down the night we'd gone to the used books store. It was wider and seemed more warehousey, though, which turned out to be the point when Simon hopped out and unlocked a tall metal door like the ones you see on storage lockers, the kind that are hinged and rolled up.

When he got back in, he parked the car inside the garage-like space, flipped a switch that illuminated a single bare bulb overhead, and dragged the metal door closed again. It didn't exactly set me at ease.

Now I was locked inside a storage facility with the stranger who'd just kidnapped me from the authorities and smashed my cell phone. Awesome.

I stayed in the car with my fists pressed tightly on top of my knees. My teeth were clenched, and my shoulders ached. Simon scraped a lone metal chair across the concrete floor to the passenger side of the car and opened my door, propping the chair in front of me.

He straddled it and leaned forward. "I guess I have some explaining to do."

I don't know why, but when his coppery eyes drilled into me, I felt some of my tension easing. It made no sense, considering the circumstances. Still, I was here now, and after a quick perusal of the space, I realized that I probably wasn't going anywhere unless he wanted me to, so I figured

I might as well listen to what he had to say.

"That's the understatement of the century," I told him at last. "So, who the hell are you, and why have you been following me?"

He smiled, revealing a set of straight teeth that flashed against his skin. "You noticed, huh?"

My eyebrows lifted. "You weren't exactly stealthy. You practically knocked me over at the bookstore." I paused, chewing the inside of my cheek. "And what about that message . . . ?" I breathed in. "How the hell did you get that on my receipt?"

His smile faded. "Let me start at the beginning. My name is Simon Davis, and I'm like you, Kyra. I was taken too."

PART TWO

Putting out the stars and extinguishing the sun.
—Ray Bradbury, *Fahrenheit 451*

CHAPTER TWELVE

FIRST OF ALL, THERE WAS NO WAY I BELIEVED A word he'd said.

Sure, he'd saved me and all. Or at least that's what he expected me to believe. But now that I'd heard him out, I was starting to suspect I'd traded whatever Agent Truman and his band of Merry Men had in store for me for a straight-up nut job.

Besides, how did I know Simon hadn't been wrong about them? Maybe they were trying to help.

It was certainly an easier pill to swallow than the one Simon was trying to shove down my throat. If only he hadn't started his explanation with the words: "I was abducted in 1981."

Uh, yeah . . .

I mean, even if I ignored the part where he'd used the word *abducted*, I could still do simple calculations in my head. I didn't have to be a math whiz to know that, if what he'd said was true, that would put old Simon here somewhere around balding and middle-aged. And there was no way in hell that Simon—*this Simon* who was sitting right in front of me—was a day older than eighteen. Nineteen at the most.

"*Sooo . . .* ," I drawled, stretching out my skepticism to epic proportions. "You were 'abducted'"—I used air quotes in case he hadn't grasped the doubt oozing from my tone—"back in 1981 and didn't return until, what, three days ago?"

But my cynicism didn't rattle him. "No," he clarified matter-of-factly, without skipping a beat. "I was only gone a day and a half. Most of us are returned within forty-eight hours."

I wilted; my hero was looking more and more like a fruitcake. "'Most of us'?"

"Kyra," Simon offered sympathetically. "I know this is difficult to believe, but you need to hear it. People—teens, mostly—have been abducted for years. Decades. I can't say why, for sure, but we believe we're part of some kind of experiment. There is a purpose—we're sure of it; we just don't know what the end goal is yet." He reached out and placed his hand on my shoulder. "Your father isn't crazy."

I flinched. From his explanation. From his touch and

from his mention of my dad. My back dug into the gearshift behind me, and I winced. "My dad? What does he have to do with any of this? How do you even know about him?"

He dropped his hand but stayed where he was, conviction written all over his face. "Your dad—his online activity—that's how we found you. That's how we knew you'd been returned. You're the first of our kind to come back after all this time. No one's ever been returned past the forty-eight-hour mark. It's unheard of. Anyone who's ever been gone that long . . . well, they're never heard from again. We've always assumed the experiments have failed after that point. That the body . . . that it didn't survive."

I heard so many things wrong with what he'd just said that I couldn't process any of them: *our kind . . . never heard from again . . . the body . . . didn't survive . . .*

I waved my hands to ward him off even though he was no longer touching me. Hysteria was creeping in on me, threatening to consume me. My throat was swelling shut, and in a matter of seconds I was pretty sure I was going to suffocate. He was literally killing me with his words. "What the . . . ? What do you mean, 'our kind'?"

My panic was obviously visible, and Simon inhaled deeply. Watching him, the way his chest was rising and falling rhythmically, hypnotically, I swore he was prompting me to do the same. "Kyra." He inhaled. "Please." He took another slow and steady breath. "Just let me talk. I'll do my best to make sense of it, and then you can ask anything you want." He exhaled calmly, easily.

211

I squeezed my eyes closed, trying to breathe the way he was. Slowly. In and out. So very, very slowly . . .

After a few seconds I felt . . . well, okay. Who was I kidding? I still felt like I was trapped in a storage locker with a maniac, but at least I could breathe again. "Fine," I muttered. "You have five minutes. And then I'm leaving." I crossed my arms and waited for him to continue. I was angry and frustrated, but most of all confused and scared.

"Let me tell you what I remember," Simon began again, not at all rushing his explanation just because I'd decided to put him on the clock. "I remember walking to my girlfriend's house; I'd just had a fight with my parents." He looked at me as if this was somehow significant, but he kept talking. "We lived in Boise, and it was August, so even though it was getting late, I remember it was still hot as hell. Man, the mosquitoes were eatin' me alive that night." He chuckled slightly, and I wondered if he thought this was funny, because I so totally didn't. I didn't appreciate his stroll down memory lane. I just wanted his five minutes to be up already so I could tell him, "Thanks for saving me from the Men in Black, but I gotta be on my way now."

Oblivious to my surliness, Simon continued, his gaze going deep and faraway, "And then there was this light . . . and it was *so* . . . I couldn't see anything but that light." He closed his eyes as if he'd gone someplace else. Distant. Another place in time.

When he opened his eyes again, he shook his head. "I was ten miles south of home when I woke up, at a place called Lucky Peak. Almost two days had passed, and I had no idea where I'd been or what had happened to me."

I stopped sulking as I broke out in goose bumps. His story was different from mine but so very much the same all at once.

Except I'd been gone way, *way* longer.

I sat up straighter, not convinced by any stretch but a little more curious. "So how'd you figure it out? And how are you still . . ." I didn't know how old I thought he was. "Shouldn't you be like fifty or something?"

"Forty-nine," he stated, as if the answer was simple. "We just don't age at the same rate as everyone else." And then his eyes narrowed. "At the same rate as normal people."

I laughed then. A small, breathy sound, and I was frowning and grinning at the same time. "Okay, *what*?" I stopped smiling then, because it really wasn't funny. "This is . . . You're just . . ." I narrowed my eyes back at him. "Did my dad put you up to this?" I wasn't sure if I was amused or pissed, or freaked out that someone—even my own father—would go to this length to prove a point. But I was definitely alarmed.

Because Simon didn't look like he was joking. Or like anyone had put him up to anything.

He looked completely, stone-cold sober and drop-dead serious.

"What do you mean 'normal people'?" I didn't use the air quotes this time, and my voice was way, way quieter.

"I'm not saying we're not normal, Kyra. I'm just saying

we're different. We can do things other people can't after we've been returned."

I spoke slowly, like he was dim-witted. "Like not aging?"

He shook his head, a patient smile replacing his serious expression. "Not at all. We age. *I* aged. I was only fifteen when I was taken, the same way you were taken."

I shook my head because what he was saying was utter-complete-*absurd* nonsense. He was nothing like me.

He only nodded in response. "I was. And you'll age too." He was speaking slowly now, as if I was the one who didn't get it. As if I was the one who was crazy. "Just way, way, *way* slower than everyone else."

I studied him and tried to see him as fifteen. He *could be* fifteen, I supposed, if I squinted just so. But more likely he was lying, and honestly, I was getting tired of being toyed with. "Prove it," I said at last, knowing there was no way he could convince me.

"Are you sure, Kyra? You want me to prove it to you?"

"Yeah. Sure. I guess that's what I'm saying. Prove it."

And then he did the absolute last thing I anticipated: he cut himself.

The knife came out of nowhere. It was one of those pocketknives, like the Swiss Army kind that has all the gadgets. Before I could do anything—stop him or escape—it cut across the soft, unblemished skin of his forearm.

I opened my mouth to say "Oh my god!" but no words came out. All I could do was pant in jagged breaths. I twisted around in my seat then, as I searched for something to stop the blood that was already spilling from the inch-long gash he'd inflicted on himself.

"No! Kyra, don't. Just watch." His other arm was on my wrist, demanding I stop rummaging for a makeshift bandage and pay attention to what was happening on his arm.

Recoiling, I reluctantly turned back and did as he said. I looked at the cut. It was wide and deep, and I could see *far too far* inside it, and I was sure it would need stitches and probably a tetanus shot, because who knew where that blade had been before he'd *shoved it into his own arm!*

I felt queasy, and the possibility of me throwing up right there in the front seat of his car skyrocketed.

And then the weirdest thing happened, and the world beneath me spun out of control. The thing started to close. The wound—it started to heal, right before my eyes.

It was still bleeding, but the flow began to subside as the blood itself became thicker, darker, and then the edges at the ends of the slash began to . . . I had to blink to make sure I was seeing it right, but they did, they began to *seal* back together.

I sat there, mesmerized, for at least five minutes, the total time it took for the process to complete. In the grand scheme of things, it had to be some kind of miracle.

But when all was said and done, his injury had spontaneously healed in mere minutes.

There was only one question left as I sat there, staring at his perfect, completely uninjured and unscarred skin. "*What . . .* are you?"

I could've used one of Cat's tequila shots right about then. I wasn't sure I'd ever felt so disoriented, not even when I'd first come back and realized I'd lost five entire years. Or when I'd gone to the dentist and learned I hadn't aged a single day during that time.

Because what Simon was telling me now went beyond far-fetched and ventured straight into *no-freaking-way* territory.

Except that I'd just watched him heal a gash that surely needed serious medical attention in less time than it took to make Top Ramen in the microwave.

"Let me get this straight. You're saying that when we're 'returned'"—I pulled out the air quotes again because it was too weird not to use them—"we're not the same as before? And you think you were taken by . . . ?" I couldn't finish the sentence. I knew how—I just couldn't say the word.

"Aliens," he filled in for me, completely nonplussed by the whole deal.

"Seriously?" I asked, my voice chock-full of disbelief.

Simon nodded, the same way he had the other three times I'd asked the very same question, trying to phrase my doubts in different ways and hoping for a different response. "I am, Kyra. I'm saying we both were. That's what happens when we're taken. We're not the same when we come back. Not the same at all."

"And when you say 'not the same,' you're talking . . . ?" I'd never had such a hard time completing sentences in my entire life.

Simon looked at me like I was being intentionally dense. "Well, *this* for one." He held his arm up for my inspection. "Have you ever seen anyone else do that? And what about sleep? I'm guessing you haven't slept much since you've been back." He studied me, waiting for me to answer, and I wanted to deny the truth.

Really. I wanted to flat-out lie to avoid feeding his delusions, but he was right; I'd barely slept, and not in the way people say that so they have something to complain about, like it's a competition.

I shook my head and shrugged. "So, I have some insomnia issues. It's been a big adjustment. I've had a lot on my mind."

"That's not it, and you know it. You're not even tired."

He didn't bother asking if he was wrong, and he wasn't. I hadn't even considered that before this minute. That it had been five long nights without more than an hour's sleep in any given night, and I wasn't the slightest bit drowsy. I hadn't yawned once.

"What about that?" I pointed at the dried blood on his arm. "*I* can't do that."

He shot me a challenging look. "You so sure about that?"

I jolted in my seat. "Are you freaking kidding me? You don't seriously want to test it out! You're even crazier than I thought, you know that?"

Suddenly I needed to get out of there. Simon wasn't just a fruitcake, he was a *dangerous* fruitcake.

But before I could open my mouth to tell him I was taking off, either with or without a ride, he'd reached out and snatched my arm, and the edge of his blade was sliding into my wrist.

This cut was longer than his, though, probably because I'd flinched and the blade had slipped. Blood spurted out, spilling onto my lap and seeping from between my fingers as my hand instinctively shot around it, trying to staunch the seemingly endless flow.

"Why did you . . . ?" I managed. But I knew why.

I continued to stare at my arm while my chest burned.

Beneath my fingers, even while Simon was trying to pry them away from my injury, I could feel something happening. There was the sensation of hundreds of needles all around the injury—not painful but prickling.

Somewhere in the back of my mind, I remembered this feeling.

"It's okay," he promised, his voice so soothing that my pulse slowed and my breathing evened out. And without releasing my grip to look beneath my fingers, I knew he was telling me the truth, because the surge of blood began to slow. Then it stopped altogether.

I waited only a few seconds before venturing a glance. I removed first one finger and then another, peering beneath, only to find my suspicions confirmed. The wound was completely healed. Or rather, *absent*. If it hadn't been for all the blood still covering my hands and my legs and the seat of the car, I would never have believed it had been there at all.

That was when I remembered where I'd felt that before, that sensation of tingling—of skin closing and healing. It was the day I'd been in the hospital and had my blood drawn, when the guy couldn't get the needle out.

Had I healed around it? So quickly that was why he'd had to yank it back out again?

"Less than a minute." Simon breathed the words as if it was some accomplishment I should be proud of.

"What are you talking about?" I shot back at him, furious that he'd cut me at all. What if he'd been wrong? What if I hadn't healed and I'd bled out, right there in his car?

"This is a new record. No one's ever healed this fast. I had a feeling. I'm sure it has something to do with how long you were gone. They've done something different to you—to make you special."

At that moment, all I really wanted to do was kick his teeth in. I'd show him how "special" I was. But for now I had to know more. For every answer he provided, I had five questions of my own.

I continued to rub the still-tingling spot where his blade had sliced me. My fingers were covered in sticky blood that settled into my cuticles and beneath my fingernails, making dark-red crescents. "You said we were 'taken' as part of some experiment; what did you mean by that? And how can you possibly believe it was . . ." I swallowed. I had to say it. *"Aliens?"*

I had the feeling this wasn't the first time Simon had had to convince someone, and a look of patience settled over his face. He sat back and nodded. "I think you already know why, Kyra. We've been tracking your father's online comings and goings for years. You don't have to pretend he didn't try to tell you this already."

I closed my eyes and wished that were enough to block him out. How could any of this—anything my dad had said—really be true?

Yet how could I argue when I'd just witnessed my own body healing itself? Simon was right; no normal person could do that.

"When they take us, they don't just take our temperatures, or poke and prod us, Kyra. They're advanced—way more so than we are. They do things to us." His eyes met mine. "We're no longer like our old selves. Our bodies heal faster and age slower. We need less sleep and sustenance. I assume you haven't eaten much either. That nothing tastes the same."

He was right about the sleep, and the food, even if I didn't tell him so.

I swallowed, trying to make sense of what he was saying.

I looked down at my hands. They were the same hands as they'd always been. *I* was exactly the same as I'd always been. I looked the same, sounded the same, had the same tan and bruise I'd had right before I'd vanished.

Which was weird. "If I can heal, why do I still have this?" I showed him my bruise, the one on my shin.

"You had it when you vanished, right?"

I nodded because I finally had him.

"Right," he said. "And you always will. I can't explain everything; I wish I could. Occasionally someone will come back with a bruise or a scar, and if they do, they'll always have it." He lifted his sleeve to show me a circular scar on the upper part of his left arm. "I still have this—from my smallpox vaccination."

I examined his scar and then leaned over and looked at my bruise, trying to decide if it had changed, even a little bit, since I'd been back. It had been almost a week, and as much as I wanted it to be different, I was pretty sure it was exactly the same as the day I'd disappeared. "So, you're saying it'll be there the rest of my life?"

Simon nodded.

"Which is going to be, like, forever?" He didn't say anything; he just lifted his eyebrows, which I took as *Yes*. "So are you *invincible*?" I couldn't bring myself to say "we" because the whole idea was so . . . out there.

"Invincible? No. We can be killed, just not that easily. I mean, cut off our heads, and I'm sure we wouldn't just"—he made air quotes to emphasize his next word—"'heal.'" He grinned at me, letting me know he had a sense of humor about all this before continuing. "Certain poisons have been known to be lethal as well."

"And diseases?" I asked.

He shook his head. "Don't really know. So far, I've never seen any of the Returned get sick."

"The Returned?" I echoed distractedly.

"That's what we call ourselves. Those of us who've been taken and sent back."

I thought about the way I'd woken up behind the Gas 'n' Sip and tried to imagine there were others like me, who had been through the same thing I had. "But you said no one comes back after forty-eight hours. What about me? I was gone five years."

Simon's head dipped forward thoughtfully. "That's why we thought you were gone for good. We'd all but written you off. Mostly, we were still tracking your dad's activity because he keeps intel on the others who've been taken. He tracks when they go missing and from where, how long they're gone, if and when they're returned. He knows ages, dates, locations, genders, religions, family backgrounds . . . he even knows what their last meal was. He documents everything about them. He never gave up on you, you know?" My heart squeezed, knowing how easily I'd given up on him. "When we saw his post on one of his message boards that you'd come back, I left camp and drove all day to get here."

"Camp?"

Simon leaned closer. I watched his hand, the one that had, just moments earlier, yielded the pocketknife, warily. But he stretched right over the top of me and grabbed something on the floor on the other side. "There are camps where there are others. Like us." He held out a pack of Wet Ones wipes to me.

I took the container and popped the plastic top, pulling out one of the premoistened towelettes while I reflected on his words. "Is that where you live?" When he nodded, I inhaled and asked, "And what about them? Can they do this too?" I glanced down at my arm. I still wasn't sure I believed him, but I couldn't deny it completely as I wiped away the blood and there was nothing but unscathed skin beneath.

"Not quite as *efficiently* as you." I was glad he didn't say *fast*, because for once in my life this wasn't a race I wanted to be in.

"So . . . how many more are there?"

"Of the Returned?" Simon shrugged. "Who knows. Hundreds for sure. But there could be thousands. A lot of us prefer to stay together. It's safer. And that way we can network with others like us." He raised his eyebrows as he kept explaining. "Some who come back prefer to remain in isolation. They move from place to place, never getting close to anyone, not even to other Returned."

I was still confused. It was too much information at once. "Safer, how? Who exactly are you hiding *from*?"

His mouth formed a hard line. "More people than you can imagine. Scientists, crackpot conspiracy theorists, government agencies. You'd be surprised how many people would like to get their hands on . . ." He stopped midsentence, and I wondered what he'd been about to say. ". . . well, on people like *us*. I'm sure that Agent Truman was able to find you the same way we did: through your dad's online chatter. That's why I couldn't approach you sooner, Kyra. I had to make sure you hadn't been compromised."

"What does that even mean?" I asked pointedly.

"It means exactly how it sounds. I wanted to make sure Agent Truman hadn't gotten to you first. That you weren't being used as bait to lure me out."

"Bait? Are you kidding me?" I crossed my arms. "You really think they'd use me as bait to catch you?"

223

Simon leaned close, his expression so grave it nearly took my breath away. "Not just me. All of us."

I stared into his eyes, noting how much more amber they were up close than I'd first guessed, flecked with chips of gold. "So how did you know I wasn't? Compromised, I mean?"

His nostrils flared as he reached out and caught my wrist. "Because I saw them coming for you. And I knew exactly what they planned to do to you when they got you."

My throat felt tight, and my chest ached, but somehow I found my voice. "You're scaring me," I managed.

Simon didn't blink when he answered me. "Good, Kyra. You should be scared. This is serious. I know it's hard to believe, all of it, but you'd better start believing it, and fast. Your dad, as well-meaning as I'm sure he is, puts you—puts all of us—at risk. Agent Truman and those NSA guys, they'd love nothing more than to get their hands on us. You saw them—all that equipment. What did you think they wanted to do, interview you?" He gave a slow shake of his head. "No, Kyra. They do their own kinds of experiments, and they're not pretty. No one ever returns from those."

"Things like . . ." I turned a pointed glance in the direction of my arm, letting Simon know what I thought of *his* tactics. "Cutting someone open?"

"Worse," he informed me, his nostrils flaring and the muscle in his jaw leaping. *"Way, way worse."*

My mind reeled with the implications. "You mentioned

224

that some people are taken and never come back. What happens to them?"

He paused, reaching for a wet wipe and absently scrubbing at the blood on his own hands. "We think those people don't survive, like failed experiments. For all we know, we're just lab rats to the aliens. Expendable. And I've never heard of anyone who wasn't a teen being returned. Maybe we're the only ones who are ever truly taken in the first place. Maybe the rest who say they are . . ." He shrugged. "Really are just crazy."

"Teens? Why's that?"

He turned his palms over and got lost in examining them. "Beats me. Maybe because our bodies are stronger and can survive all that shit they do to us." Sitting straighter, he rubbed his hands over his knees, his eyes searching me out. "Or maybe it's just that teens are more disposable. You can yank them out of their lives for a few days and then drop them right back in, and it's just a blip on the radar. Younger kids get AMBER Alerts and milk cartons. Families send out search parties because they were likely abducted by some psycho sex offender. People are quick to give up on teens, to call them troubled or runaways . . . especially those who've been fighting with their parents." He raised his eyebrows at me.

My dad and I had been arguing.

"When we turn up again and can't remember what happened, either no one believes us or they suspect we've had some sort of drug-induced blackout." He shrugged. "You know, because that's what teenagers do." Something flashed behind his unusual eyes.

"Is that what your parents thought happened?"

"They never came out and said it, but I knew they never bought that I didn't know what happened to me." He shook his head, shrugging it off. "It doesn't matter anymore. It was a long time ago."

"Where are they now? Your parents?"

His brows squeezed together, and this time his pain was evident. "I couldn't stay. Eventually I had to distance myself from them to keep them from asking questions about why I wasn't getting any older."

"Why didn't you just tell them?" I couldn't imagine not telling my parents something so huge.

But then I knew I was lying. That had been the old me. The me from five years ago who had parents I could confide in and trust, and whose dad was her number one fan.

Now . . . I wasn't so sure.

Simon wrung his hands in front of him, and I realized the subject was just as touchy for him as it was for me. Families were a complicated matter. "I tried once." He exhaled. "I tried to tell my dad because we were close like that and I used to be able to tell him anything. But when I tried to explain . . . to tell him I'd changed . . . he wanted nothing to do with it. He said it was crazy talk, and if I ever said it again, he'd have to send me away . . . to get help." His copper-colored eyes sought mine. I thought of the way I'd shunned my dad when he'd tried to share his theories

226

with me. "We never mentioned it again, but my dad . . . he never looked at me the same after that." He curled his fingers around his knees and squeezed them while he leaned back. "I'm not the only one with a story like that, or with no place to go once the lack of aging becomes too obvious. The camp gives us a place to go and others who understand what we've been through."

The sound of a car's engine beyond the metal door made us both freeze. I held my breath as my gaze shifted between the entrance and Simon, wondering what we'd do if the NSA had somehow followed us here and was surrounding us at that very moment. From what I'd seen, there wasn't another way out.

When the car kept going, passing us by entirely, I released the breath I'd been holding.

Simon voiced the concerns I'd been keeping bottled up inside. "We can't stay here. I have no idea how long it'll be till they figure out where we are. If we leave now, we can be back at my camp sometime after midnight."

I nodded, but only because he was right about leaving. The storage space wasn't a good place to hide out.

He went to the bay door and opened it, the noise echoing off the walls around us. He checked both directions before coming back and getting in the car.

"I'm not going with you," I told Simon when he started the engine. "I have a family here." I was surprised to hear myself say the words, surprised by how strongly I felt about the thought of abandoning them again: my dad, my mom, even Logan. "And someone else."

"Yeah. Tyler Wahl. I saw you with him, at the coffee shop." He grinned at my surprised expression. "I've done my homework. I guess I also expected you to say that." Shaking his head, he forced me to meet his gaze. "I can't make you come with me, but you're taking a huge risk, Kyra, and, to be honest, I think it's a big mistake." He reached into his glove box and dug out a new cell phone. This one was way less fancy than the one he'd destroyed. "It's a burner, but it'll do the job. Plus it can't be traced to anyone. Only turn it on when you need to use it—my number's programmed."

I took the phone, relieved that he wasn't trying to stop me.

"I'll drop you someplace safe," he went on. "But you have to promise you'll be careful. You can't go back home, even if your family insists. The NSA will be waiting for you, and no matter what they or anyone else says, they can't be trusted. Understand?"

I nodded numbly.

"Be careful, and trust no one." He nodded toward the car door, indicating for me to close it. "I'll stay in town for the next twenty-four hours. But I definitely think you should reconsider coming with me. It's the safest option—for everyone. There are things about us, Kyra, that make us dangerous to be around—and I'm not just talking about the NSA. Call me when you're settled somewhere."

Simon's idea of a "safe" place was literally a travel agency called Safe Travels that he dropped me off in front of. If we'd been playing a game, which we weren't, I'd have given him minus five points for lack of creativity.

But he'd earned at least fifty bonus points when he handed me a wad of cash stuffed into a manila envelope along with a fake ID that, when I saw my face staring back at me, was so convincing I almost believed that my name really *was* Bridget Hollingsworth. As cool as the whole false-identity thing would have seemed at any other time, it was less cool right now, while I was still attempting to process what he'd just told me. About me being *different* from every-one else.

I tried to convince him there was no way I'd need the driver's license *or* the three hundred dollars he'd given me, although, to be perfectly honest, I didn't *hate* the driver's license.

But Simon had insisted I keep them both, and ultimately I'd agreed to hold on to them for the time being, with the promise that I'd give everything back once I could convince my parents to square things away with Agent Truman, which shouldn't take long. Regardless of what Simon had told me about what I could or couldn't do now, I was counting on them to clear up this whole mess with the NSA.

And then I'd start fixing things between me and my dad.

My dad, who wasn't as crazy as I'd believed. Who hadn't been wrong about aliens and abductions.

It was all still so hard to believe.

Healing within a matter of seconds. Barely needing sleep or food. Aging at a snail's pace. *Crazy.*

I caught a reflection of myself in the glass exterior of an insurance office as I strolled along the sidewalk. Slowing,

I scowled at the girl staring back at me, a girl who wasn't Bridget Hollingsworth . . . but wasn't really Kyra Agnew either. She still looked like the same girl she'd always been: dishwater-blond hair, freckles splashed across the bridge of her nose, and eyes that were too big—no matter how Tyler saw them.

I didn't want to be an anomaly. I just wanted to be the old me again.

I searched the other side of the glass, hoping to find a clock, just to get a glimpse of it so I could ground myself in the time, but there were none. Reaching up, I tucked a piece of my ordinary hair behind my ear before I turned the corner. Keeping my head down, I tried to maintain a low profile, the way Simon had warned me. It was harder than it seemed, considering my jeans were covered in smears of drying blood. When I came to a bench, I perched uneasily on the edge of the seat and pulled out my new phone and powered it on.

I called my dad three times, because he seemed most likely to believe me, but each time it went straight to voice mail, and I didn't leave a message. I didn't text him either because I didn't want to take the chance that Simon had been wrong about the burner not being traceable. I figured I'd try him again later.

My knees bounced up and down nervously as I punched in a different number, waiting for someone to answer on the other end. I was afraid that what Simon had told me would change everything. But I was afraid, too, that everything had already been changed because of Agent Truman and his men.

"Hello?" The voice was tentative, and I hoped it was just because I was calling from an unfamiliar number.

I hesitated, but only for a second before exhaling into the mouthpiece. "Tyler?"

He didn't say anything at first. There was a pause, and shuffling. It stretched out, and after a minute I started to worry about whether he was coming back at all. Then I heard him, his voice a sharp whisper. "*Kyra? Where are you? I've been trying to reach you. What's going on?*"

I shook my head. "I can't explain right now. What's going on over there?" My palms were sweaty, which seemed like a "normal person" thing to do. "Are those people . . . are they still at my house?"

"Most of them are gone now." His voice was still hushed but insistent. "But they were here, and they were asking questions about you, asking my parents and me if we knew where you were. What did you do?" He stopped talking, and then, with just the barest hint of a laugh because I swear he couldn't help himself, he added, "You know I was only joking when I asked if you were planning to knock off a bank."

I wanted to laugh, too, but instead I groaned. "I wish it was that simple," I admitted. "Can you get away without anyone knowing? I'll tell you everything if you meet me."

"My dad would shit a brick if he knew I was even talking to you. He got all 'yes, sir' and 'no, sir' when he was talking to that douche bag agent guy." My heart sank. I'd been sure I could count on Tyler. And then his voice, husky and absurdly beautiful, found me from the other end. "So of course I'll be there. Name the place."

And despite the whole crappy situation, I smiled.

CHAPTER THIRTEEN

I KNEW THE SOFTBALL FIELD WAS A BAD IDEA.
Agent Truman had already followed me there once; it made
sense he'd think to look there again, waiting for his chance
to pounce on me.

That was why I didn't choose the softball field. I picked
the bookstore instead.

I had a hard time believing Agent Truman knew anything about Tyler's bookstore. Still, I couldn't afford to take
any chances. I stayed hidden behind one of the gross, garbage-
filled Dumpsters in the alley, waiting until I was sure Tyler
had come alone. And until I couldn't stand the stench of

warm rot emanating from inside the giant metal bin any longer.

When he got out of his car, I made the *psst* sound at him until I got his attention.

Despite the cloak-and-dagger circumstances, a spark lit up his face when he saw me, making me realize he had been the exact right person to call. At least until he got a good look at me.

"What the hell?" The grin fell from his face as his eyes raked over my blood-covered jeans. He gripped my arms, making it impossible to avoid his inspection.

"Don't worry. It's mine." I tried to laugh it off. "I'm fine. Really."

But my explanation had the opposite effect, and his expression shifted from frown to scowl. He reached for my hand and dragged me toward the bookstore's back entrance, again not bothering to knock, just letting us inside. "What the hell happened to you?" he demanded. "First those government guys surround your house and ask a shitload of questions. And then you turn up covered in . . ." His eyes were so much softer than his tone as they captured mine. It would have been impossible *not* to see the fear in them. ". . . It is blood, right?"

I nodded, guilt welling up inside me. He didn't need to be involved in my mess.

I guess I do have another option, I thought, feeling the manila envelope crumpled up in my back pocket. I could always run away with Simon and actually *become* Bridget

Hollingsworth. Essentially, I could start over.

The idea had its merits.

But so did staying here.

Because *here* meant Tyler.

Tyler, who was watching me with his incredibly sympathetic green eyes and who had a dimple to die for and kisses that made me forget my name—the real one and my fake one. And who was reaching for me now in spite of the fact that I had blood smeared all over my clothes.

When his arms circled me and he pulled me up against him, his chin settling on top of my head, I breathed in and braced myself. I could do this.

"Remember when you said if I believe it, you believe it?" I raised my eyes to his. He frowned back down at me, the weight of that look like lead settling over my chest. "You might want to wait till you hear what else I have to say."

Tyler was a way better listener than I had been. He didn't interrupt me the way I had Simon. In fact, the only interruption to my explanation had been Jackson, who'd come into the back room to locate a book he'd put on hold for a customer. He offered us a sheepish apology for the disruption, even though *we* were the ones hiding out in *his* bookstore. He cast a few awkward glances my way, making me even more uncomfortable about the fact that we'd made ourselves at home in the dark recesses of the cluttered storeroom.

Tyler didn't seem at all uneasy and was so focused on me that he barely registered Jackson's presence at all. He offered his friend a quick nod but impatiently waited for me to continue my explanation after Jackson slipped back into the front of the bookstore once more.

Relaying the things Simon had told me was harder than I'd expected, and I'd expected it to be damn near impossible. I'd worried that Tyler was going to up and bolt at any second, because hearing myself repeat the information, hearing the way it sounded coming out of my mouth, it seemed even stranger and more far-fetched than it had when I'd been in his shoes.

I was sure I was forgetting to relay some vital piece of information, something that would convince him I didn't deserve to be carried away by Agent Truman and his agents in one of their black vans with the tinted windows. I tried to make it sound somehow logical that I was going to age slower than everyone else and that I no longer needed normal amounts of sleep or food.

Tyler didn't comment.

Heck, he barely blinked.

He just did that thing where he went all silent and introspective, as if he was assessing every word. Every syllable while I sat there, terrified I was losing him.

My chest tightened as I waited for his verdict. And then I realized what it was I'd forgotten.

"Here. Let me show you." I rotated on the overturned crate I was sitting on across from Tyler.

I spied the box knife on top of a stack of old magazines. It was the kind with one of those razor blades that can be raised and lowered with just the flick of a thumb. I snatched it and, before I could chicken out, took a deep breath and flipped my wrist over, ready to slice into my own flesh.

But before I could prove I wasn't lying about my ability to heal—that what I'd told him was the God's honest truth—Tyler's hand shot out and snagged mine. "Have you lost your mind? There's no way I'm letting you cut yourself."

I looked up, searching his earnest green eyes. I wished I knew what he was thinking, wished I could see inside his head.

I lowered the blade, nodding considerately. Because I didn't have to be a mind reader to recognize that look: I'd pushed him too far.

"I understand," I said at last when I couldn't take another minute of his placating gaze. It was the same look I'd given my dad when he'd first tried to tell me where he thought I'd been for five years. Humor mixed with pity. "I get it. It's too weird. Accepting that I'm still sixteen is one thing, but this . . . that I was abducted and experimented on . . . by aliens . . ." I made a face to drive my point home. "It's too much. I know how it sounds, and if I were you, I wouldn't want anything to do with me. I mean . . ." I looked down at myself, at the blood on my jeans and at the box knife in my hand, and let out a derisive laugh. "*So crazy*, right?" There was nothing more for me to say. Nothing I could do but wait for him to make up his mind about whether he was okay with this. With me.

Tyler's grip on my hand tightened. "You think I won't

believe you unless you cut yourself? You think you have to prove yourself by showing me what you can do? Jesus, Kyra. *Jesus.* Haven't I already convinced you . . . I *trust* you." He loosened his hold, and without thinking, I did too. The box knife dropped to the floor between us.

Tyler got up and stared down at me. "You're stupid," he stated matter-of-factly, and I shot to my feet, immediately taking offense.

"*You're* stupid."

He laughed then. "No, I mean you're stupid if you think I'd give up on you that easily."

My voice lowered to barely a whisper. "But even if you believe it . . . how can you even want . . . ? God, it's just so . . ." I exhaled, trying to get rid of all the awkwardness bundled up inside me, vibrating my every nerve fiber. "I'm not going to age, Tyler. I'm a freak."

"Okay, now you're just insulting me." Tyler reached over and put his finger beneath my chin, dragging my eyes to his. Not that I'd want to look anywhere else. I could stare into those eyes for the rest of my life—which, evidently, was a lot longer than his would be. "God, Kyr. I don't care about any of that." His finger moved away from my chin and lingered near my jaw, caressing, stroking, making it hard to pay attention to his words. "I care about you. *You*, Kyra. The you I know. The you I might be falling in love with. It doesn't matter to me how old you are or *will be*; all I care about is *who* you are, and that hasn't changed from this morning. You can't stand there and tell me you're not that same girl, because I'm telling you, *you are*. You're more perfect than anyone I know." His hands slid up to my cheeks until he was holding my face. His mouth was mere millimeters from mine, and I could taste the intensity behind his words as his breath fused with my own. "The person you are has nothing to do with anything you've just told me about healing or aging. It's your memories and life experiences, your hopes and fears and dreams and passions that make you who you are, and none of those things have changed, have they?"

I shook my head, fervently wanting to feel half his passion as our lips nearly brushed. My breathing was already coming in shallow gasps, and my eyes stung as I blinked to hold back my tears. It hadn't escaped my notice that he'd said he might be falling in love with me.

His grip on my face remained secure. "I'm glad. I'm glad you're back here with me. I'm glad you're mine instead of Austin's." His lips were soft as they grazed mine at long, *long* last. "And," he said, pulling away just enough so he could add one more thing, "everyone else will feel the same way I do if you just give them a chance. If you don't believe that, then you're underestimating them. They're your family. They love you."

I grinned, unable to stop myself. "They'll be glad I'm yours?" I teased.

He dropped his hands to my waist and tugged me until my hips were pressed against his. "You know what I mean. I think you need to tell your parents the truth. What you told me. They'll help you figure out how to handle that agent guy, and if he's really as dangerous as you say he is, they'll keep you safe. That's they're job. That's what parents do."

Tyler stopped talking, and his eyes flicked down to my lips, lingering and clouding over. He inhaled, as if it was taking every last ounce of will to keep from kissing me, and I didn't want him to hold back. I wanted him to give in. I wanted to feel like a normal girl. Like me. So I stepped up, balancing on my tiptoes, and wrapped my fingers around the back of his neck.

He surrendered easily, lowering his head in an instant. A sound somewhere between a growl and a moan escaped his throat the moment his mouth covered mine.

And then we were lost, the two of us. And I no longer cared about whether I was a normal sixteen-year-old girl . . . or something different. Because I was Tyler's.

He'd said as much with that amazingly perfect, ravenous kiss.

It was that very same kiss, though, that masked the footsteps. And it was the kiss, too, that kept me off guard, making me unaware that we were no longer alone.

It wasn't until I heard the click—until we both heard the click—that we jumped apart. My lips were still swollen and pulsing, but my heart raced like mad.

I fixated on the gun, so when the guy spoke, it took me a second to realize it wasn't Agent Truman talking. "Don't move." The voice—and the gun too—crushed any hope I'd had that everything was going to be okay, that I would just go back to being plain old Kyra Agnew, regular girl. The guy behind the gun was a younger, fresher-faced version of the stiff NSA agent who'd been shadowing me wherever I went.

Like the others back at my house, this agent had one of those walkie-talkie things, and he lifted it to his mouth and pressed a button. "I found her," he spoke into the crackling radio. "We're at . . ." He shot a quick glance at Jackson, who was cowering in the doorway behind him. "Where are we?"

"Second-Chance Comics and Books. On Pine," Jackson answered, keeping his gaze on the gun in the agent's other hand, the one he was holding on Tyler and me.

The agent repeated what Jackson said into the radio and then told Jackson, "Good. Now go out front and wait for someone to arrive so they know where to find us."

Jackson flashed Tyler an I'm-sorry expression even though he didn't say a word. He avoided my gaze altogether and did as he was instructed, leaving us alone with the young NSA agent.

"What do you want?" Tyler asked the agent, taking the lead and moving to stand in front of me, putting me out of the path of the gun.

I didn't have a plan—everything was happening too fast to think. But I didn't stay where Tyler put me. Instead, I reached down and snatched the box knife off the floor, clutching it in my palm.

The agent saw what I'd done, probably because I hadn't been exactly subtle about it, but he stayed where he was, his gun still cocked and trained on the two of us. I didn't blame him, really. I guess he'd heard the expression "You don't bring a knife to a gunfight."

"Son," the agent said to Tyler like he was decades older than we were, even though he looked like he'd barely graduated from whatever training academy the NSA sent their agents to. "You need to step away from the girl. You have no idea what you're dealing with here. She's putting you in danger."

That was when I realized it, the way the agent held the gun. He'd never really been pointing it at me at all.

He'd kept it aimed at Tyler the entire time. And the way he looked at me, all meaningful, the way he challenged me with his steady gaze, made it more than clear that he was in on my little secret, and he suspected the same thing I did: that it wouldn't do any good to shoot me.

Not that I was immune to pain or anything—I'd definitely *felt* the blade when Simon had cut me. But I'd healed all the same. And, most likely, if what I'd learned then was true, I'd probably heal from a gunshot too.

Tyler . . . not so much.

"Turn yourself in," he told me, "and no one has to get hurt."

"Don't do it, Kyr," Tyler ordered, his eyes never straying from the agent's. He reached into his pocket and tossed me his keys. "Run." He said it so calmly it was hard to believe he'd even noticed the gun at all. "Get out of here. Now!"

I looked from Tyler to the agent with the gun and down to the gun itself. There was no way I was leaving him.

It was over. The NSA had found my Achilles' heel.

Still clutching the box cutter, I held up both hands, showing the agent that I surrendered.

Grinning with a kind of condescending arrogance, the agent took a step toward me. "I knew you'd make the right choi—" He stopped then, right where he was, midsentence and midstride. His eyes flicked down to my right arm, falling to my wrist.

I looked too.

A trickle of blood made its way down my arm from my closed fist where I clutched the razor-sharp blade curled against my palm. I recoiled, opening my fingers, but it was too late. The blade had already done its job, cutting a wide trench across my hand.

The pain was there again, a sting that started in the cut and burned all the way up my arm to my shoulder.

"Kyra!" Tyler started to lunge for me but stopped himself. His eyes were trained uncertainly on my injury, and I suddenly hoped he wasn't one of those people who fainted at the sight of blood.

"It's okay," I told him, nearly forgetting we weren't alone. "Wait . . . watch." Already I could feel the telltale prickling sensation that told me the wound was beginning to heal. The tingling that meant my body was working. "It's okay. It'll heal."

But he was shaking his head, his actions slow and skeptical. Despite everything he'd said, he hadn't been entirely convinced. He remained where he was, transfixed, and he saw the same thing I saw.

It did heal. Same way as before. First the flow of blood around my palm became a mere trickle. And then the wound began to mend itself. To close, until there was nothing but the streaks of blood to indicate it had ever existed at all.

Tyler was still shaking his head when the agent lifted the walkie-talkie to his mouth. "We have a situation here," he stated numbly, his eyes as wide as Tyler's. *"I repeat,"* he said, this time taking an entire step back from us, "we have a . . ." His eyes dropped again to the blood that had dribbled down my arm. I didn't know this guy, but if I had to guess, I'd say something about me or my cut had frightened him. "We have a Code Red," he finished.

He lowered his weapon. "Come with me, son," he said to Tyler, using the barrel of the gun as a pointer, indicating Tyler should step away from me too.

When we heard a door opening at the front of the store, the agent stopped backing up and whispered to Tyler, "It's too late for both of us." And then he closed his eyes and lifted his gun to his temple.

I gaped at him, at the scene unfolding in front of me, wondering what the—

But Tyler didn't hesitate. He grabbed my hand, the one without the newly healed cut on its palm, and he dragged me. We were running when we reached the door that led to the alley, and were still running when we spilled out into the narrow, garbage-filled street, to his awaiting car beyond.

Running away from the earsplitting sound of the gun-shot that came from the bookstore behind us.

★ ★ ★

We sat dazedly in Tyler's car while we tried to collect ourselves after what we'd just witnessed, which we still weren't entirely clear about. Had that agent really just shot himself?

Tyler recovered before I did. I wiped the blood on my already-stained jeans and stared blankly out the windshield at the quiet street beyond, trying to take a page from Tyler, the way he seemed to be able to channel that silent inner calm whenever he was thinking. It was hard, though. I wasn't like him.

Are you sure? I silently asked, my brows pinching together as I nervously gripped the cell phone he'd handed me. I'd already tried calling my dad again, convinced it would be easier to explain things to him since he already believed half the stuff I had to say.

Turning to my mom was an entirely different story. She'd always been more practical than he was. She was all about facts and numbers and puzzles—things that made sense. Things that were normal and fit and didn't disturb the status quo.

Things *unlike* my dad and his alien conspiracy theories. And surely unlike a daughter who was no longer like everyone else.

Tyler clutched my hand. *It'll be okay,* his squeeze assured me.

I glanced down at the scribbling on my damp palm—the one I hadn't cut—surprised that the marker had survived all the perspiration and blood and scrubbing with Wet Ones.

The numbers were blurred around the edges, but it was still my handwriting, exactly the same as it had always been—reassuring considering so much else about me wasn't.

I checked the time and then dialed hastily, before I could change my mind. Holding my breath, I waited to find out if Tyler was right or not.

Even though no one said hello when the phone stopped ringing, I knew it had been answered. "Mom?" My voice was timid and shaky.

"Kyra? Oh my god, where are you? I told you to stay home." Her words came out in a rush, her relief audible.

"Mom, I need you to listen to me. There were these guys from the National Security Agency who came to the house—you can't trust them. I can't explain why right now, but you have to believe me. They're after me, and they want to hurt me." I looked to Tyler for strength before going on. I choked on a breathy chuckle. "I know it sounds like I've been drinking from Dad's crazy Kool-Aid, but what I'm saying is true. These guys are bad, Mom. Don't tell them anything." When she didn't respond right away, I asked uncertainly, "Mom? Did you hear me?"

There was a pause, and then my mom repeated, her voice quieter, more hesitant than before, "Where are you now? I . . . I can come get you."

I heard someone else then, in the background. It was Tamara Wahl. "Is Tyler with her? Ask her if Tyler's with her. Is he okay . . . ?" It was strange, the way her voice warbled, and I knew even without seeing her that she'd been crying.

The end of her sentence trailed off, like she'd been dragged away from the phone.

It was all so weird, I wasn't sure what to make of it.

"I—I can't tell you where I am right now." I shifted, intentionally avoiding Tyler's attentive gaze. And then things started to click into place. "He's . . . he's not there now, is he? The NSA guy I was telling you about?"

"Kyra, please. He says you need help." Her voice cracked when she tried to talk this time, and I could hear her trying not to fall apart the same way Tamara Wahl had. "He says you were infected with whatever that guy from Skagit General Hospital had. He says you're contagious." She was shouting now, and I didn't know if she was shouting at me or just shouting because she wanted me to pay attention to her. "He says you're a danger to others, Kyra! He says you need to come in right away to be treated—" Her voice broke, and I could picture her covering her mouth.

Contagious? No wonder Tamara Wahl had been crying— she probably believed it, too, that I was out here infecting Tyler as we spoke.

I shook my head. "He's lying, Mom. I'm not infected with anything. That's not what he wants from me. He wants to do experiments—to hurt me."

But when she answered me, there wasn't a hint of flexibility, and she no longer sounded like she was losing it. "No, Kyra, you're wrong. You're confused. You need to turn yourself in so he can help. That's all he wants, is to help you. They all just want to help before it's too late."

My face fell as I turned to stare out the side window. "Mom—"

I thought about the message she'd left me, the text that had been on my phone right before the people from the NSA had pulled up in front of our house: *Don't go anywhere. I'll be home soon.*

She hadn't been on her way home. She'd known then. Agent Truman had gotten to her and filled her head with lies, and she'd given him permission to come and take me. To "help" me.

For all Tyler's words about family and that it was a parent's job to protect us no matter what, my mother had been willing to hand me over to a bunch of strangers who'd lied to her, without even talking to me.

Simon was right; I couldn't trust anyone.

Not even my own mother. *My mom.*

I hung up on her and sat there clutching the cell phone in my fist while tears streamed down my face. I wondered why—when I'd been taken—they couldn't have stripped me of my emotions too. Because it sucked to feel this way: betrayed and alone.

Tyler didn't move or say anything right away. He knew, of course. It was written all over my tear-streaked face.

And then the phone in my hand made a strange, clicking sound, and my eyes flew wide as I gaped at it. The call was over. But the phone had come back to life, and the screen was all lit up.

The message on the face flashed: CONNECTING . . .

CONNECTING . . .

"Dammit," I cursed, throwing the phone—Tyler's phone—away from me. How had I been so careless, so stupid? Of course they'd traced the call. Agent Truman had probably been there the whole time, standing over my mother's shoulder as he listened in on us, tapping the phone line to find out exactly where we were. *"Dammit, dammit, dammit!"*

Tyler was reaching for his keys now, too, understanding clear on his face as he snatched the phone and chucked it out the driver's side window. "Let's get outta here."

Standing at the open door to my dad's trailer, it was hard to say for sure if his place had been trashed or not.

Using the disposable cell phone Simon had given me, I had dialed my dad's number at least half a dozen times on our way to his place. When he didn't answer any of my calls, I'd finally turned off the phone and thrown it on the seat between us.

"It's gonna be okay," Tyler had offered consolingly. "When we get there you can talk to him in person. If anyone'll understand, it's him."

"Yeah?" I'd challenged, in no mood to be comforted. "That's what you said about my mom."

I'd shut down for the rest of the drive, sulking because I was good at it—always had been. It wasn't Tyler's fault, but it was easier to be pissed at him than to admit how terrified I was. I didn't want my dad to turn on me the way my mom had.

"Looks like they've already been here," Tyler said when

we saw the wreckage, which would have been stating the obvious if I hadn't already seen my dad's place on a "normal" day.

"I don't know . . . it's hard to tell." I had no way of knowing whether the unlocked door should alarm me, but I stepped inside cautiously, kicking scattered newspaper out of my way. There were dirty dishes piled in the sink and on the countertops, and stacked on the kitchen table.

I assumed Tyler picked up on my meaning and wisely chose not to state the obvious, that my dad's place was gross.

But beyond the grossness of it, something felt off. The skin at the back of my neck stretched tight, and the tiny hairs at the nape stood on end. "Nancy!" I called out, wishing more than anything that the mutty dog would lope in and greet me sloppily with her molten-brown eyes and her big, fat, juicy tongue. I thought about the way she'd placed her head in my lap and stared up at me all dreamily. She wouldn't spurn me just because some stupid agent told her I was no longer who she thought I should be.

My hopeful plea was met with silence while that something-is-off feeling nagged at me.

I walked warily toward the hallway, kicking more and more of the litter out of my path, until it no longer seemed like just the clutter of a drunken slob. I looked down, paying more attention to the debris in my way, and recognized the papers I was wading through.

These were my father's files and clippings, his maps and charts and missing-person fliers, all leading the way to his room like a haphazard trail. The door at the end of the hall-way stood ajar, but it was the handprint on the door that made me stop dead in my tracks.

"Dad?" I called out, dread snaking its way around my windpipe. I was terrified about what I might find on the other side of that door.

Behind me, Tyler reached for my hand, and every muscle in my body tensed. "You stay out here," he whispered, but I shook my head vehemently.

"I need to know." And even though my voice shook, I'd already made up my mind. I needed to see for myself if that was my dad's bloodied handprint. To know without a doubt if he was in there. Because if he was, it was all my fault.

I reached out and pushed the door open. I went into the tiny bedroom that my dad had been using for five long years to track others like me . . . those who'd been taken.

Once inside, I turned all the way around so I could see into every corner and every crevice of the tiny space.

The small bedroom-turned-office had been destroyed. Pictures had been ripped from the walls and were strewn across the desk and floors, some intact and some ripped to shreds. Same thing with the maps and charts. It was in a state of shambles.

But I didn't give a crap about any of that. All I cared about was that my dad wasn't there.

He was gone.

"Where do you think he is?" Tyler asked, and I jolted, nearly forgetting I wasn't alone.

I knew, too, that I could no longer put Tyler at risk simply because I wanted his help. I'd already put him in too much danger.

I shrugged and shook my head at the same time, hoping more than anything that my dad had managed to get someplace safe.

Tyler held his hand out to me, and I took it, our hands fitting together seamlessly. The idea of leaving him was nearly unbearable, like losing part of myself—something I understood all too well.

As I let him pull me along, something in the wreckage caught my attention, and I hesitated.

"Hold on a sec." I pulled my hand from his, reaching for the picture that was jumbled in with all the rest. A photograph.

I bent down, brushing aside broken glass to pluck it free. Beneath the first photograph was another. And beneath those, another and another.

I recognized all the images despite never having seen anything like them in real life. Fireflies. Picture after picture of fireflies.

There were faraway images of swarms and incredibly detailed close-ups. Others were artistic—shots taken in the night sky, making the fireflies look like stars against the black canvas of night—and others still that were clinical feeling and stark, in which you could make out each and every detail of the insects, right down to their delicate antennae and bulging round eyes. It was as if my dad had been studying the insects.

At the bottom of the haphazard pile was an image I'd seen before. I hadn't made the connection between it and the nocturnal luminaries, with their delicate, vein-laced and swirl-tipped wings.

My fingers traced the image as I tried to recall the first time I'd seen it: the beetle-like version that depicted what a firefly looked like at rest . . . and burnished in gold.

Just like it had been in the center of Agent Truman's badge. It hadn't been a golden beetle at all. It had been a firefly.

My thoughts were interrupted when a single drop of blood fell onto the photo from above me. It landed right in the center of the picture and splattered outward, blooming like a flower. A feeling of icy alarm settled over me as I turned to glance over my shoulder.

I'd half expected to find my father there, with his bloodied hands outstretched to me.

But it wasn't my father. It was Tyler, standing above me and studying the same images I was.

"Your nose." I let the picture flutter to the floor. "Tyler, you're bleeding."

He frowned at me before using the back of his hand to check for himself. "You've got to be—" He shook his head, perplexed. "I haven't had a bloody nose since I was a kid."

But I was already on my feet and running toward the bathroom, kicking litter out of my way. When I came back, I handed him a wad of toilet paper. "I think you're supposed to lean your head back. And pinch your nose. I think you're supposed to pinch it."

He did as I said, and without taking the paper away, he dropped his gaze and grinned at me. "So you're saying I'm *not* gonna miraculously heal the way you did? I thought maybe some of your superpowers might rub off on me."

I rolled my eyes, wondering how he could possibly make jokes during a situation like this. It would be hard to leave him when the time came. "They're not superpowers." I smirked back at him. He sounded ridiculous with all that toilet paper bunched up and plugging his nose. I grinned. "And I'm pretty sure they don't work that way." I nudged him with my shoulder as I shoved past him back into my dad's room. "I just want to grab a few things and then we need to get out of here before anyone catches us. I was hoping my dad would be here. I have so many questions, and I think he might have some of the answers I need." It felt so strange to admit that out loud, that my dad had been right after all. I looked around at the room. At the ripped papers and broken glass. Even the computer monitor had been smashed. I couldn't bear to think that he might've been harmed because of me. "I just hope he's okay."

"Me too." Tyler's voice came out muffled by the toilet paper.

I began collecting what I could find, anything that looked even remotely useful, although most of it looked like junk. I gathered the firefly images and a map with a bunch of colorful dots and lines my dad had drawn, along with the one missing-person flier I couldn't ignore: the one of me.

While I was searching, I found the ball from the first

baseball team I'd ever been on, back when I was in the first grade—when the boys and girls still played together. Our parents had signed Austin and me up for the same team, and my dad had volunteered to be our coach.

This was the very same ball Austin had hurled through my bedroom window after I'd accused him of throwing like a girl. His parents had grounded him for a whole week for breaking my window—one day for every year he'd been alive on this earth.

And for an entire week I'd regretted taunting him, because for seven painfully long days I'd had to come home from school and play all by myself. I'd lost my best friend because I'd made fun of the way he threw.

My dad, though, had saved that ball. He said it was one of his favorite mementos. I used to think he meant because it was from our first game—his as our coach and mine as a player. But now that I thought of it, I wonder if it was more than that. I wonder if it was because of the lesson I'd learned, about how to treat those I cared about.

My dad had always been big on the power of words and respect.

"The tongue pierces deeper than the spear," he'd told me when I'd complained about Austin's punishment. And even though I knew he was trying to teach me some sort of lesson, all I could remember thinking was that it was too bad it wasn't true, because how cool would it be if our tongues really were spears? First graders thought of things like that, I guess.

"We better get moving," I told Tyler, putting the ball back. He had his own collection of things, and I appraised his findings with a dubious eye. His nose had stopped bleeding, and his toilet paper compress was gone.

"What do you think?" he asked, holding up a fanny pack by its strap. "You think your dad would mind if I kept this?"

I made a face at him. How long had my dad been holding on to that relic? "Are you kidding? You're not seriously planning to wear that thing, are you?"

"You never know when you'll need both hands free." He strapped it around his waist and started filling it with the things he'd gathered: some newspaper and magazine clippings, a USB thumb drive that had been lying beneath the papers on the floor, and a CD with a handwritten *2009–2014* scrawled across it.

"This isn't a looting mission."

He looked meaningfully at all the junk in my hands. "Are you sure about that? Here, I bet you can fit all your stuff in this thing." He held the pouch open for me.

"I'm not letting *my stuff* touch *that thing*. My hands work just fine. You know your nerd status just shot up like a million points, don't you?" I didn't tell him the real reason I wasn't sharing space in his fanny pack, that I wasn't planning to go with him.

He shrugged like it was no big deal, but I loved that he didn't care that he was making a fool of himself with that ridiculous pouch.

His eyes shot skyward as his body went entirely rigid.

"*Shh!*" The crooked grin melted from his face. "Did you hear that?" His head cocked slightly, and he strained—we both strained—to find whatever it was he thought he'd heard.

"No," I whispered, slightly thrown by the sudden shift in his demeanor. "I don't . . ." But I'd spoken too soon. It was there, and now, just barely and so faraway, I could hear it too. My throat ached, and I nodded this time. "We're too late."

The *whomp-whomp-whomp* sound of the approaching helicopter pounded within my chest and beat through my veins. I felt more human in that instant than I had in my entire life. More mortal. More defenseless and exposed, even within the suddenly-too-cramped walls of my father's trailer.

"I have to go," I said. I bundled the missing-person flier and the map and the prints of the fireflies into a roll and stuffed them into my back pocket, right next to the envelope Simon had given me.

I made my way to the front of the trailer, where it was gloomier now that the sun had set. I didn't turn on any lights along the way. Tyler was right on my heels, following me closely, and he'd noticed my slip. "You said 'I.' You said '*I* have to go,' Kyra, and I don't care what you think, but you're not leaving me behind."

Reaching the front door, I pulled back the musty-smelling curtain that drooped limply over the glass and realized how useless the curtains in my dad's crappy trailer were. They were textured. The surface of the glass was bumpy, meant

257

for privacy rather than for visibility. He might as well have covered the windows with newspaper or tinfoil. All I could make out was the darkness beyond.

"I don't have time to argue," I shot back. "But you can't go with me. Stay here and tell them this was all some sort of mix-up. That you didn't know anything about me and what I am." I dropped the curtain, ignoring the dust that puffed up when I did.

Tyler grabbed my arm and forced me to face him. "Kyra, stop being so stubborn." When I opened my mouth to argue, he cut me off. "No. I mean it. You're being stupid again, and this time not the good kind. You're out of your mind if you think I'm not going with you."

Bright lights filtered in through the impractical privacy windows and filled the darkened trailer, casting blurred beams along the wood-paneled walls. Others came from above, accompanied by the louder, and much closer, *whomp-whomp* noises of the helicopter, which was right on top of us now. They came from the window over the sink and the opaque skylight that was obscured by layers of fir needles and caked-on dirt.

I reached for Tyler's hand, deciding that now wasn't the time to argue over whether I would let him stay with me or not, because I didn't think either of us was getting out of this mess anyway.

Red and blue lights washed over Tyler's skin as his lips tightened. "Come on." He hauled me back toward my dad's trashed office. He ripped the curtain rod off the wall, where it had hung above the window, and pressed his face to the rough-surfaced glass. "I don't see any lights out there. If we hurry, we might be able to slip out back before they catch us."

"And then what? What will we do? Where are we gonna go?" I hated that I was saying this, but it needed to be said. "Tyler, *please*. Just stay here. You'll be safer that way."

He ignored me. Flat-out acted like he hadn't even heard me.

"Here," he ordered, tugging the crank on the window, because that was the kind of window it was. It didn't move, not even an inch, as if it were glued in place. "Shit," he cursed, growing more agitated by the second. The helicopter sounded like it was right on top of us now, making it almost impossible to hear ourselves.

No longer uncertain, Tyler reached for the broken computer monitor. Without skipping a beat, he hurled it through the window. The noise of shattering glass was swallowed by the helicopter that was right overhead. I kept looking behind us, checking the hallway, and the door beyond, waiting to be swarmed by the agents outside. My entire body was shaking, and I thought I was going to hyperventilate as I wheezed for each breath.

Tyler, though, was single-minded. Shielding his eyes, he used a heavy book to break out the remaining shards and then pulled off his hoodie, spreading it over the bottom edge of the opening.

"Come on," he told me, cupping his hands together

beneath the windowsill and motioning for me to step into them so he could hoist me over the edge.

Without the window's glass in place, the sounds from outside echoed all around us. Not only could we hear the helicopter, with its constantly rotating blades, but we could make out voices shouting and car doors slamming. They were coming.

Behind us, the sound of the trailer's front door crashing made me jump, and without waiting, or looking back, I went for it, lunging toward Tyler. I dropped my foot into his hands and let him throw me through the broken window. I didn't have my balance, though, and when I landed on the other side, I fell on my hands and knees in the pool of broken glass. My heart was trying to pound its way out of my chest, and I barely had time to glance at my hands to see if I'd been hurt when Tyler was coming through the window right behind me, landing more gracefully than I had.

Somewhat shakily, I stood upright, relieved that we'd made it.

Until I heard Agent Truman, and my skin prickled. "We've got you surrounded. There's no point trying to run."

Even if he hadn't said we were surrounded, I saw his gun. And he aimed it the same way the agent from the bookstore had. At Tyler.

I sagged, letting his frigid words settle over me. Letting the weight of their meaning—like an iceberg—crush me.

This was it. There was no more hope of leaving Tyler behind, because now all I could do was turn myself in and hope Simon was wrong.

"Kyra!" Tyler had to shout to be heard above the helicopter overhead.

When I turned to him, in the darkness behind the trailer, I was confused about why he'd said my name in the first place, because he wasn't even looking at me. His eyes never strayed from Agent Truman.

Yet all the same, I felt him slip something into my hand. Agent Truman continued to stare Tyler down, unaware of what had just passed between us.

And then, buried in the constant *whomp-whomp* of the helicopter's blades, I thought I heard Tyler say, "You know what to do."

I wasn't sure I did at first, but then I squeezed my fingers around the laces of the ball Tyler had placed there, and I remembered that night at the ball field, when I'd tossed the ball at Tyler . . . when I'd nearly ripped a hole through the backstop.

Without a word, Tyler's eyes slipped to mine. I don't know how he conveyed it, or even if he did, but I swear he told me *You can do this* with that look.

And I believed him.

Agent Truman's expression narrowed suspiciously as he surveyed us, and his gun moved to me. "Don't do anything stupid," he commanded. "I won't shoot you," he added, making a disgusted sound like a grunt. "But I *will* kill him." The light from the helicopter landed on us, falling in a wide, spectral circle that encompassed all three of us, and Agent Truman moved the gun then, aiming it directly at Tyler's head while a ruthless expression distorted his face, and I had no doubt that he meant what he said.

I didn't think then; I only reacted. Like when I was on the mound. Like when the stands were filled with people cheering but I couldn't hear a single one of them because all that mattered was me and the person holding the bat.

I focused on the gun.

The gun and the ball in my hand and the beating of my heart.

I breathed, and then I moved.

And I was fast. Man, was I fast.

Agent Truman couldn't have dodged the ball even if I'd have given him fair warning. It was out of my hand like a shot. And any control I thought I was lacking had all been in my head.

I was precise. Crazy, uncanny, laser-like precise.

The ball, when it hit Agent Truman's gun, and the fingers he had wrapped around its grip, exploded. It came apart—the laces, the leather—exposing the layer of worm-like yarns underneath the leather skin.

Agent Truman's face went ashen as his knuckles exploded as well. Even above the helicopter, I was sure I hadn't imagined hearing that sound.

And then he crumpled to his knees, and before anyone else could stop us or before he could pick up his gun with his other hand, Tyler and I ran. . . .

Disappearing beneath the canopy of trees into the jet-black forest behind us.

CHAPTER FOURTEEN

I WAS STILL SHAKEN, BUT I KEPT RUNNING, WITH
Tyler right behind me. My legs and my lungs were burning
even though it didn't seem like we'd gone all that far. But the
woods kept getting deeper and denser and darker.

The helicopter overhead made it impossible for us to stop
to catch our breath. It zigged and zagged, its light never
pinpointing our location, but it was up there all the same.
Which let us know they hadn't given up on us.

We stayed as close as we could to the thicker patches of
trees and brush, trying to keep low and out of sight. The
leaves above us were thrashed by the blades, and pieces of

projectile branches and dirt whorled around us whenever the helicopter came too close. Most likely they were tracking us on foot, too, and we had no idea how much of a head start we had on them.

"Here." Tyler pulled me down beneath a layer of thick brush. "Let's see if we lost them."

I dropped in front of him. "How did you know I could do that?" I asked, panting. "Back there, with the ball?"

"You kidding? I saw you throw that night. I figured that was one of your new superpowers."

"I don't have powers," I countered.

He shrugged dubiously. "Did you see the way you threw that ball—you have powers." I couldn't deny his accusation entirely. Simon might not have mentioned anything like that, but it would be one giant coincidence if my new ability to throw stupid-fast wasn't somehow linked to everything else that made me . . . well, less than normal.

Reaching up, Tyler plucked a twig from my hair. "How you doin'?" he asked. "You okay?"

Nodding, I found my heart beating for a different reason now. "You?"

A lazy grin tugged at his lips. "Hell no. But you're still not ditching me."

"It's not funny."

His hand dropped to my side, his fingers interlacing with mine. "I know it's not. And I'm serious. You're the most amazing thing that's ever happened to me. I just don't want you getting any crazy ideas about losing me out here."

My heart faltered. Losing him was the last thing I wanted.

When the spotlight from the helicopter came too close again, it jerked us back to reality. We jumped up, breaking free from the bushes like startled animals, and darted across the overgrown forest floor. Branches whipped and pulled at us, snagging and ripping our clothes and skin.

"This way." I clung to Tyler and towed him along, toward a stand of trees ahead of us. The glowing halo of the spotlight bobbed behind us, moving drunkenly in our wake.

Tyler stumbled again and again, and I wondered at how he couldn't see the branches and vines he continuously tripped over. I tried to warn him whenever I remembered, but it was hard, and my words got lost in my gasping breaths. When his toe landed solidly against a large rock in the path, he staggered, dragging me down with him.

"It's okay," I panted, pulling him back up before he'd actually hit the ground. "Keep going. See?" I pointed toward the trees. "We're almost there."

The spotlight was nearly to us, trailing us like an unnatural shadow.

"No! I can't see it," he shouted back, fumbling for me once more and finding my hand. "I can't see anything out here. Nothing but that stupid light."

I dragged him along, pulling him out of the reach of the light that veered too far left to find us. "Nothing?" I managed to pant, still running.

Ahead of us there was a tunnel between the trees. I was almost certain we could squeeze through it. I had no idea what was on the other side, but I didn't think the searchlight could find us there.

When we slipped inside, I exhaled heavily, collapsing on the damp ground. I surveyed our temporary hiding spot—essentially an opening in a blackberry thicket. If we moved too far in any direction, the pointed thorns would lance us. "You can't see anything at all?"

"Shit!" Tyler cursed, brushing against one wall of the treacherous spikes, and then, trying to escape them, he lurched too far the other way and backed into yet another wall of them. He extricated himself carefully this time, cursing the entire time. I helped by pulling stray barbs from his T-shirt and hair.

"Are you saying you can?" he asked when the worst of his swearing had faded to a stream of unintelligible mutters. "See, I mean? That it's not pitch-black to you?"

I blinked, looking around at our surroundings. At the thick vines and the jagged-edged leaves. I saw the angry red scrapes running down his right arm and on his cheek from the blackberry vines, and that he was frowning at me even though he wasn't actually looking directly at me.

I reached out and moved a stray vine he was dangerously close to tangling with, saving him from more of the welts and scrapes.

I could see. And he couldn't.

Tyler grinned then. "You have night vision," he said to no one in particular, since he was staring directly at a wall of bushes. I could practically see his thoughts then, too, mentally chalking that up to yet another of my new "super-powers."

"I think we should call Simon," I told him, digging for the envelope in my back pocket. "Here." I reached for the fanny pack I'd made fun of him for wearing. I unzipped it and stuffed the cash and the things I'd taken from my dad's place inside.

I kept the phone.

As soon as I powered it on, light filled our hiding space, and I immediately covered the small screen with both hands. If there *was* anyone following us on foot, we'd just given ourselves away.

I dialed the only number that was programmed and waited. I had to cup my hands over the receiver to hear, even though the helicopter had veered away from us.

When Simon answered, his tone was clipped, and he got straight to the point. "We've already heard you're in trouble. Where are you now?"

I kept my voice low. "We're in the woods behind my dad's place. I don't know where exactly, but they're follow-ing us. I don't know how long we can hide."

"We?" Simon started, but then he let it go. "Keep your phone on. We'll find you."

When I hung up, I flipped the phone closed and dropped it in the fanny pack too.

Above us, the helicopter was circling around. Coming back to where we were hiding.

I glanced up, looking at the jumble of vines and thorns.

What I'd initially believed might be a tunnel was, in reality, a dead end. We would be trapped if they found us now. "We can't stay here. There has to be a way out of these woods."

"You'll have to be my eyes," Tyler said, holding out his hand to me.

"Great," I muttered, taking it and wishing I'd shown a little more interest in Girl Scouts. Instead, I'd given up when it was time to graduate from Bluebirds because I thought the Girl Scout uniforms were too . . . *green*. "It really will be the blind leading the blind."

When we reached the river we stopped. We were at a dead end. The waters were fast and dark, and rushed wildly past us in frenzied surges with fat whitecaps that knocked the breath out of me just to witness.

But right now this river was our only way out.

"We can do this."

I wasn't sure I agreed with Tyler's little pep talk, but those NSA thugs were approaching too fast to argue. The helicopter was whipping the treetops and making them lash wildly, as its searchlight flickered here and there, trying to locate us.

But it was the dogs that were likely to find us first. And I could hear them, their incessant barks and growls growing closer and closer to where Tyler and I stood on the ledge, our hands clasped together so tightly I was sure I'd left fingernail marks in his skin.

"This is the craziest idea ever," I shouted, easing closer to the rocky threshold.

Tyler smiled, and I thought it was the most amazing smile I'd seen in my life. I hoped it wasn't the last time I'd see it. "Or the best." He squeezed my hand in return.

The dogs and the agents and the flashlights all broke through the tree line behind us at the same time. Their lights bobbed frantically, converging on us in unison.

I wavered, scrambling to decide which fate was worse. But then Tyler squeezed my hand again, and I counted to three. And as if he'd been doing the same, we both leaped at once.

When the icy waters enveloped me, I forgot how—or why—to breathe.

There were only two things I knew for sure.

One, that I was trapped.

And two, I was going to die at the bottom of this effing river.

Most people talk about how their lives flash before their eyes right before they die. That didn't happen for me. All I could think of, all that kept going through my head, was that it was a fanny pack that had gotten me killed.

And instead of spending my last minutes reflecting on the bucket list of things I should have done, or the things I wished I'd done better, or all the people I wanted to make amends to, I was pissed that I'd gone after the stupid fanny pack in the first place.

What had I been thinking, going after it to begin with? The current had been too strong, dragging the pack along until it had gotten caught in a tangle of fallen trees at the bottom of the river.

And here I was, my foot snared by that same twisted gnarl of branches. At least if Tyler finally decided to give up on trying to save me, he'd have the pack, because it would be clenched in my cold, dead fingers.

My chest ached as I desperately kicked and kicked and kicked again, trying to free my ankle. I was no longer cold, even beneath the freezing waters, which I was sure was because of the panic that sent white-hot jolts of adrenaline surging through me every few seconds. The river's currents continued to pull and drag and suck at me, although less so down here, so far beneath the surface.

I reached down and tried to wrench my foot free, but my hands were useless. I could see the way my ankle was wedged beneath the massive trunk, caught between the twisted branches, and I wondered how I'd managed to get it so lodged in the first place.

If I hadn't been at death's door I would've been impressed that I could see it all so clearly in the dark and murky riverbed.

I saw Tyler too. Swimming toward me from the water's surface. I don't know why he kept coming back down; I was a lost cause, but he refused to quit.

Again I tried to wave him away, gesturing for him to give up on me, but he ignored my flailing protests and went straight to work on my ankle instead. This time, the fourth time he'd come down for me, he had a hefty section of branch in his hand.

He used it like a tool while bubbles rose from his mouth, and from mine. He had to be tired from fighting the currents and from exerting himself time and again, but he refused to quit, stabbing at the branches and trying to free my ankle.

I reached for his shoulder, grasping a handful of his shirt and signaling for him to leave me. It wasn't going to work, and I didn't have much time left. He'd already had to go back up for air three times; how much longer could I possibly last?

He jerked away from my grip and positioned the sturdy piece of wood beneath the tree trunk that was pinning my ankle. He was crazy; there was no way that thing was going to budge. But he was more stubborn than I'd given him credit for.

He leveraged his branch, which was far flimsier looking than the trunk he was determined to move, and when he put his weight on it—all the weight he could manage in the water—it moved all right. It shifted.

But in the wrong direction.

The weight of the trunk rolled even farther onto my ankle, shattering the bones with a crunch that may or may not have been audible beneath the water. All I knew was pain like no other.

I opened my mouth to scream, fire bursting in my foot and spreading everywhere. Bubbles and muted sounds rushed from my throat as the last of my air reserve burst out of me. It took everything I had not to inhale then. Not to gasp in huge lungfuls of the frigid river water in my next breath.

Black crept in around the edges of my vision.

Tyler's face registered his mistake for only a second before he threw himself on top of his makeshift lever once more. Adrenaline and pure determination were propelling him now, and somehow, someway, that combination was enough, because that one last effort did the trick. The trunk rolled away from me.

Barely, but enough.

My foot, the bones crushed and still throbbing, slipped free from its trap.

Lying on the shore, Tyler and I stretched out on our backs and stared up at the sliver of a moon making its appearance between clouds that moved like tiny, silver-tinged vines, creeping in and over and across the sky.

Tyler was panting and breathless, while I shivered, my teeth chattering in an endless rhythm, waiting for the tingling in my ankle to subside.

It was the strangest sensation, the awareness of my own bone re-forming beneath my skin. I could feel the broken pieces moving and shifting, remodeling themselves. It pricked and itched and tickled and stung. I didn't move. I just let it happen while I lay there, wondering at it all because it was too new and strange and unusual to do anything else.

I thought about Agent Truman and his shattered fingers,

and guessed at how long it would take *them* to heal.

When the process was complete, when the last fragment of bone had knit itself back into place, I could roll my ankle without so much as wincing.

After what felt like an eternity, and when I was sure we were both still alive and relatively unscathed, I held up the fanny pack, still dripping with river water, and announced, "Got it."

Tyler rolled onto his side and glared down at me. "You scared the shit out of me. You were down there way too long." He cupped my chattering jaw. "How did you do that, Kyra? Could you . . . *breathe* under there?"

My eyebrows lowered. "*Breathe?* No!" But I thought about it. Tyler had gone back up for air three times while I'd been forced to hold my breath the entire time. "Of course not," I maintained.

"Do you have any idea how long you were down there?"

I shook my head. I didn't. I'd lost all sense of time.

"It had to have been ten, maybe even fifteen minutes."

I let my head fall back until I was staring at the sky again, watching the viney clouds part and shift and reveal pieces of the moon. Behind us the river, the place that should've been my tomb, continued to gush and flow.

Fifteen minutes was forever. In fifteen minutes I should've been dead.

But here I was.

Tyler appeared above me then, his eyes glittering mischievously. "I'm glad you didn't."

"Didn't what?" I asked, nearly forgetting to breathe again.

"Die," he clarified. "I'm really glad you didn't die on me." His fingertips brushed my lips, and my pulse quickened.

I laughed, wishing I had half the control over my reactions to being near him as I did when I threw a ball. "Thanks. Me too." And then I shot upright, my brow wrinkling. "Tyler? Your nose. It's bleeding again."

CHAPTER FIFTEEN

MY ANKLE WAS GOOD AS NEW. ESPECIALLY FOR having been crushed beneath a giant tree. Unfortunately, the phone hadn't fared as well.

We'd learned that fanny packs were not, in fact, water-proof. After having been submerged in river water for nearly fifteen minutes, its contents had gotten soaked. Enough to short-circuit the phone, which made it impossible to call Simon and let him know where we were.

In my estimation, that meant we were screwed. It was unlikely that Simon and the others from his camp were tracking us at that moment.

Tyler and I were on our own.

Fortunately for us, though, cash *was* waterproof, and so was the fake ID, both of which came in handy when we finally staggered out of the woods and found ourselves standing on a nothing of a road in the middle of Nowheresville, USA. But it was a nothing of a road that had a crappy little motel, and that crappy little motel had a VACANCY sign that blinked more brilliantly than any fireworks I'd ever laid eyes on.

Halle-freaking-*lujah!*

The girl behind the counter was considerably too young to hold a job, maybe too young to make it into a PG-13 movie, which meant she was probably the owner's kid or grandkid. It also meant she didn't raise an eyebrow over the fact that I was walking—rather than driving—and she barely seemed to notice that I was dripping wet from our river adventure.

I counted out my damp bills, which she also didn't question, and signed the registration book. It was strange signing Bridget Hollingsworth's name, and I wondered if I could just as easily slip into this other girl's life.

As easily as waking up behind the Gas 'n' Sip.

Tyler was waiting for me outside the motel's office, and I handed him the key that was suspended on a red plastic chip that read #110.

We stopped at the vending machines on our way to room 110 and used the quarters the girl had traded me for my wet bills to pick up a couple cans of Coke, a pack of chocolate chip cookies, some Doritos, and a thing of beef jerky—all the major food groups.

The room itself was stale smelling and brightly colored. Orange, mostly. Orange bedspread and orange shag carpet and a bright-orange lampshade that was shaped like a pear. *Supersweet.*

Mostly, though, it had heavy orange curtains that were perfect for privacy, and a queen-size bed.

But that was the thing—I'd asked for two beds, and room 110 had only one.

I eyed Tyler, and he eyed me back.

"I like the way you think," he finally threw out there, wiggling his eyebrows comically.

"Uh, yeah. I didn't do this." I wandered to the bed and sat on the end of it. *Awesome*—it squeaked too. "But we have to keep it. I don't want to draw any more attention than we already have."

"Suits me just fine," he said, leaning against the wall and crossing his arms over his chest. "I just hope you can keep your hands off me."

I rolled my eyes. "I'll manage." Another shudder gripped me. It had been like this since we'd gotten out of the water onto solid land. I couldn't shake the bone-deep cold.

Tyler eased away from the wall and dropped down next to me on the bed. He dragged me against him and tried to rub the chill from my arms. He regarded me seriously. "You should jump in the shower. It'll warm you up."

"You'd say anything to get me out of my clothes, wouldn't you?" I accused.

"Well . . ." He grinned. "You're not wrong. But in this

case, I think saving you from hypothermia comes before seeing you naked." He paused a second and then added with a wry look, "Although seeing you naked runs a close second."

He winked at me as he got up from the bed and then sauntered into the bathroom to start the water, as if he hadn't just set my entire body on fire. It was hard to imagine I even needed that shower now.

If I ever had a daughter, I swore I would warn her about boys like Tyler—the kind who could turn you into a puddle of mush with a wink and a grin. And an innocent-looking dimple.

When he came out, steam was already wafting from the bathroom behind him. "There are towels and those little minibottles of shampoo. I'll be back in a few. I'm gonna see if I can scrounge up something dry for you to put on." He took the key and a couple of the bills we'd set out to dry, and left me to get naked.

I looked ridiculous in my men's triple-XL Asplund Motor Inn souvenir T-shirt, even though I was grateful that the owners thought enough of their crappy motel to have souvenir T-shirts made in the first place. The giant shirt fit more like a dress on me, falling to my knees, which was a good thing since they didn't sell souvenir boxer shorts or anything else for the lower half, and I'd been forced to put on my wet underwear beneath it. My jeans were hanging over the heater, which seemed to blow only lukewarm air, alongside Tyler's clothes.

This was one of those moments in life when I wished I were more disciplined. When I had to bite my lips against the images the sounds of his shower were producing in my head. Images of *him* naked. But instead of mountains of self-control, that was all I could think about.

Tyler undressing.

Tyler getting wet beneath the stream of steaming hot water.

Tyler lathering up.

I was worse than a fifteen-year-old boy whose hormones had kicked into overdrive.

To distract myself from thoughts of Naked Tyler, I started sifting through the things we'd salvaged from my dad's place, even though there wasn't much left to salvage after the river fiasco.

The fanny pack had saved things from drifting away, but that was about all it had done.

I took the phone apart, removing the battery in hopes that once all the parts had dried, it might power up again, at least enough so I could get Simon's number off it.

"Dream big," my dad always told me.

Most of the things, though—the photos, the missing-person flier, the map—were a soggy mess. I did my best with them, but I finally gave up, tossing everything but the map into the wastebasket. The map I'd painstakingly spread over a table until it looked a little less like something Logan had chewed up and spit out. I could still make out some of the diagrams my dad had drawn on it, but most were smudged beyond recognition.

I had no idea whether the USB stick had survived being plunged into the river; but like the phone, I hoped it would dry out and might eventually be useful, so I set it aside with the CD.

The last thing I pulled from the fanny pack was the last thing I'd expected to find in there: the giant button of my fourth-grade picture that my dad used to wear. I hadn't even seen it in the mess at my dad's place.

"I couldn't resist," Tyler said from behind me.

I turned and saw him scrutinizing me from the bathroom, a towel wrapped strategically around his waist, blocking all the interesting stuff. Well, most of the interesting stuff.

My eyes traveled over the defined planes of his chest and down his muscled arms. His skin was damp still, and my fingers itched to dry him off the rest of the way. Any red-blooded American girl would've had the exact same thought.

"Um, yeah," I said, averting my gaze back to the plastic-coated button in my hand. "It's me, when I was little." I smiled coyly, feeling silly that a trinket from my past had made me so happy.

He grinned. "Yeah, I know. I sorta recognized you."

A flush burned my cheeks and made me hot all over again. "Thanks. That was sweet of you."

Tyler coughed, and at first I thought I'd just made him uncomfortable with my praise and he was trying to cover it up by clearing his throat. But then he kept on coughing.

"Shit, Tyler. Your nose."

And then there was that. He was bleeding again.

Snatching up the box of tissues from the nightstand, I rushed over to him with a wad already in my hand. He was as stunned as I was and pressed the tissues to his nose.

I knew then that something was wrong. Tyler had said it himself; he hadn't had a bloody nose since he was a kid, yet this was his third one today.

My mom's words rose up in my head: *He says you were infected with whatever that guy from Skagit General Hospital had. He says you're contagious.*

That was the second time Agent Truman had brought up that lab tech from the hospital—first sending me his picture and then telling my mom I'd been infected by him. But now the lab guy was dead; that's what it said on the news, right? That he'd been found dead in his apartment, and the cause of death hadn't been determined yet.

But what if it had been?

I tried to make sense of it. What if I really was contagious, like Agent Truman said I was?

It would explain what was happening to Tyler, wouldn't it?

And then I thought about that other guy—that agent at the bookstore. I'd seen the look on his face when he saw the blood trickling down my wrist. The way his hands shook, and his eyes had been filled with indecision and panic.

The lab guy had been exposed to my blood too.

I lifted my hand to my mouth. "Oh my god. It's me, isn't it? I'm the reason all those agents were suited up in biohazard gear."

Tyler fumbled for me, his hand finding my cheek. Even

behind the tissue I saw his lips quirk. "Don't do this. Seriously, Kyr."

My heart raced over the way he said my name.

"Think about it. I wasn't infected, Tyler—I *am* the infection. Remember that agent? He was all set to shoot you, right up until I cut myself. What if it's something *in* me that makes people sick—something about my blood? What if he shot himself because of me?" I was frowning so hard my head hurt, but I needed Tyler to take me seriously. "And what if that same thing is causing your nosebleeds?"

"Stop it," he said through the filter of the tissues. "You're making way too big a deal about this. It's a nosebleed."

But I stood there, watching him as he held the compress to his nose. I'd been so focused on drooling over his pecs and abs that I hadn't really noticed the shadows beneath his eyes.

I reached up and pressed the back of my hand to his forehead.

Tyler grinned. "On second thought." This time when he coughed it was totally and completely fake. He grinned some more. "If you want to play nurse, I'm all in."

I didn't share his enthusiasm, though. Because when I felt him, the moment I laid my hand on his skin, I knew . . . Tyler was sick.

"You're burning up."

"That's what I'm saying. I need medical attention." He refused to give it up. "See what I did there? I made you all worried, and now you sorta have to be nice to me."

"Tyler. Don't. This is serious. What you need is to lay down and stop acting like this is no big deal. I don't know what's going on or why this is happening, but we have a problem. I need to figure out how to get us some help. I think Simon might know what to do; I just have to find a way to get ahold of him." I went to the bed and peeled back the tacky orange covers and gave him my best I'm-serious face, waiting for him to quit pretending this was some sort of game.

He tried. He wasn't great at it, but at least he tried, pasting on a solemn expression for my benefit. He still held the tissues, but with one hand he reached out and stroked my arm. "It'll be okay, Kyr. I really believe that. Everything'll work out. I'll get some rest, and I'll feel better in the morning. And then we can find your dad, and you can explain your side of things to him, and you two will work things out. Your mom . . . well"—he winced—"I'm not sure about her. But everything else . . . things always have a way of working themselves out. You'll see."

He eased down onto the bed, getting beneath the covers. "How 'bout this? I'll make you a deal. I'll stay in bed if you promise not to worry." He stretched out. "Come here," he said, reaching for me, and I flushed all over again. When I hesitated, he grinned. "I know you don't need much sleep or anything, but it'll make me feel better just having you next to me. Humor me. Pretend you're tired too." He yawned, and I ached to feel that way again. To feel my eyelids grow sleepy and let my thoughts drift until dream was impossible to differentiate from reality.

I missed dreaming.

More than anything, though, I wanted Tyler to be right. I wanted whatever was wrong with him just to be exhaustion and for him to wake up feeling refreshed.

I frowned at him as I settled onto the side of the bed, testing the feel of it. "Just sleep," I insisted, ignoring the way my body reacted to being so near him. To knowing what he was, *or wasn't*, rather, wearing beneath the covers.

He caught me the second I was within reach and hauled me against him. I was hyperaware of every single thing about this moment. His skin, which was too hot and too dry and too tempting, and how badly I wanted to run my fingers over every inch of it. The tang of motel soap that clung to him, and the way it smelled different on him than it did on me. The itchy comforter I was lying on top of and how it kept us apart. The thrum of my heart and the sound of his breathing.

"See? This isn't so bad."

I grinned reluctantly, shifting my gaze to his, and he tightened his grip on me. "How's your nose?" I asked.

He peeled back the tissues and checked it. "What did I tell you? Nothing to worry about. Just a bloody nose."

I didn't know how to tell him I thought he was wrong.

Tyler talked in his sleep.

Like *talk*-talked. In full, coherent sentences.

Of course everything he said was out of context and

made no sense, but it was more amusing than any late-night talk show or infomercial on TV.

He talked about washing his car, something about "wrong soap" and "scratching the paint." And later there was muttering about a dog. Whose dog, I didn't know. He just said, "You can't bring that dog in here." He must've been serious about it, because he repeated it more than once, each time more forcefully than before.

I bit back my laughter, not wanting to wake him, until he said the one thing that made me freeze. Just a single word, but it sent shivers racing up my spine.

"Kyra."

I stayed where I was, wanting desperately—so damned desperately—for him to say my name again. I probably would've waited all night, except that was about the time he started to shiver. The same way I had shivered after we'd climbed out of the river. I forgot all about my name on his lips and slipped back into Florence Nightingale mode, jumping up from where I'd been lying next to him, and pressed my hand against the side of his cheek.

If I'd thought he'd been burning up before, he was downright sizzling now.

Panic overrode logic, and I tried shaking him awake. "Tyler. Wake up. Your fever . . . it's worse."

He mumbled something less coherent than his dream babbling had been, something I couldn't make out, and I shook him again. "Wake up," I demanded, getting right in his face now. "I need you to wake up!"

When he didn't respond, I went to the bathroom and ran a washcloth under cold water. I brought it back and laid it across his forehead. I wouldn't have been surprised if steam had risen from the compress. It didn't, but it also didn't rouse him.

"Dammit."

I grabbed the key and the ice bucket, not bothering with pants, and hurried out of the room.

When I came back, he was in the exact same state as when I'd left him: burning up and delirious. He responded, at least, to the ice.

"What the hell!" He shoved at me lethargically. "Stop. I'm fine." His "I'm fine," however, was less than convincing, and I was stronger than he was in his fevered state.

"Here . . . ," I said, my voice gentler as I wrapped the cubes in the washcloth and pressed them against his neck.

With the ice buffered by the cloth, he stopped thrashing against me and let me leave it. When the ice melted, I replaced it.

But I needed to do more.

"I'll be back," I whispered against his ear, and felt the heat coming off him in rippling waves.

The lady who staffed the office for the overnight shift was nice enough, if a little hard of hearing. Apparently they sold T-shirts but not Tylenol. Go figure. She didn't "believe in the stuff," she explained, so she couldn't help me out.

I did my best not to roll my eyes, but it took every ounce

of self-control to stop myself. Who didn't *believe in* Tylenol?

She did, however, point out that there was an all-night gas station just "down the way a bit," and she aimed a crooked finger indecisively. I assumed she knew by then I was on foot since there weren't any cars in the parking lot, so I started jogging in the direction she'd indicated.

She was right. It didn't take long to find the small, four-pump station, which was good since by the time I got there my not-yet-dry jeans were starting to chafe. Also because I was out of my mind with worry over Tyler.

The station was open but deserted at this hour. And it wasn't the convenience store kind of place that had aisles of snack foods and miscellaneous household supplies and motor oil and beer. Instead, there was one lone attendant's stand in a center island that overlooked all four gas pumps. Behind the glass there was a limited assortment of sundries: cigarettes, condoms, cough drops—that sort of thing. I could see the display rack of individual packets of pain relievers sitting plain as day on the back counter.

Problem was, the attendant was nowhere to be seen.

If I'd wanted breath spray or condoms, I'd have been in luck. I could have busted out the BACK IN FIVE sign that blocked the small opening where people passed their cash and made a run for it. No such luck.

"Hello?" I called out, hoping that the cashier was right around the corner, maybe taking a smoke break or something; and when no one answered, I tried again, louder this time. *"Hello!"*

I paced nervously, chewing on my lip and then on my fingernail, trying to decide what I should do.

I didn't want to go back empty-handed. Tyler *needed* this medicine.

I went to the glass and pressed my face against it. It was right there. Right in front of me. If I had the balls—or the ovaries, in my case—I'd break the damn glass. I was already on the run from the law, wasn't I? How much worse could my situation get?

Just one packet of Tylenol or Excedrin or ibuprofen. I wasn't choosy.

I pounded my fists helplessly against the glass because I knew I'd never do it, even if it had been right where the breath spray was. I wasn't a thief.

"Hello?" I yelled again, my eyes never leaving the display as anxiety made my voice crack. *"Is anyone here?"*

And that's when it happened.

The display of pain relievers . . .

. . . it moved.

Moved, as in wiggled. Enough that all the packets swayed side to side. A miniature earthquake.

Except it was only the pain reliever rack that was affected. Nothing else. Not the ground beneath my feet or the counters inside the booth or the condoms or the cough drops.

Just the pain relievers I'd been staring at longingly.

Shut. Up.

My eyes widened, and my fists fell to my sides. My throat tightened as I tried to make sense of what I'd seen. I looked behind me to see if anyone else had noticed it, but I was still alone.

All alone.

I turned back.

Nuh-uh . . . not me . . .

It wasn't . . .

I glanced down at my hands—ordinary, normal hands. *No way!*

I curled my fingers back into fists and lifted them to the glass, mimicking my previous actions.

Nothing happened. There was nothing but me and the empty booth and all those pain relievers I couldn't reach.

I stared. I stared hard.

I concentrated.

And then . . .

. . . still nothing.

I banged my fist on the glass, releasing a gust of frustration as I swore under my breath. "Dammit. *Dammit!*"

All at once the entire pain reliever display shot across the booth and crashed against the glass, scaring the crap out of me.

I jerked away from the explosion, my heart crammed in my throat and my eyes so wide I felt like they'd pop out of my head. "Holy . . ." I gasped. "Oh my god, oh my god, oh my god . . ."

But there was no one there to see. I checked.

I almost wished there had been. Someone to say, "I saw it too." Or "Holy crap." Or "Dude, you did it."

Somehow, someway, by some freaking miracle I had just managed to move—like levitate or something—that whole entire rack across the attendant booth.

With my new superpowers.

When I finally recovered from what I'd done, when I'd accepted it was real and come to terms with it, and when I realized I'd better get the hell out of there before someone else showed up and figured out I was the one responsible for all that damage, I jumped into action.

It was all there, all the medicine I needed; I just had to shove—fine, break—the BACK IN FIVE sign to get it out of my way. It was a small feat after what I'd accomplished with the display stand, and it took me only a second. Hard to believe the cashier had left this place unattended in the first place.

After I'd filled my pockets with as many packets as I could carry, I laid three twenty-dollar bills on the counter inside, more than enough to pay for what I'd taken and to make up for the mess I'd made. Because, I might be desperate, but I certainly wasn't a thief.

I ran the entire way back, anxious to get out of there before someone spotted me, and even more anxious to get back to Tyler. I stopped running, though, almost tripping over my own feet, the moment the Asplund Motor Inn came into view.

Not because I was winded or because I was no longer in a hurry to get back, but because of the car in the parking lot. The one that hadn't been there before.

Black. Nice and shiny, polished black.

I felt sick. Not like Tyler, all fevered and nosebleedy, but straight-up, gut-puking sick.

If it hadn't been for Tyler—Tyler who was still in there, still burning up, probably all because of me—I would've turned tail and run. Right back to the gas station, past it, and into the woods.

I would have disappeared forever this time.

I squeezed my eyes shut, pressing my fists into the hollows of my sockets, and did my best to come up with some sort of plan. But there was no good plan for how to get Tyler out of there. Not now.

As I passed the office on my way back, the old lady inside met me at the door. "Oh good, you're back. Nice man's been waitin' on you."

I ignored the woman, my stomach roiling as I kept walking. I glanced toward the black car parked right in front of room 110.

It was empty, I noted. Whoever was here was probably already inside the room. Waiting for me.

My heart climbed into my throat as I stood outside. My key felt heavy and my fingers too clumsy to work it. It took me forever to screw up the courage to slip it into the lock. Closing my eyes, I knew this was probably my last chance to change my mind.

I could still run.

I could still disappear and be Bridget Hollingsworth.

Instead, I turned the key.

The room was dark, but I could see everything clearly.

Tyler was out on the bed, curled in a ball, delirious and shivering. I wanted to shout at him to run, but it was no use. All our things were exactly where I'd left them, untouched and spread out to dry. The light from the bathroom was on, and the door was ajar.

The agent was in there.

The silence was palpable; each second I stood there waiting for him to make his appearance was physically painful.

When I couldn't take it any longer, I finally let the door close behind me. "I know you're here."

When the bathroom door opened, I felt like I was going to jump out of my skin.

And when I saw who was standing there, framed by the light spilling out of the bathroom, my heart nearly stopped.

"Simon?" I breathed. "What the—? How did you know . . . ?" I looked to the electronic components that had once been a cell phone. "The phone you gave me was ruined when we jumped in the river."

Simon's eyebrows rose up a notch. "You jumped in a river?"

"To get away. The agents from the NSA were after us, and we didn't have any other choice."

Simon frowned and then nodded toward Tyler. "Did you cut yourself? While you were escaping?"

So that *was* it then. It was all the confirmation I needed. Bile rose in my throat, stinging all the way up. "It was me? I did this to him—*my blood*?"

"I don't have time to explain right now. We need to get you both out of here. I can explain on the way." Simon went to the bed. "Come on. Help me get him to the car."

As if he'd heard Simon, Tyler moaned.

Ignoring Simon because he didn't matter for the moment, I went to Tyler and stroked his face. "It's okay," I whispered, pulling one of the hijacked packets from my pocket and ripping it open. I eased his head off the pillow. The back of his neck was slick with sweat. "Take these," I ordered, dropping the Tylenols into his mouth and grabbing the open can of Coke from the nightstand.

I was grateful for the pills he managed to swallow, and I prayed they did the trick.

I was suddenly unsure about what the right thing to do was. I wanted to take Tyler, to keep him with me and try to make him better. But what if being around me only made him worse.

"Maybe we should leave him here," I told Simon. "Call 9-1-1 or something."

Simon grabbed my arm, his grip firm. "I won't stop you if that's what you decide, but just be clear about what you're setting him up for. If you do that, he won't be getting the *help* you think he is. Those NSA guys, they *will* find him. And when they do, they'll figure out why he's there—what happened to him and why he's suddenly so sick—and then they'll cut him open—same way they would you and me."

I jerked away from his grasp, rubbing my arm. Glaring at Simon, I lowered my voice and asked the question I *so* didn't

293

want to ask. "Why? Why would they do that?" I thought of that guy—the agent from the bookstore who'd raised his gun to his own head after being exposed to my blood. Suddenly the gunshot we'd heard made sense. He didn't want to be a science experiment. "Why wouldn't they just cure him?" I refused to think of the lab tech from the news.

Simon stared at me for a long, long time. His lips pressed together, and his expression shifted all the way from determination to compassion. It was the compassion that did me in.

I shook my head, denying what I saw in that look. "No," I insisted. "There has to be something. Some way to fix this . . . to make him better." I looked back to Tyler, and hated him for abandoning me like this. For being completely-totally-utterly unavailable when I needed him most.

I hated Simon, too, for telling me the last thing in the world I wanted to hear.

But most of all, I hated myself for being a toxic, fucking mess.

CHAPTER SIXTEEN
Day Seven

I RODE IN THE BACK OF SIMON'S CAR WITH
Tyler's head in my lap.

It had taken nearly twenty minutes after Tyler had swallowed those first two Tylenols for his fever to finally break. When he was alert enough, I was able to persuade him to swallow two more and then managed to sit him upright so we could get him dressed and into the car, where he collapsed again.

We talked for a while—Tyler assuring me still that he was all right and me knowing differently but keeping my mouth shut because inside I was barely holding my shit together.

When he finally admitted that his head was killing him, I didn't have the heart to tell him it wasn't his head that was killing him; it was me.

The entire time it was hard for me to maintain eye contact with him, yet I couldn't stop myself from touching him. My fingers were everywhere, stroking his cheeks and his forehead, his shoulders and his hair. "I'm so, so, *so sorry*," I whispered beneath my breath whenever I thought he wasn't listening. I repeated it inside my head, too, hoping there was some penance in the words. That I could somehow absolve myself for being an accidental murderer.

If Tyler heard me, he never mentioned it. His hand continued to clutch my knee, his fingers occasionally caressing my thigh, as if it made him feel better just holding on to me. Reassuring himself that I wasn't going anywhere.

And I wasn't. I swore I would never leave him again.

When he started mumbling, I knew he was dozing, and I turned my attention back to Simon, who kept casting uneasy glances in the rearview mirror, checking on how we were doing back here. "Whose car is this anyway? You know, it scared the hell out of me when I saw it in the parking lot."

The sun was starting to rise, casting a golden glow over his dark skin in his reflection. "Sorry about that. The car . . . well, let's call it a loaner."

I shook my head, sighing. "So it's stolen. Great, Simon. How long are we supposed to drive around in this thing before someone notices it's missing and calls the cops? Then what? We can't let them take Tyler." When I said his name,

Tyler shifted in my lap. I smoothed my fingers over his hair to settle him down again.

Simon dropped his eyes back to the road in front of him. "Don't worry about it. We're almost there. Willow is meeting us, and we'll ditch this car. No one's gonna catch us." I didn't ask who Willow was. I assumed it was another one of Simon's *Returned*, from the camp he'd told me about.

I sagged back in my seat, letting my fingers sift through Tyler's sweat-dampened waves. I couldn't help being pissed at Simon. I blamed him. He should've warned me. I would never have risked cutting myself around Tyler—or anyone else—if I had known my blood was somehow toxic.

"You got it all figured out, don't you? You still never answered me. How'd you find us anyway?"

Stupidly oblivious—or maybe just plain stupid—to my irritation, Simon grinned. "It wasn't that tricky, just a little time-consuming is all. It would've backfired if you hadn't checked into a motel or if you hadn't used the ID I'd given you. After calling about fifty places, I finally found a Bridget Hollingsworth at the Asplund Motor Inn."

"And they just gave you that info over the phone? I didn't think they could do that."

I don't know why I was blaming him. Before he'd shown up, my entire goal had been to get ahold of him. Yet now that I was sitting in the exact place I'd wanted to be, the very sight of him made me want to puke.

Or maybe it was everything he represented.

Everything I hated about myself.

I shrugged and looked out the side window. *Same difference.*

We were in the mountain pass now, and I could see the summits in the distance where the snow still hadn't melted and probably wouldn't, even when the summer temps hit their highest. I wondered how far we'd be traveling, but I was too stubborn to ask.

I continued to run my fingers over and through Tyler's hair, trying to calm myself as much as to soothe him while he slept. When I finally trusted myself to be reasonable, I leaned forward, closer to the front seat. "Are you sure, Simon, that there's nothing . . ." Tears crowded my eyes, and I blinked furiously, swallowing hard to get my words out. "That there's nothing we can do to help him?"

Simon's golden-flecked eyes sought mine. He didn't have to answer, but he did anyway. "I'm sorry, Kyra. I know it sucks. I didn't tell you everything when I told you why I left my family. It wasn't only because my parents were asking questions about why I wasn't aging. There was more to it than that."

I wasn't sure I wanted to hear what he had to say, but I needed to know. "It was my sister. I mean, I didn't know at the time . . . that it was me. But we were fishing . . . I was teaching her to fish, of all things, and I cut myself. I didn't even know about the healing thing. But she was there and saw the whole thing. She'd sworn she'd never tell anyone." He cleared his throat. "Turns out that wasn't really an issue. Shortly after I'd cut myself, she got sick. We thought it was the flu at first—she had a fever, was vomiting, had a bloody nose. But then she lost all her hair. Within a day she was dead. My folks are Christian Scientists. They don't believe in doctors, just the power of prayer, so they never even bothered calling for help." His voice was hard now. Bitter. "They tried to pray the evil out of her."

I wanted to catch his eye again in the mirror, but he refused to look at me. I wasn't sure what I felt then, if I hated him still or if I wanted to hug him because he was the only person I knew who understood what I was going through.

I didn't get the chance to decipher my feelings because that's when I noticed it, the clumps of hair in my hands.

Tyler's hair.

I was right about Willow being one of the Returned.

She was also crazy badass. Not like Cat, who gave off a take-no-crap vibe, but more like an I-could-rip-your-throat-out-and-leave-your-carcass-in-a-ditch kind of thing.

Add to that the fact that she had tattoos blanketing both arms and wore sleeveless leather like a biker chick, I was terrified of her. I was also glad she was on our side.

Or on Simon's side, at least.

She and Simon did this half-handshake, half-shoulder bump thing when we got out of our car at the rest stop and they greeted each other.

Willow eyed me up and down. "That her?" she asked, spitting sideways as she checked me over.

Seriously? She chewed tobacco too?

I'd tried it once, on a dare from Cat because she'd said all the big leaguers did it. I'd swallowed more of the stuff than I could keep between my lip and my gums, and ended up feeling both dizzy and nauseous. After that I decided to stick to sunflower seeds.

As much as Willow scared me, I was far more scared for Tyler, and about losing him. "Help me," I shouted to both of them. "We need to get going." I didn't care that she raised her eyebrows at being bossed around, or that she could easily do that leaving-me-in-a-ditch thing.

Simon nodded to her, indicating that she should do as I said, and she followed his lead. He was definitely the one in charge.

She stopped cold when she bent over and looked inside. "Holy mother of . . . Is he . . . ?" She stood upright again, her arm resting against the top of the car as she eyed Simon. "Are you sure we're bringing him? What's the point?"

Simon made eye contact with her over the roof of the car in a way that made it clear they understood each other, and I got the feeling it was for my benefit when he said, "Because Kyra says so."

Tyler was more alert after he got out of the backseat and puked.

I've never really been good around sick people, I guess because I've never had much experience with them. But I stayed with him while he gripped his knees for support and heaved over and over and over again.

What came out of him was black and thick and sticky, and I tried to imagine what combination of food had caused that mess. I had to assume it had more to do with whatever poison or pathogen I'd inadvertently passed on to him and was now working its way through his system than anything he'd ingested.

The whole experience probably only lasted thirty seconds, but it felt like hours.

I rubbed his back and said things like "It's okay" and "It'll be over soon" and "You're doing good," which was a strange thing to say because it sounded like I was cheering him on. Like he was competing in the Puke Olympics or something.

When it was over and he'd wiped his mouth on his sleeve, he leaned on me while he stumbled to the ginormous purple truck Willow had brought to meet us. I wasn't sure how we *weren't* supposed to draw attention in that beast, but I didn't bother mentioning it as I helped Tyler step onto the running board so he could climb inside.

The engine, when she started it, was ridiculously loud, giving the NSA's helicopter a run for its money. Everything about this truck made me uncomfortable, right down to the fact that we had to shout to be heard, even from inside the oversize cab.

Willow drove, and when she jammed the truck into gear, we lunged from the rest stop parking lot and onto the highway, making our way out of the mountains and into the eastern side of the state, which was flatter and browner and more desertlike than where we'd just come from.

Willow kept her suspicious gaze directed at us from her place in front, as if she expected Tyler—who was sitting upright now—to suffer another bout of stomach-blasting nausea. I couldn't say she was wrong—he was pale and had a sheen of perspiration across his forehead—but it irritated me, the way she watched us all the same.

"I have the bags," I snapped, even though she hadn't said a single word. I waved the plastic grocery bags she'd forced on me like flags, hoping she'd get the point and stop giving us the evil eye.

When she went back to watching the road, I turned to Tyler. My chest tightened painfully.

He was still achingly beautiful, his eyes even more green against the washed-out pallor of his skin, but already his cheekbones were more defined than they should be—even more than they had been just yesterday—and his lips were cracked and peeling.

"Tyler," I started, but he reached across the space and gripped my hand.

"Don't," his voice rasped urgently. He squeezed my fingers tighter than I thought he should be able to, and I felt somewhat better, even if it was foolish to let myself hope. I leaned my head against his shoulder.

Willow interrupted from the front. "So Simon tells us you mend at crazy speeds—that so?"

It was the last thing I wanted to do—make small talk with Willow—especially about myself, but Tyler seemed to perk up just a little. "She totally does. And she can hold her breath forever."

Simon twisted around so he was facing me, his arm resting on the back of his seat as his eyes devoured me. "Really? How long's *forever*?"

"At least fifteen minutes. That's how long she was trapped in the river." Tyler met Simon's eyes, his cracked lips attempting to grin. I hated how breathless he sounded. "She can see in the dark too. Can all of you do that?"

"No," Simon answered Tyler firmly. "We can all regenerate—heal," he explained. "And we age more slowly and are more resistant to disease, but I don't think any of the other Returned have shown signs of night vision or the ability to go long periods without oxygen." He and Willow exchanged another look, sharing another of their secrets. "Have you heard of that?"

Willow gave a decisive shake of her head.

"Anything else?" Simon probed, this time directing his inquiry at me.

I thought about the gas station, and the way I'd moved an entire display of pain relievers—sent it shooting across the attendant's stand until it smashed into the glass—simply by concentrating on it. I wondered if any of the Returned could do that. Move things with their minds.

I shook my head and shrugged. "Not that I know of."

There was a brief silence, and then we were back to front-seat and backseat conversations when Willow dropped her voice and told Simon, "I talked to Jett while we were stopped, and he said there was chatter about the No-Suchers widening their search. We were hoping they'd pack it in when they lost her, but I don't think they're letting this one go."

Since I was sure the "her" in question was me, I didn't feel bad for eavesdropping.

I glanced curiously at Tyler and then, tilting my head sideways, I interrupted them. "The No-Suchers, who're they?"

"The NSA, or as some people call them, the No Such Agency because everything they do is on the DL."

"So what's the deal with them? They just go around chasing those of us they think were experimented on?" It was still almost impossible to say the part about us being "alien" experiments out loud, so I didn't try.

"Officially, no. *Officially*, they were never even here." He lifted a shoulder noncommittally. "Unofficially, you're the biggest prize they've had their eyes on in years. Maybe ever. If Agent Truman can get his hands on you . . . you're what they call a 'career maker.'"

Inwardly I shuddered. The idea of Agent Truman, or any of those guys in hazmat suits, hunting me was disturbing. "Aren't you afraid of them? Doesn't having me with you put you all at risk?"

Willow lifted her chin. "We're not scared of them. Buncha grade-A pussies is what they are." I wasn't sure about the "pussies" part, but I doubted Willow was used to being messed with. "Besides, they'll never find us." She grinned at me through the rearview. "Not unless we want 'em to."

"So what happens now?" Tyler asked. "How long do we have to hide before they give up?"

A long silence engulfed the cab. Willow shifted her gaze away from us as if suddenly the road was the only thing worth noticing. Simon didn't ignore us exactly. He continued to dart nervous gazes back and forth between us and Willow. But he'd gone all radio silent too.

Finally I said what neither of them would, because they were too afraid to say what we all knew. "Forever," I answered. "We have to stay hidden for the rest of our lives."

I didn't say the part where Tyler's life would be way shorter than it should be.

Three hours after we left the rest stop we were at Simon's camp.

It was in the mountains, too, but these mountains were less snow-capped peaks and densely packed fir trees than the Cascades we'd just traveled through and more like scrubby sagebrush and rocky outcroppings and spare-looking pine trees that might burst into flames if a match were lit anywhere in their vicinity. This was what my mom had always referred to as "rattlesnake country."

By late morning the temperature was already approaching the eighty-degree mark. It was hard to imagine what it was like out here in July or August.

I wiped the sweat from my upper lip as I climbed down

from the truck, kicking up a cloud of dust as my feet hit the gritty earth.

Tyler was asleep inside the cab.

He hadn't thrown up again, but he'd bled. Not from his nose this time but from his right ear. I'd dabbed at it while he slept. I didn't say anything but caught Willow watching me as I swiped at the trickle.

He was getting worse.

"We've got a place for you two already set up in the bunkhouse. We can get him in there, and then we should talk," Simon told me, coming around behind me while I watched Tyler sleep. "I know this is hard, Kyra, but there's nothing you can do for him. He's only got a day or so left." He put his hand on my shoulder, and I shrugged it off, not wanting to hear what he had to say. "We'll make him as comfortable as we can. We have drugs we can give him—they won't cure him or anything, but they'll . . ." He faltered, just like he should falter, I thought. Because this was bullshit. It shouldn't be happening. ". . . they'll make it easier on him."

I clenched my jaw, biting back every terrible thing I wanted to say to him because I knew he was right; it wouldn't do any good.

The bunkhouse we were taken to was rustic to say the least: four walls and a few cots, which looked barely used and smelled like deep-rooted dust. With the windows closed it was even hotter in there, and I had to prop them all open just to get the scant breeze moving through the ramshackle building so Tyler wouldn't suffocate when I laid him down.

I sent Simon to get us some water and a washcloth so I could sponge Tyler's burning skin.

When a boy came back with what I'd asked for, he offered me a grimy-looking water jug and a worn-looking rag. "I'm Jett," he explained, pushing a mop of sandy-brown hair out of his eyes. "Simon had to take care of some things and asked me to look after you." His eyes drifted to Tyler, to his limp form on the cot, and then skittered away from him again as if looking at him for too long was difficult. It was, really. I was the only one unwilling to admit it. "Can I get you anything else?"

I shook my head, turning back to Tyler and ignoring the boy.

After a minute I heard footsteps and knew the boy had left us alone. *Good,* I thought. I didn't want him here anyway. I didn't want anyone here unless they knew how to fix Tyler.

I dug into my pocket and pulled out another packet—Advil this time. I tore it open with my teeth and forced Tyler awake again. It was getting harder and harder to keep him conscious. "Tyler . . ." I tried not to sob when I said his name, but that was harder too. Guilt shredded me from the inside out. "Take these," I ordered.

He opened his mouth listlessly but not his eyes, and I let the pills fall on his tongue, which didn't really look like a tongue should—not pink and soft and moist. Instead, it was desiccated, like leather. Pretending not to notice, I lifted the jug to his lips and trickled the water into his mouth.

After he finally swallowed, I thought he'd go back to sleep. Instead, he moved his lips to talk. At first all that came out were these garbled, whispering sounds, like muffled breaths, and then I heard him.

"'Stuff your eyes with wonder,'" he croaked. "'Live as if you'd drop dead in ten seconds. See the world. . . .'" He paused, taking a breath. I tried to figure out what he was saying and wondered if he was hallucinating. But he wasn't finished. "It's more . . . 'more fantastic than any dream made or paid for in factories.'" I recognized it then. It was from *Fahrenheit 451*, the book he'd shared with me. His favorite one.

My eyes burned, and then that burning gave way to the tears, because I understood what he was saying. I bent over him, weeping as I clutched his hands, desperate to make him know how sorry I was. "You . . . you . . . know?" I managed to say between choked gasps.

Tyler's face remained still, his eyes closed. When he breathed, it sounded like it was coming from too far down inside his chest and each breath had to be dredged up. Labored for. Speaking was an effort. "I heard you . . . when you were talking. I know . . ." He paused to take a long, determined pull of the dusty air around us. "I know I don't have long." He strained to open his eyes, and again it was a struggle, that task that should have been so incredibly simple.

Yet when he did, I nearly lost it.

His eyes . . . oh my god, his eyes . . .

What had once been beautiful and green, and had

sparkled when he smiled, were now completely and totally devoid of all color. As if black ink had been spilled within them, blooming from the pupil and diffusing outward.

"I wish I could see you," Tyler said, lifting his hand feebly and reaching for my face.

Trembling, and unable to stop myself from crying openly, I moved so he could find me, letting the tips of his fingers graze my cheeks until even that effort was too much for him and his hand fell back down. I captured his hand then and crushed my lips to it.

"I don't want you to blame yourself, Kyra. Not ever." He wheezed, and before I could stop him, he spoke again. "It was worth it, you know. I would trade a million lifetimes for the one I've had with you."

"You're wrong," I insisted. "I would trade anything to give you your life back. Anything."

I felt him then. Going quiet, completely motionless, once more. Exhaustion overtaking him.

I hovered above him, listening to the sounds of his breathing and hating how much I feared that this might be it. The way my stomach clenched at the rasping sound he made as he fought for each and every breath like it might be his last. I had a hard time swallowing as I willed his lungs to find a rhythm, for him to hang on.

When he found that calm at last, I relaxed, easing back and letting go of his hands.

"Simon wants you to come with me."

The voice startled me, but I recognized it. It was Jett,

standing in the doorway behind me.

"What? I can't leave him," I said, getting to my feet.

"He'll be okay for now," Jett explained, nodding toward Tyler, who was out cold. "He won't even know you're gone. Simon wants me to show you around." When I looked like I might argue, which I considered, unable to bring myself to leave Tyler alone, Jett added, his voice quiet and persuasive, "You'll want to see this. I promise."

CHAPTER SEVENTEEN

IT WAS HARD TO LEAVE TYLER IN THE FILTHY, rundown cabin while I followed Jett into what I could only describe as a maze of tunnels that extended far below the hot and dusty surface of the camp.

"What is this place?" I ran my hand along the cool concrete that made up the underground walls. I'd let Jett lead me down into what I thought was a sewer opening in the middle of the soil, one that had been concealed by a heavy iron cover that he had to drag off it, and once we'd dropped all the way to the bottom, I found myself surrounded by darkness. The tunnel we walked through seemed endless, and, unlike me, Jett needed a flashlight to find his way.

"Used to be part of the Hanford operation—the nuclear facility. They haven't used this place in years, though. I'm not sure this bunker is even on the map." He stopped in front of a closed metal door that blended into the cement wall around it.

"Nuclear facility? Is it safe to be here?"

Jett flashed me a boyish grin, and I wondered just how old he was. He looked younger than both Simon and Willow. Younger than me and Tyler, at least in human years. I had no idea how that translated in *replaced* time. At the delayed aging rate of the Returned, he could've been back for mere weeks or as long as decades. "It is for us," he bragged.

Goose bumps broke out over my skin at his answer. He worked to unlatch the door, which involved rotating a handle the way you did with submarine hatches. "Okay," I said, rubbing the chill from my arms. "But what about Tyler? He's not . . . like us?" The seal popped with a hiss, and the door burst outward.

Jett shot me a look that told me I was being unreasonable. "He's also been exposed," he said. "He can't survive."

I hated him for being so matter-of-fact about it, even if it was the truth.

Jett frowned at me. "I'm sorry," he explained. "We've all lost people we cared about."

I kept rubbing my arms, my skin no longer chilled but wanting to ward away the feelings that overwhelmed me. I turned my attention to the room in front of us.

Jett lifted his chin toward the opening, his eyes sparkling. "Welcome to my lair."

From the other side of the open door came the hum of
electricity, the buzz filling the air with its static charge. Jett
stepped over the threshold, which was several inches high,
and I leaned in closer to see what it was he was hiding in
there.

Computers. There was a hodgepodge collection of
computer workstations—monitors and keyboards and rout-
ers and modems of various sizes and designs—like they'd
been salvaged from junkyards and thrift stores and yard
sales—anyplace he'd been able to get his hands on a piece
of equipment. There were printers and cords and discs too.

And then there were the maps. Walls and walls of maps.

It was like the military version of my dad's place. More
organized and state-of-the-art, but it had that same feel to it.
A similar command-center vibe.

"What do you do down here?" I questioned, taking a
step inside and feeling slightly claustrophobic once I was on
this side of the metal door.

"This," Jett declared, interlacing his fingers and flipping
his hands over, and then he cracked all his knuckles in front
of him at the same time, "is where the magic happens." He
hit a power button on one of the computers, and at once they
all crackled to life, monitors blinking furiously through a
series of synchronized commands.

When they finished flashing the sporadic lines of script
on their screens and came fully ablaze, there was a single

glowing logo in the center of each and every one of them—
a logo I recognized all too well—and the dusting of goose
bumps that had prickled my skin when Jett had mentioned
this was a nuclear facility came back with a vengeance.

It was an electronic image of a firefly.

"What the holy mother of . . . the fireflies . . ." I shook
my head. "What are those . . . what does that mean?"

Jett flashed me a curious look. "Have you seen that
before?"

"Yes. I mean, maybe not this one exactly, but ones like
it. My dad had all these picture of fireflies at his place."

He nodded. "That makes sense. Your dad would probably know."

"Know what?"

"About the fireflies, and what they represent."

"And that is *what* exactly?" I asked, blowing a strand of
hair out of my eyes irritably.

Jett laughed at my reaction. "Oh yeah, I keep forgetting
you're new to all this." He sat down at one of the computer workstations and twisted his chair back and forth, like
a restless schoolkid. "There have been stories of UFO sight-
ings that date back hundreds—maybe thousands—of years,
but it wasn't until the 1950s, when there was this Brazilian
farmer—a guy named Antonio Vilas-Boas—who claimed
he'd been taken on board one of those alien spaceships and
ordered to impregnate"—he wiggled his eyebrows when he
said the word *impregnate,* making me think he was as young
as he looked—"this hot 'humanoid.' When he was returned,

he was in pretty bad shape, like they'd beaten the crap out of him. And even though authorities *claimed* they didn't buy his story, it caused a flood of other people to start reporting that they'd been abducted too. The thing is, some of these claims had certain things in common. Things that didn't get reported to the general public." He leaned back while he continued to twirl in his chair. "Wanna guess what those things might be?"

I raised my eyebrows, pretty sure the answer wasn't rocket science or anything. "I'm gonna say *fireflies?*"

Jett gave an exaggerated nod. "Bingo! And not just a firefly here or there. According to those 'abducted,' for lack of a better word, or witnesses, there were always lots of them—swarms of them."

"And you think the fireflies have something to do with the taken?"

"Oh, they have something to do with it, all right. We're sure of it. And so were the government agencies and the scientists who were tracking the activity at the time. It wasn't the No-Suchers . . ." He paused to clarify, unaware that I'd already heard the term. "I mean the NSA, who tracked that kind of thing back then. Rumor has it that after working with Winston Churchill during World War Two to cover up a UFO sighting in England, President Eisenhower had these covert meetings that were called the First Contact meetings with the aliens to forge a treaty with them. He also formed his own agency to look into these so-called 'abductions' as well."

"This sounds like the kind of crazy conspiracy stuff my dad would spew." I sighed, crossing my arms and feeling somewhat defensive.

He sat up straighter. "Anyone can Google it, but from what I know about your dad, he's not all that crazy. There's some truth to this. At least part of it. I don't know much about the First Contact meetings or about who was really behind this new agency that was formed, but I do know that they got wind of people claiming to be returned, and of witnesses stating that they'd seen huge gatherings of fireflies around the time those people had been taken. Once it was proved that the Returned had the ability to heal, a plan was devised." He winced. "A really terrible plan, somewhere along the lines of torture. But it got the job done."

Cocking my head, I took a step closer, almost afraid to ask. "What did they do?"

Jett pulled up his sleeve and showed me his arm. "They used the whole firefly thing against us. They tracked us down and captured us. They questioned us, and if we didn't admit to being one of these so-called Returned, then they would use this thing that looked kind of like a car cigarette lighter, but it was more like a brand, really. It had a symbol in the center of it: a firefly." He shrugged, as if it wasn't a completely barbaric thing he was describing. "Since they couldn't risk exposing themselves to our blood by cutting us, they used it to sear our skin instead. To test us."

I frowned as I leaned closer, trying to figure out what I was missing. "But . . . there's nothing there," I stated solemnly, hating that someone could do something so vile to another person—human or not.

His voice lowered. He was quiet, so quiet, when he answered, "That's how they knew. If you healed, you'd been returned."

I closed my eyes. I felt sick. I didn't say anything for a very, very long time. Finally, when I trusted myself not to throw up when I opened my mouth, I whispered, "I'm sorry."

Jett looked up at me with eyes that couldn't decide if they were blue or green or shades of gold. It was like staring into cut glass.

Or into the iridescent wings of a firefly.

"It was a long time ago," he recalled with a faraway look in those mosaic eyes of his.

"This is what it looked like," he said, pointing to the golden-beetle image on his screen.

"They were a different agency back in WW Two—I'm not even sure what jurisdiction they fell under. But the guys who are after you now are a part of the NSA, at least indirectly. They're an offshoot agency that operates under the radar of the rest of the organization. The government doesn't sanction what they do, and if the public ever discovered their true purpose, it would be denied. They're kinda the Area 51 of agencies. Officially, they don't exist . . . except that they totally do."

I turned away from the screen, unable to stomach the idea of anyone, especially people in authority, doing the things Jett was talking about. It was barbaric.

I inhaled, still trying to steady my stomach. "How old are you, Jett?"

He came back to the present then, dropping his sleeve and offering me a small smile. "Twelve when I vanished." He counted on his fingers then, his smile growing. "But now . . . sixty-four years young."

"So how did you escape?"

Jett lifted his chin. "My pops wasn't the kind of guy you messed with, not even if you were a GI." He closed out the image with a sharp click, and though I wanted to ask more about it, I got the feeling the discussion was over.

"What did I miss?" Simon asked, ducking through the doorway as he joined us. Willow was right behind him, and I wished she didn't make me so uneasy. She just had that energy about her, like she was hoping a fight would break out at any second just so she could let off some steam.

Like punching was her hobby.

"I was just about to show her the Sats," Jett said, turning to face one of the monitors.

"Sats?" I asked.

"Satellite images." His fingers danced over the keyboard, and a series of images flashed up on the screen. At first it was like looking at Google Earth: generic images I'd seen searching the Web. But then they became more specific as he refined the shots, honing in, until I recognized the city . . . the street . . . the house he was converging on. The image was crystal clear; there was no mistaking it.

It was my mom's house. The very house I'd grown up in.

Except that it looked so strangely different now, covered almost completely in plastic. Enclosed the same way my mom had wrapped the leftovers she'd set out for me. Surrounding the property, all the way around the yard, there was a tall chain-link fence that hadn't been there before.

"Quarantined?"

It was Simon who answered me. "They're probably searching for evidence as well as contaminants. I wasn't lying when I said they'd do anything to get their hands on you."

"Assholes," Willow growled, reminding me that we had an enemy in common.

"What about my dad? Has anyone heard from him? Did they get to him too?"

Jett went to work on the keyboard. "We've been following the online chatter—his message boards and chat rooms, all the places he usually frequents. So far he hasn't made an appearance. But we also haven't heard anything on the police or No-Suchers' frequencies to make us think he's been taken in for questioning either. He seems to have gone off the grid for now." A satellite picture of my dad's trailer popped up, and it was like looking at my mom's house. It, too, had been quarantined, tented in plastic sheeting and enclosed by a chain-link barricade.

This time I could read the signs that were hung on the fencing: WARNING: RESTRICTED AREA

And at the bottom of the sign, in bold red letters: USE OF DEADLY FORCE AUTHORIZED.

The whole thing—the signs, the fencing, the quarantine—it was all insane.

"So I never asked this, but when we were at the bookstore, Tyler and me, there was an agent who . . ." I stopped because it was hard to find a way to put the words together just right.

But I didn't have to finish my thought, because Jett turned around to look at Simon—another silent exchange. They already understood what I wanted to know.

"He killed himself," Willow answered before either of the two boys had a chance. "Shot himself. That's how we knew you were in trouble; their frequencies blew up with word of an agent being exposed to a Code Red and offing himself."

Code Red. So that's what he'd meant.

I turned to Willow, who didn't seem to have any qualms about answering my questions. "And Jackson?"

"Was that the other guy's name?" She shrugged, and again I was struck by how easily they accepted all this. "They got him. He was exposed, too, I guess. Must've been fresh blood still on the floor when he came in to see what happened."

I shifted on my feet. "How do you know he was exposed?"

Simon and Jett exchanged a look again, and again it was Willow who didn't mince words. "We already got confirmation that he died."

"Died? How?" I asked, ignoring both boys and turning

all my attention to her now.

"How do you think?" she answered as if I were dense.

My voice cracked. "Already?"

Simon pushed past Willow to stand in front of me. "He probably touched it—the blood. If it made contact with his skin, it would have reacted more quickly."

But that didn't make sense. "It was on my clothes," I explained. "Tyler . . . he touched me after I saw you. He should've—"

Simon interrupted. "It wasn't fresh then. There's only about a sixty-second window when contact makes a difference. Airborne's bad, but skin contact's worse."

I don't know if that was supposed to make me feel better, that Tyler would outlive Jackson because he hadn't touched my blood within that sixty-second window, but it didn't. Dead is dead.

I shook my head, not wanting to be like them. Not wanting to be okay with all this, to accept death so willingly. Already, though, I could feel the hollowness consuming me, and I wondered if this was how it started. The carving out of your emotions. If I would soon be empty, a shell. "There has to be a way," I murmured, collapsing bonelessly into one of the chairs.

And then it was Jett—Jett who'd only been twelve when he'd been taken but was now sixty-four years old. Jett who looked at me with those confusing, kaleidoscope eyes when he said the words that gave me back some of myself. "Maybe there is a way."

I shot to my feet. "Wh-what are you talking about? What are you saying?"

Simon looked as confused as I felt, and behind me, Willow was silent.

Jett blinked rapidly and pushed his hair out of his eyes. "What if . . ." He rubbed his hands on his pants. "What if he could be one of the Returned?"

It was as if Jett had poured gasoline on an open flame.

"What you're suggesting is crazy!" Simon shouted, waving his hands as he spoke. "No one's ever done that. Not on purpose. Even if we wanted to, there's no way of even knowing where or when one of these 'takings' might occur."

"Besides," Willow added, a million times more subdued than Simon was but just as convinced. "There's no guarantee he'd even come back. Most don't."

I didn't know that. I knew *some* didn't, but not *most*. It didn't matter, though. What Jett was suggesting, it was crazy. Beyond crazy.

It was as good as murder as far as I was concerned.

It was taking a normal, living, breathing human and turning him into something . . . *less than human.*

I'd be sentencing Tyler to a life where he would no longer be normal. Where he'd be a walking time bomb because his blood was toxic to everyone around him. And where he'd never age like other people, so he'd be forced to give up all his friends and family in order to keep his secret.

He'd be a freak, like me.

"Think about it," Jett went on. "What if we can figure it out? What if we can pinpoint a location and take him there?"

"How?" Simon interrupted. "Where?"

Encouraged by Simon's questions, Jett sprang into action. He went to one of the walls where he'd already hung the mostly decimated map I'd taken from my dad's place. He tapped it, looking at me. "I enhanced the map we got from you. . . ." He went to the nearest workstation and pulled up an exact replica of the map, only this one was easier to read, the smudged lines clearer and more legible. "I also tried the USB, but it's too damaged. I couldn't get anything off it."

Impatient, Willow chimed in. "Will you *please* just get to the point?"

"The CD was another matter," Jett continued, oblivious to Willow's short temper. He grinned like a kid on Christmas morning. "It held a lot of your dad's backup files for the past five years, and your dad is one righteous record keeper. Most of what he had on that disc we already knew: names, dates, locations—that kind of thing."

"So?" Simon interrupted. "What's your point?"

"The point is, there's one place that comes up in his files numerous times as a *taking* site. One place that's shown up again and again and again and again in the past five years that we've never been able to pinpoint."

Jett jumped up from his chair and tapped a spot on the map with the tip of a pen. "And it's not that far from us."

I stared at the distorted map of Washington State. "Where

323

is it?" I asked, because even if I wasn't willing to entertain the idea of letting Tyler become like me—*like us*—I needed to hear Jett out.

"It's called Devil's Hole." Jett breathed the name, filling it with as much wonder as he could manage.

"Devil's? Hole?" The skepticism in Willow's voice was obvious.

Again Jett didn't seem at all discouraged by her cynicism. "It's here, not too far north of the Oregon border," he explained as he traced a path from where we presumably were—in an abandoned nuclear bunker below the ground—all the way to the place where Jett believed Tyler had a chance of being taken.

"There's been a lot of talk about it being just an Indian legend. In fact, there was this Native American shaman named Red Elk who once told reporters that his father had first taken him to see the hole back in 1961. He claimed that not only was the hole 'endless' but also that strange things happened whenever he went near it. He never really said what those strange things were, but there were others who swore that animals refused to go anywhere near the giant crater. Some have said it's the gateway to hell." He flashed a crooked smile.

"Of course, none of these things was ever confirmed. At least not for the general public. But here's the interesting thing. . . ." He raised his eyebrows. "No one's ever really known the true location of Devil's Hole. But there are those who believe the government knows exactly where it is and that it's always been a source of alien activity, and they've been trying to conceal the location for years. According to your dad"—he was looking at me again—"those people are right, because he seems to know *exactly* where it is too."

He took off the pen's cap and circled a pinprick of a spot on the map, making it clear that this was the location in question. I studied the distance between here and there. He was right; it wasn't far. A couple of hours at most.

"And what? You think we can just show up there, and they'll take Tyler and *heal* him?" I couldn't help it. The idea was preposterous.

"Not just heal. *Restore*," Simon corrected.

"But if his body's already damaged, won't he come back that way too? Like me, with my bruise and my tan lines?"

Jett was already shaking his head. "That's not usually how it works. We've seen cases where people with cancer were returned completely healthy, and people who'd had gruesome scars came back unblemished."

It was so incredibly, unbearably, outrageously tempting—the idea of saving Tyler's life.

But it wasn't really *his* life I'd be giving him back. It was a new life.

I knew because I wasn't the same anymore. As much as I wanted to believe I was still the same Kyra Agnew from five years ago, I couldn't keep living that life anymore. How could I possibly subject Tyler to that? How could I take away his life like that?

He still had a family who loved him.

I shook my head, more confused than ever. "I don't know. How can I force him to become one of us?"

Willow scoffed at my reluctance. "What choice do you have? If you don't, he'll die."

I spun around to face her. "If I do, his old life is over. Isn't that the same thing?"

No one stopped me when I left the underground bunker and made my way to the surface once more. I had to see Tyler.

Either way I was a murderer; there was nothing I could do to change that fact. But this way at least he could die with dignity. He could leave this world the way he was meant to go—as himself.

Still, knowing it was the right choice didn't make it any easier when I knelt beside him and saw the blisters that had broken out over his lips and cheeks, spreading down his neck. I wanted to touch him, to feel his heart beating beneath my palms; but I was afraid my touch might somehow hurt him, so instead I whispered his name into the chasm between us.

"Tyler," I breathed, holding back the flood of emotions that hearing his name stirred within me. A name I'd forever equate with humanity. A name that would forever brand me—the way the fireflies had been seared into the skin of those suspected of being returned—a killer. "Tyler, I'm here. I promise I'll stay with you."

His head lolled my way, and spittle foamed at the corner of his mouth. I shouldn't have disturbed him. I should've left him in peace. "K—K—Kyra," he finally managed.

"Yes. It's me." I reached for his hand but stopped myself before I grabbed it. The outer layer of his skin was peeling away. At this rate, even if what was inside him wasn't killing him, he was sure to get an infection from the pollutants in the air around us. "Don't say anything. You don't have to say anything."

But he struggled anyway, trying to talk. "K—Kyra." He panted my name. Panted. And I physically ached at the effort he put himself through. "I w—want you to . . . know . . ."

"Tyler, don't. Just . . . *shh* . . ."

He reached for me, blindly, clumsily. His raw fingers searched for me. And I wanted to touch him so badly that when they found me, I fumbled for them, clinging to them, unable to stop myself. Unable to care that I might be hurting him. Maybe he was past hurt. Maybe I didn't even care anymore. I wanted to stroke him. Kiss him. To breathe him in so I could remember that smell forever. "I . . . love . . . you . . . ," he gasped at last.

That was it. He undid me with those words.

It would have been better if he'd said nothing at all, because I could live with nothing. Love . . . well, love was another matter altogether.

Love required sacrifice and making hard choices and doing things that were bigger than just you.

It wasn't something you asked for, or could control or change. It was something you accepted.

Love was a force of nature.

Lifting his hand to my trembling lips, I remembered

when he'd told me that he might be falling in love with me. I remembered exactly what he'd said to me.

"You can't stand there and tell me you're not that same girl, because I'm telling you, *you are*. You're more perfect than anyone I know."

Tyler thought I was perfect. And even now, knowing that I was the one responsible for doing this to him, he was able to say those words to me: *I love you*.

He understood, maybe better than I did, what it meant to love.

I searched his face, wondering how I could possibly let him go when he had so much left to do. Even if his family turned their backs on him, or if he had to walk away from them, didn't he deserve a chance? Was it really up to me to decide who was, and wasn't, *normal enough*?

I got to my feet, easing his hand down and squeezing it as gently as I could. "I love you, too, Tyler. So goddamned much it hurts."

CHAPTER EIGHTEEN

I RAN OUT OF THE DUSTY CABIN, YELLING ALL their names. Screaming for Simon and Willow and Jett. There were other Returned living in the camp, and they stopped what they were doing to watch me, none of them looking alarmed by the stranger in their midst. But I didn't know any of them, and I didn't care that I was drawing attention by my hysterics. I only cared about one thing now.

Without pausing, I plunged, feetfirst, through the opening in the ground. I was still shouting for the others as I sprinted down the concrete corridor, their names echoing off the walls and bouncing back at me.

But they were already halfway to me when I nearly barreled into them.

"We need to go." I was breathless and panting. "I changed my mind. I want to take him. To Devil's Hole. I want to try to save him."

"I'm not sure that's possible now," Simon said, pulling me aside. "We . . . have a situation."

"What? *No.* We need to take Tyler. We don't have time—"

"Kyra . . ." Simon didn't lower his voice, but he gripped my arm, and it was clear from his tone that whatever was wrong, it was serious. "We have to get out of here," he confided. "Somehow they know where we are."

"Who knows? The NSA? How?" I turned to Willow, remembering what she'd said when she'd picked us up, that there was no way we could be found here. "I thought you said this place was safe?"

Willow took a step toward me, her shoulders hunched as if I'd just declared war with my accusation.

Jett jumped between us. "We don't know how. Maybe your dad knew about us. Maybe there was something in his files—a map or a diagram with our location—and they found it." He shrugged as if it was impossible to believe, even for him. "I thought we were more careful."

Simon waved both Jett and Willow away. "Doesn't really matter now. What matters is, they're coming. And if they know where we are, it's just as likely they'll figure out about Devil's Hole. It might not be safe to go there."

I shoved Simon, pushing him against the wall. I couldn't let him give up that easily. "Nuh-uh. No way. I won't let you do this. You said it yourself—what choice do we have? If we don't take him and at least try, he'll die for sure." I could feel my decision, and Tyler's last chance, slipping like sand between my fingers, and I was desperate to keep hold of it. "We have to take a shot." I lowered my hands. "Simon, please," I begged. "Please. We have to try."

Simon closed his eyes, clearly struggling with what to do.

My gut twisted, and I chewed nervously on the inside of my lip while I waited for his answer.

When he opened his eyes, he looked past me to Willow. "Stay behind with Jett and organize the retreat. Gather as many supplies as you can." He turned to Jett then. "Collect all the hard drives, and any paper and electronic files we have. Don't leave them *anything* they can use to track us. Understood?"

"Of course." Jett nodded, and then took off back toward the computer room to start stripping it down.

Simon turned back to Willow. "When we're done, Kyra and I will rendezvous with the rest of the group at the Silent Creek camp. I'll radio ahead and let them know to expect us. They'll take us in, at least until we can find a new place to call home."

"And Tyler," I added, relief overwhelming me.

But Simon just shook his head. "No, Kyra. Tyler will either be gone by then—taken by them—or he'll be dead. We can't wait around to find out which. Once we get to

Devil's Hole, we'll have to leave him there. Even if we had the luxury of waiting around for the next day or so to see if he's going to be returned or not, people are rarely returned to the same place they're taken from." He ignored me then and looked at Willow once more. "We should be meeting you there by morning."

If it hadn't been for the morphine, I definitely would've changed my mind.

As it was, the screaming had stopped once the drug had finally entered Tyler's system, which was just about the time we reached the long, barren stretch of highway on our way to Devil's Hole.

But the screams still echoed inside my head, as did the implications of what I was about to do.

Playing God.

Still, I prayed it worked. That we weren't chasing a pipe dream. That I wasn't pinning all my hopes on the impossible.

Next to me, in the driver's seat, Simon gave up trying to find a decent station on the radio. "Jett was trying to help, you know? That's just his way," he explained. "He grew up in Vegas. He was young, but his old man was a bookie, so numbers—odds—come second nature to him. He thinks everyone gets the same comfort from them that he does." I thought about what Jett had told me, about his dad not being the kind of guy people messed with, and I guess it made some sense.

With the radio off, I could hear Tyler's gurgling breaths coming from the backseat. It wasn't that I'd wanted to be in front with Simon, but I'd been too afraid to sit in back with Tyler. I didn't want to accidentally brush any part of his skin, which had broken out in large lesions. My jaw tensed as I turned to check on him.

"Well, Jett and his stupid statistics only made me feel worse," I shot back under my breath, not wanting to disturb Tyler. "Now it's all I can think about."

And it was true, I kept turning the numbers over in my head.

Most people who were taken were never returned, that much I'd already known—Willow had said as much—but Jett had hammered the point home. He didn't have any hard numbers, but his best guess had been somewhere around 33 percent. That was one person returned for every three taken, he'd clarified.

I hated to think what might have happened to the other 67 percent.

Maybe they were returned, too, and had never come forward. Or maybe they were failed experiments. Maybe they hadn't survived whatever torture we'd been put through.

Maybe we were all expendable.

I couldn't afford to think that way, not when I had Tyler's life in my hands.

According to my father's records, Jett explained, the likelihood of being taken from Devil's Hole was higher than anywhere else. In the past five years there had been seven people reported missing from that area. That was the highest incidence of repeat "takings" ever recorded if that's really what happened to them.

Seven people missing. It made sense that Tyler had a chance of being taken if we could just get him there in time.

The problem was, of those seven people, only one had returned.

One.

That was only 14 percent, Jett had explained. Considerably lower than the 33 percent average. The idea of subjecting Tyler to those odds made me sick.

But listening to Tyler breathe now, I knew time was against us. Devil's Hole was his last chance.

"Can I ask you something?" I probed, trying to push aside numbers and statistics because Tyler was more than that. "Why do you think they're doing it? The experiments, I mean? What's the purpose? What are we being put back here for?"

Simon stared out at the road for a long, long time, and for a long, long time I waited. After a while I gave up, turning my attention to the road, too, convinced he had no intention of answering me.

And then I heard him. "I ask myself that every day. Every day since I realized what I was. We all have. A lot of what Jett does is search for theories. He coordinates with other camps and even tracks down the lone Returned, trying to come up with some . . . *reason* for what's been done to us." He went silent again, and I remained rigid. Eventually he sighed. "I think there must be a reason; we just don't know what it is yet. But it's something big, and I think the No-Suchers think so, too, and that's why they want to get their hands on us so badly." Swallowing, he looked over at me. "I believe there's a reason you were gone so much longer than the rest of us before you were returned. That they're perfecting what they do to us, preparing for something. And those things you can do that we can't, I think they're important."

I shook my head, afraid he might be able to see how much he was scaring me with all his talk of plans and something coming. "I think you're wrong," I denied in a whisper. "I think we were just in the wrong petri dish at the wrong time."

Simon smiled at me. "Maybe you're right. I think that, too, sometimes. That they're just fucking with us because they can. That it's all just a game, and we're the pawns."

I turned away. I hated to think my life had been turned upside down for some cosmic chess match. "How much longer till we get there?"

Simon looked at the gauges in front of him. "About two and a half hours. Three at most. It'll be dark by then." He cast me a wry look, and I knew he was making a mental list of things I could do that the other Returned couldn't. "But that shouldn't be a problem for you."

I leaned my head against the window, wondering how I'd last for three more hours listening to the labored sounds coming from the backseat and wishing I could stop myself from asking "How much longer do you think he has?"

Simon didn't stop to ponder his answer the way I would have. He didn't candy coat it either. "He might not survive the trip."

It was a strange location. Not as hidden or off the beaten path as I'd expected, considering all the weird things Jett had told us about the place.

Because he was so into legends and facts, and where the two intersected, Jett had given us the exact coordinates, along with driving directions for how we could find the *real* Devil's Hole.

The directions, however, were relatively simple to follow, and like Simon had predicted, it was just starting to get dark when we pulled off the main highway and onto the gravelly side road that Jett had marked for us.

After a couple of turns, we found the place at the end of a dirt road. No warning signs—no signs at all.

The only thing that struck me as unusual were the crickets, which shouldn't have since we were out in the middle of the desert. Even with my window up I could hear them, giving the whole scene—the dry, weedy grasses and scrub brush for as far as I could see—a poetic vibe.

I twisted around in my seat as we came to a stop at the top of the short hill where the road ended. I was relieved that Tyler was still breathing.

Reaching out to Simon, I let out a shaky laugh. "We did it."

Simon shut off the engine, his expression reserved. "Let's

not get ahead of ourselves. We haven't done anything yet."

I frowned at him, wanting him to be more optimistic. This *had* to work.

Glancing back at Tyler once more, I bit my lip. He was still unconscious, and I told myself it was the morphine. "Hang in there," I whispered softly.

Beside me, Simon reached over and pressed his hand over mine. "I'm sorry. I just . . . I don't want you to get hurt." He withdrew his hand. "You need to be prepared, because this might not work, Kyra. He might not be taken. And even if he is . . ." He didn't finish.

I swallowed. "I know."

Simon opened his door and switched on his flashlight. "Don't let your guard down," he said in the same voice he used when he spoke to Willow or Jett. I wondered if that's who I was now, one of his Returned. "The last thing we need is to be caught unaware."

Caught. My mouth went dry at the reminder that the NSA might know about this place.

I searched the spare terrain, looking everywhere the flashlight couldn't reach—all the places *Simon* couldn't see. The car had kicked up a cloud of fine sand behind us, dust that would take several long minutes to settle. And our tracks, if someone was looking for them, would be easy enough to find.

I joined him, pretending I was interested in the map, even though the lines and squiggles, the keys and symbols, and the scales were complete gibberish to me. "Where is it?"

He looked around and then pointed off to the right, just beyond a cluster of flat rocks past the end of the road. "About twenty meters that way. We'll have to carry him the rest of the way."

I nodded mutely.

From inside the car, Tyler coughed. A wet, hacking sound.

"We need to hurry," Simon told me, throwing down the map and shoving the flashlight into his back pocket. "We're almost out of time."

Even though Simon carried most of Tyler's weight, I was sweating by the time we reached the top of the short hill. My job was to hold Tyler's feet and serve as lookout, but Tyler was more alert now, moaning every time we bumped or jarred him, which was pretty much always, making me cringe inside. The coughing was worse, too, growing deeper and wetter sounding by the second. I worried he was drowning in his own fluids.

"Simon," I rasped, unable to hold back my tears. "We found it. This is it."

He grinned back at me, and for the first time I thought he might feel it too. Hope. "Just a few more steps," he beamed.

When we reached the edge of the legendary crater, we set Tyler down and I collapsed. Wiping my cheeks with the back of my hand, I approached the brick wall that surrounded the rim. Someone had gone to great care to look after this place. Even the perimeter was well manicured. The grasses and brush were trimmed back so they didn't crowd the wall or the area surrounding it.

At my feet, Tyler wheezed, a rheumy sound that made my skin crawl. "Now what?" I turned to Simon fearfully.

He looked back at me, and I could see it . . . in his eyes. The look that told me he had no idea.

We'd been waiting for almost an hour.

Waiting for the taking. Or, it seemed more likely at this point, waiting for Tyler to die.

I was okay with that now. I just wanted him out of his misery already. It was too hard to watch him suffer. Too hard to listen to his pleas for relief.

The morphine was wearing off, and he'd begun clawing at his own skin—at the blisters we could see, and the ones we couldn't. It was like watching him try to rip away his own flesh.

"Try singing to him again," Simon said from his place near the edge of the cavernous pit, where he'd been chucking rock after rock into the hole. "He seems to like that."

Simon was right; the singing had worked . . . for a while. I'd tried everything I could think of to keep Tyler calm: whispering, cajoling, soothing.

"It's not working," I shot back. "He's in too much pain." My face crumpled. "Are you sure this is the right place?"

He paused, his arm cocked midthrow. "I'm positive. How many giant holes could there be?" He flung the rock to emphasize his point, and I knew he was as frustrated as I was.

I didn't want to freak out, but that's exactly what I was doing. "Maybe we're scaring them. Maybe they won't take him with us sitting right here, in plain sight."

His shoulders fell as he stepped away from the rim. "Kyra," he explained, and even in the dark I could make out those eyes of his, the same way I had that first time I'd seen him, in the bookstore. "People have claimed for years to witness the takings. Obviously bystanders have never stopped them before."

"Then what?" I complained. "What are we doing wrong?"

The sound of tires rolling over gravel stopped us both cold. My head snapped around, in the direction we'd parked, while my heart beat once . . . twice . . . and once more, hammering agonizingly, thunderously inside my chest. "It's them, isn't it?"

Simon lunged for the flashlight on the ground, and he switched it off, ignoring me as he scurried to the ridge to get a better look. He gave me his answer the second he dropped down again, his back pressed against the wall of rocks and his fingers to his lips. There was nothing I could do about Tyler's whimpering.

"What do we do?"

He pulled a knife from his back pocket and rolled up his sleeve. "I don't want to do this, but if we have to, I'll infect them."

"Simon, no . . ." I jumped up from my spot next to Tyler, meaning to go to him, to convince him that was crazy

340

talk. How could he be willing to use himself—his blood—as a weapon like that?

But I stopped, unable to speak or think or breathe the moment I saw it . . .

. . . *them*.

So very many of them.

It was like looking at a constellation.

A radiant, sparkling, living constellation.

"Oh my god . . ." I covered my mouth with both hands and gasped between my fingers. Tears blurred the lights, blending and distorting them until they were one giant mass in my eyes. "They're so . . . *so beautiful.* . . ."

Simon looked at me, confused. He lowered the knife and let go of his sleeve as he turned to see what I had. To know what I knew.

That we'd been in the wrong place all along.

"Fireflies," he breathed.

They weren't amassed near the mouth of Devil's Hole like we'd believed they would be but were gathered at the top of a rugged stone peak instead. The site of them, with the moon hanging high above and the outline of local wild-flowers and brush below, was picturesque, and almost made me forget what they foretold . . . and the reason we were here in the first place.

I knew for certain then that I'd never seen anything like them before, not in real life, because if I had, if I'd ever wit-nessed anything like their spectral presence, I would have known. I would have remembered. They were as out of place as they were haunting, and I fell to my knees as I realized what seeing them meant.

Because they were too far away.

We could never reach them, not in time.

Tyler was going to die.

Tyler passed out the moment we tried to lift him, as if he'd just given up.

As if even he knew we were too late.

Everything inside of me knew the same, but I couldn't afford to stop trying. Not when we'd come so close.

But when I heard the last voice I ever expected to hear all the way out here, in the middle of the night near this strange place called Devil's Hole, I froze, my eyes prickling with tears and my throat squeezing tight.

"You have to put the boy down, Kyra."

I turned to watch the man approach, and I had to blink several times because I was blinded by the approaching flashlight.

But as the light bobbed away from my eyes, I saw him clearly. I would have recognized that flannel shirt and scruffy beard anywhere. "Dad?"

It was true. My dad was there, but he was with Agent Truman—the starched man in the starched suit—who stood just behind my dad.

"Kyra," my dad said to me, his voice all rough around the edges, like it was hard for him to talk.

That was when I realized I had no family left to go back

to. Agent Truman had convinced my mom I was dangerous and turned my dad against me too.

Blood pulsed behind my ears while my eyes slid to the thick Ace bandages wrapped around the agent's right hand.

Seeing Agent Truman's lopsided wrap job made me feel a million times better. I hoped he ended up needing surgery that involved metal pins and rods and lots and lots of recovery time, the same way Carrie Dreyer had when that broken bone had come through her skin.

"Do as he says, and your dad here doesn't have to get hurt," Agent Truman snarled at me over my dad's shoulder.

I looked down then and saw the gun in Agent Truman's good hand—his unbandaged one. He held it awkwardly, his grip unnatural, pointing it directly at my dad's back.

My dad lifted his hands in the air, showing me he was the same as me—a pawn. "I'm sorry, Kyr," he said hoarsely.

My gaze slid out of focus as tears welled fatter behind my eyelids. My dad hadn't turned on me. He was still my number one fan.

Simon gave me a meaningful look, and we did as we were told, easing Tyler onto the dusty ground. I took extra care to make sure we weren't laying him on any rocks, and then I turned to my dad.

I struggled to find the right words, but everything seemed wrong and not big enough, and definitely not sorry enough for the way I'd turned my back on him. "No . . . Dad . . ." I shook my head, wishing more than anything I could run to him so I could feel his bear-like arms around me. "I'm the one who's sorry. For everything. For not believing you in the first place." Then my gaze shifted to Agent Truman. "You can't do this," I told him. "It's illegal. He hasn't done anything."

His mouth twisted into a snarl. "This isn't about legal or not legal." He lifted his bandaged hand. "You have no idea how special you are, and I'm not about to let you get away again."

I'd been so focused on my dad that I'd nearly forgotten all about Simon.

"I don't think you have much choice," Simon stated. His voice was subdued when he spoke. *"That,"* he said, nodding at the poorly wrapped Ace bandage. "That's nothing." He clutched his knife in his fingers, clenching and unclenching his fist.

Agent Truman's eyes narrowed as they fell on the knife, but he didn't even flinch. "You wouldn't. Not with Kyra's old man here." He lifted his gun then, holding it to the back of my father's head, and my heart nearly exploded.

Simon's eyes slipped to my dad and then to me. I could see the conviction fade from his eyes even before his chin dropped and he, too, lifted his hands in the air. And then, as if all the will had been drained from him like a deflated balloon, he opened his fingers and let the knife slip to the ground.

But Agent Truman didn't back down as easily. He shoved the nose of the gun hard against the back of my dad's neck. There was something in the agent's expression, the wild look in his eyes and the firm set of his jaw, that made him look determined. He settled his gaze on me. "The easier you make this, the less likely dear old daddy won't end up at the bottom of that pit over there."

"Let him go." I couldn't tear my gaze away from the gun. I couldn't go with him, but there was no way in hell I was letting him hurt my dad. "Drop the gun," I warned, trying to sound reasonable. "I mean it." I concentrated, my hands curling into fists so tight my fingertips ached. A throbbing started in the back of my head.

I thought about the way I'd felt when I was at that gas station, when I wanted—when I *needed*—those pain relievers for Tyler so he wouldn't die from fever.

And now what I needed was for Agent Truman *not* to kill my dad.

I blinked slow and hard. I forced all my attention on the gun, on the barrel.

I clenched and unclenched my fingers, balled and unballed my fists. "No!" I screamed. "Let! Him! *Goooo!*"

When the gun jerked from his grasp, it flew end over end so fast that I could barely track it. It was that fast. A blur.

But I did see it, and so did everyone else, watching as it hurtled like a rocket toward the crater.

We never heard it hit the bottom.

For a moment I just stood there with my mouth hanging open. I'd done it. I'd actually moved something with my mind . . . on purpose. And this time there were witnesses.

Simon didn't take as long to react, and he turned to me

in an instant, his copper eyes finding me as he demanded, "You . . . *you* did this." It wasn't a question because, of course, he'd seen the truth with his own two eyes.

He looked stunned, and maybe a little pissed that I hadn't told him everything I was capable of, when we heard Tyler. He exhaled, releasing a gut-wrenching gurgle.

And like that, I was no longer concerned with Simon or Agent Truman or even my dad. I dropped beside Tyler as blood trickled from the corner of his mouth. *This was it,* I thought, even as I was silently screaming *not yet . . . not yet . . . not yet!*

"Tyler," I whispered, leaning as close to him as I could get so no one else could hear us. My windpipe felt crushed, and it was hard to swallow. My eyes ached.

He was burning up again, but I guess none of that mattered anymore. It would soon be over. He'd be at peace. "I'm here. I'm staying right here." I reached for his hand, no longer worried about hurting him, and his eyelids fluttered open.

He tried to focus, but his sightless eyes made it impossible, and his gaze darted wildly about, making him look lost and confused. I finally gave myself permission to cry, because there was nothing left to do. I'd taken him to the wrong place.

Maybe, I thought desperately. *Maybe if we all tried . . . maybe there is still time.*

I petitioned Agent Truman, who was just standing there, gaping at his empty hand. "Please. If we can just get him up to that hill. If you help me, I promise I'll go with you." I pointed to the place where the fireflies had been just a few short minutes ago.

But the rocky peak was dark now. The fireflies were gone.

Beside me, Tyler sputtered, and I turned to see blood spewing from his mouth and trickling from his nose too. When he gasped, he choked on it, and then choked some more.

He really was drowning, and soon it would be over.

"What the—"

I didn't know what Agent Truman was trying to say, but Tyler's hand suddenly went weaker in mine, his fingers going limp as his gasps grew frail and reedy.

"Kyra." My dad tried to get my attention, but it barely registered. How could I care? How could anything else matter when Tyler was dying? When I was losing him?

And then a cloud of light passed over the top of me.

I wanted to ignore it, but it was far too radiant to be overlooked. Still holding Tyler's hand, because I wasn't ready to say good-bye, I glanced skyward; and when I did, my chest tingled and I felt light-headed.

They were amazing this close-up. The fireflies. They were so close I could single out individual clusters of the tiny, glowing insects. It wasn't like before when they'd appeared to be one enormous knot. Rather, they were like a collection of several groups that had all come together. Like tribes working in unison.

And they were positively breathtaking.

Dropping Tyler's hand at last, I stood up as I watched while this swarm—this giant, undulating cloud—began to break apart. Beyond me, at the crater, something was happening, and there was light pulsing up from below, from deep down inside Devil's Hole.

Whatever was down there was alive. And it was coming closer. It was bright and fast, and loud, and it sounded vaguely like the fireflies above us—like the millions of wings that beat. Only louder. Angrier.

And when they were finally there and we could see them at last, we knew what they were. They were fireflies too. But there were so many more of them as they emerged from Devil's Hole. So many it was impossible to see anything *but* them. They were everywhere. All around us. Eating up all the space until there was no room, no air, no *nothing* left at all.

I would have run, but I didn't know where to go. I couldn't move or breathe without touching wings and legs and antennae. I could feel them crawling and fluttering and bumping into me, tangling in each and every strand of my hair, creeping beneath every layer of clothing, crawling up my nose, and nesting in my ears.

I slapped and scratched and flung them away from me, knowing it was useless because there would only be more to take their places but totally unwilling to accept their infestation all the same.

The flash, when it came, was nothing like the first time,

when I'd felt it throughout my entire body. When I'd tingled and been weightless and felt tugged by whatever force had been pulling me from the ground.

This flash was the same, but different.

It was blinding, exactly the way it had been the night I'd disappeared from Chuckanut Drive while my father had watched helplessly. Blinding to the point that I couldn't see, or sense, anything for several long minutes. I tumbled to the ground, entirely disoriented. I couldn't tell up from down or left from right.

I opened my mouth to call for help, but no sound came out. I was speechless, sightless, helpless.

And then, like before, on that fateful night on Chuckanut Drive, there was nothing. . . .

EPILOGUE

SEVENTEEN DAYS. THAT'S HOW MUCH TIME HAD passed since I woke up beneath the scorching sun near the mouth of Devil's Hole.

Just me and Simon.

We'd stayed there for nearly an hour—maybe less, maybe more. It was hard to know for sure. Time felt irrelevant after everything we'd been through. We'd searched for the others—Tyler, my dad, even Agent Truman—but they were nowhere. I tried long after Simon had given up on them, convinced they were gone. Convinced they weren't coming back anytime soon.

I'd shouted for them until I was hoarse and scrambled up

the rocky hills to get a better view of the desert landscape. I skinned my knees and cut my palms, but there was no one there who could be infected by my recklessness.

I even crawled to the edge of Devil's Hole and screamed their names into the void.

The only evidence that they'd ever been there at all was Agent Truman's sedan, still parked behind our car, and his badge, which had been lying on the ground right where he'd once stood.

Even the fireflies had vanished.

"It's not healthy, you know? Drawing bugs all day long." I jerked my head up to find Natty grinning at me. She sat down, sliding a small plate of fruit in front of me. "Here, eat. It won't do you any good to starve."

Natty was sweet like that, the only kind-of friend I'd made since we'd arrived here at the Silent Creek camp, where Simon and his band of Returned had taken up refuge after the NSA had discovered their location.

Simon had tried to talk to me over and over again after that morning when we'd driven all the way from Devil's Hole. I knew he thought I was avoiding him, and maybe I was, but it wasn't about Simon, not really.

I just couldn't bear to face him, to be reminded of what I'd done to Tyler, and to my dad as well. If I hadn't been so selfish, if I had just been able to let Tyler go peacefully—the way he should have—my dad would still be here.

Not . . . *vanished*. Maybe forever.

And Simon was just another reminder of what an idiot I'd been.

It hadn't been all that hard to avoid him, though. Simon's group—Jett and Willow included—kept to themselves for the most part. It was like the two camps were rival high schools, coming together only for important meetings but staying segregated whenever possible. When they did sleep, they slept in different quarters; and when they ate, they made sure it was in different shifts.

But I wasn't tethered by whatever pecking orders had already been established. I was like the new girl at school, able to choose for myself. And once we'd arrived at Silent Creek and I'd met a few of the Returned here, I'd immediately gravitated toward their way of life. They lived peacefully in this place, no guns or satellite trackers. They tended to their vegetable gardens and raised chickens and washed their clothes in the stream near the edge of camp.

Like the Returned from Simon's camp, these Returned were young, so it was strange to see the way they worked so efficiently, delegating chores and responsibilities, and voting whenever an issue arose. There was a leader of the Silent Creek camp, but not the way Simon was. Thom was more of a chairman than he was a strategist or final decision maker.

But being in a new place, with new people, didn't make it any easier to forget those I'd left behind.

If, or rather *when*, from what I'd gathered, Simon and his Returned moved on, I wasn't sure what I'd do—stay here in the mountains of central Oregon with Natty and Thom and the other Silent Creekers or move on with Simon and Jett and Willow, and the rest of their Returned.

Natty would be hardest to leave if I did go. Mostly she

stayed quiet and didn't ask a lot of questions, just made sure I ate every day or so and kept me company. Even when I didn't feel like talking.

I glanced down at the doodles on the edge of the page—the fireflies—and flipped my journal closed. I smiled weakly at her while she slid in silently beside me, not asking more than I could give.

The fireflies. They still took up too much space in my thoughts, still made me shudder, even seventeen days later.

I'd never get rid of the sensation of a million legs climbing over every square inch of me.

It shouldn't have happened that way. Simon told me so. None of it. The way the fireflies had engulfed us. Or the fact that they—whoever they were—had taken my father and Agent Truman along with Tyler.

Simon didn't have to tell me the rest—I had Jett's statistics to rely on for that. The Returned were usually young, in their teens.

It didn't bode well for my dad.

But honestly, at the seventeen-day mark, it didn't bode well for any of them.

Still, I refused to give up hope. Not yet. I was desperate to know if any of them—if Tyler or my dad, at least—had survived.

Both camps had their own information networks in place, yet so far neither one of them had heard so much as a peep about anyone, *anywhere*, being newly returned. And that lack of news was . . . well, it was killing me.

"I wasn't drawing. I was . . ." It didn't matter. Natty

didn't need to hear that I was trying to write it all down so I could find a way to make some sense of it, because it would never make sense, even if it *was* on paper.

"You're crying again," Natty said quietly, and I blinked, wiping my eyes on my sleeve.

I was past being embarrassed over my outbursts, which were happening more and more frequently as I tried to cling to hope. "Sorry," I offered halfheartedly.

She shrugged and picked up a slice of apple from my plate.

"Kyra!" It was Jett who'd come bursting into the dining room of the old mountain church house the Silent Creekers had taken over. "Kyra, come quick!" His cheeks were flushed, and his eyes were overly bright. "There's something you should see."

I jumped up and reached for the hand Jett held out to me. We ran across the small courtyard to the temporary communications room Jett had set up using some of the equipment he'd brought with him.

Like everything else, the communications equipment for both camps was kept separate, and Jett had a no-share policy about his stuff. I was clearly an exception to that rule.

"Someone reported a Returned?" I asked, knowing I sounded desperate and not caring in the least. I wanted it to be true so bad.

Jett's eyebrows lowered. "We're not sure exactly," he hedged, and my stomach dropped. "We intercepted a report of a teenage boy the No-Suchers picked up. They suspect he's one of us."

I frowned at him, refusing to let myself be crushed again.

"So? That could be anyone. What makes you think it was him?"

"Here. See for yourself." He handed me a laptop that was so bulky it felt like it could withstand an atomic blast.

I took it, my stomach doing crazy flips as I glanced tentatively down at the screen. I wanted to give myself just a few more moments of believing it could be Tyler before finding out it for sure wasn't. Sometimes those few seconds of hope were worth the crash back to reality, and I didn't want to lose that feeling—not just yet.

When I finally dared to peek, there was an email already cued up, and from the looks of it, it was definitely need-to-know information only. It had the word CLASSIFIED written all over it.

I skimmed the body of the email, my heart soaring with each passage I read:

On June 10 at 18:47 . . . Washington State Patrol reported an unidentified male between the ages of 16 and 20 years old at a rest stop just south of Olympia, Washington . . . subject was carrying no identification and refused to reveal his name to officials. Subject is currently being held at the Tacoma facility for my inspection.

"I don't get it. This could be anyone." I started to close the laptop, but Jett stopped me.

"Read who sent the memo."

When I did, my stomach tightened, and I had to reread the signature line several times.

It was right there, in black-and-white. Agent Truman was back, and he'd sent the email about a boy he wanted to "inspect."

"Jett? What was he talking about? What's the 'Tacoma facility'?"

It was Simon who answered my question as he came into the room. "It's exactly the kind of place we've been avoiding. And if that's him, if it really is Tyler and he's been returned, we need to get him the hell outta there."

I turned to Simon then, wishing I could take back every second I'd avoided him over the past seventeen days, because now when I needed him most, he was right here for me. I was almost afraid to ask: "Can we do that?"

Simon pushed away from the wall, grinning daringly at me. "We can sure as hell try."

"Kyra," Jett half whispered from his spot beside me, and I whipped back around to face him.

He was pointing at the screen again, only this time it wasn't the email he meant. "Look," he breathed, his mouth hanging wide open.

It took me a second to process what had gotten him so worked up, but on the screen a message had popped open, obscuring everything else. In it there was only one word, blinking at us.

Supernova16?

I stared at the mysterious message for several long seconds, my heart sliding into my throat.

Beside me, Jett's voice rose excitedly. "It's him, isn't it?"

My hands shook as my fingers touched the keyboard.

What if it was a trap?

On the other hand, what if it wasn't?

I had to know, so I tapped in the single word message and hit ENTER: *Dad?*

ACKNOWLEDGMENTS

I cannot even begin to express my gratitude to the many, *many* people involved in getting *The Taking* into the hands of readers, but I'm going to give it a try anyway.

First off, I want to thank the world's best critique partner, S. R. Johannes (aka Shelli). Thank you for never thinking any idea is impossible—no matter how obscure and far-fetched it sounds when I'm trying to explain it. My go-to man in blue, police chief Bryan Jeter, thank you for lending your serious law enforcement expertise to my not-quite-so-serious hypothetical cases. And thanks also to Dr. Michael Long, my longtime dentist—who really does hum under his breath while he works on my teeth—for helping with the ins and outs of dental X-rays and chipped molars.

One thing I like to do when writing is to take a real place—in this case it was Burlington, Washington—and then build a fictional world around it. So to the people who live in and around Burlington, thank you for letting me rearrange and re-create your city to suit my purposes. And for letting me abduct some of your citizens.

As always, there were so many people who worked diligently behind the scenes before *The Taking* ever made its way to bookshelves. First and foremost, my incredible agent Laura Rennert—not to mention the entire crew at Andrea Brown Literary Agency. I feel fortunate to have all these strong and brilliant ladies in my corner!

Everyone at HarperTeen, including my enthusiastic publicist Mary Ann Zissimos—you make juggling look easy!—as well as my insanely creative cover designers Sammy Yuen and Laura DiSiena from the Harper design team—can I just say how much I love this stunning cover? My editor, Sarah Landis, who is always awesome to work with but somehow managed to get *inside my head* on this book. Thanks for helping me get what I wanted to say out on the page precisely the way I wanted to say it. (I probably should have asked for your help on that last sentence, Sarah!) To all of my foreign publishers and readers who have made a place for my books overseas, how can I thank you all enough? And a heartfelt thank-you to Alicia Gordon and the dynamic duo of Erin Conroy and Ashley Fox at WME for all of your tireless efforts in a world in which I'm utterly clueless—you ladies make everything clearer, and that's saying something!

I'd also like to thank all my friends from the Arizona writing retreat, during which I wrote the very first words of *The Taking* but refused to share what it was about because I was convinced I would "jinx" its mojo. Just being around that much incredible writing energy was all the spark I needed to get things rolling for this book. You ladies are seriously the best!

And again, to my family and friends for tolerating my weird, writerly ways, and for forgiving me when I come out of my cave and announce that I'm ready to join the real world again.

Lastly, to Josh, my partner in crime. Thanks for reading endless iterations of every manuscript I've ever written, and offering suggestions and advice, and never once complaining even when I'm less than pleasant about, well . . . everything. I love you more than I can probably ever express.

THE ACTION CONTINUES IN

How do you move forward
after someone steals your past?

THE

REPLACED

sequel to THE TAKING

KIMBERLY DERTING

PART ONE

CHAPTER ONE
Day Twenty-Five
Silent Creek Camp

DEAD.

Or rather, like I was dying.

That's the way I felt, watching the screen go all black like that. Like my lungs had gone from two functioning things that were pink and plump and filled with life, to shriveled-up hunks of useless meat that could no more pump air from them than I could sprout wings from my back and fly.

It had been seventeen days since I'd watched the guy I love be plucked from the ground by aliens, and then vanish in a blaze of light. The same night I'd lost my dad in that very desert. And now the first actual hints of the two of them being out there had just flashed across the screen, right before the computer shut down.

"Does someone want to explain what the hell just happened?" I was surprised I'd even been able to force the words from my mouth at all, considering those messed-up lungs of mine. I whipped around to face Jett, who was already leaning over my shoulder and punching frantically at the keyboard in front of me. He tried his best to boot the computer back up, but I could already tell there was no point. Everything we'd been looking at a moment earlier was just . . . gone, and now we were left staring at a big empty field of nothing.

He shook his head. "Someone shut us down," he muttered, but he wasn't talking to me now—his comment was directed at Simon. He lifted the computer from my lap and dropped it onto his own as he hunched over it, his fingers gliding in a way that made it look effortless while he got lost in a series of commands and functions I'd never understand. Jett handled a keyboard the way I handled a softball, like it was second nature. "They knew we were in their system and they locked us out." He unconsciously rubbed his arm and I recognized the gesture. It was Jett's tic whenever he mentioned the No-Suchers, as he called the NSA. Even though they hadn't directly been responsible for branding him back in the day, when the government had begun covertly hunting for the Returned, and even though he'd healed from the firefly image they'd scalded into his skin—the way we all healed from our injuries—his hand instinctively stroked the spot.

"They," I repeated. Of course it was them. We'd intercepted one of their classified emails right before that cryptic message had popped up, and somehow they'd caught on to us.

That dying sensation was back, rendering my lungs utterly ineffective, and even though I wanted to talk, the words were stuck so far down in my windpipe I practically had to cough them out. "But . . . he . . . he was right there," I sputtered, and even that came out sounding like someone had just punched me in the throat. I pointed at the deceased computer Jett was furiously trying to revive.

Even though it had only been a single word, that message from my dad had flipped my entire world upside down. For a split second I'd actually allowed myself to believe this seventeen-day nightmare had finally come to an end. Now, with Jett's computer struggling to come back to life, I had no idea if, or when, I'd ever see my dad again.

"Kyra," Simon tried. "We're not even sure it was him. It might have been *them* all along."

"Yeah. Coulda been a trap," Jett paused to interject.

I glanced down at the gibberish-looking commands that filled the screen, and felt a flare of hope when I saw that he at least had the thing rebooting. I held my breath, hoping against hope that the pop-up message we'd seen right before the whole computer had shut down might somehow—yes, miraculously, I get that—still be there after Jett was done working his magic.

But I knew better. It was gone for sure.

"Shut up," I insisted to both of them. Then I sighed because I knew they'd never help me if I didn't at least *try* to be nicer about it.

I hadn't been all that nice to Simon since he and I had had to leave Devil's Hole all by ourselves, without either Tyler or my dad. I'd avoided him whenever possible, even though I wasn't sure if it was because I was ashamed of what I'd done by poisoning Tyler with my blood, or because I was mad Simon hadn't warned me in time to stop it all from happening in the first place. The only thing that was clear was that I hadn't wanted to talk to him about any of it. And even though I didn't particularly want to be nice now, it wouldn't do any good to alienate them when they were only trying to help. "You're wrong, both of you. It had to be him." I exhaled, scowling now because they'd seen the same thing I had, my nickname—*Supernova*—clear as day in that message. "Who else would call me that?"

Simon's black brows met over the bridge of his narrow nose, and he was so close I could make out the golden-y flecks that seemed to float in his copper-colored eyes. "You know that was your dad's online handle the entire five years you were missing." It wasn't a question, and he wasn't wrong.

Supernova16. It had been plastered all over my dad's crazy internet message boards for years. Anyone who wanted to could have sleuthed that mystery out on their own.

He held my gaze, and for a minute I thought he was waiting for me to back down, to admit there was at least a possibility I might be wrong, because there was always a possibility, wasn't there? And when I didn't—not so much as a blink, since there was no way I thought I was mistaken, not this time—his gaze dropped to the screen and he studied

Jett's impressive recovery of the laptop with just a little too much interest.

But it was too late because I'd already recognized the look in his eyes.

Pity.

Simon hadn't for one second believed it had been my dad who'd sent me that message. And now, because he knew I did, he felt sorry for me.

I stormed away from Simon and Jett, leaving them alone with their stupid computer . . . and all their stupid unwanted pity. I wasn't sure why I was so pissed that neither of them came running after me, especially since I hadn't really expected them to, but I still totally was. And since I was the heroine in this melodrama in my head, I could be as pissy as I wanted.

But even if they'd tried to stop me, I'd have been pissed about that too, so they couldn't win for losing.

I was surprised to find Thom, the leader of the Silent Creek camp, waiting outside the temporary communication base, looking like he had something to say. But carrying on an actual conversation was the last thing I wanted to do, so I lowered my gaze and bulldozed past him, feeling only the slightest stab of guilt.

Mostly I was aware of how loudly I'd been muttering beneath my breath, and even as I kept moving, determined to make a quick getaway, I uncrossed my arms and tried to look a little less crazy, hoping that, at the very least, he hadn't heard the foul things I'd been saying about Simon and Jett.

In Silent Creek, we didn't have girl residences and boy residences. We had the Silent Creek campers' residences—entire houses where Thom's Returned dwelled, sometimes *with* roommates and sometimes being assigned the entire homes to themselves—and the two small rooms we'd been allotted when Simon had ushered us here after his camp had been disbanded. After the No-Suchers had discovered his hidden fortress at the abandoned Hanford site back in Washington.

But two rooms were all we needed. It's not like we slept or anything, not really. It was just nice to have a place we could call our own, even if we had to bunk with our fellow Returned. Willow's bed was directly across from mine, and even though I knew she didn't like anyone touching her things, I nudged her storage container—one of those plastic bins—with the toe of my shoe, pushing it back beneath her bed.

Apparently, having a few minutes to myself didn't just make me calmer, it made me bolder.

Unfortunately, I wasn't alone for long.

When Simon finally found me, I was still sitting there, staring sullenly at the floor. I glanced at the bedside clock, and an uneasy jolt rippled through me as I realized that over an hour had passed—sixty-six whole minutes, to be exact—while I'd been sitting there, brooding over Simon and the lost message and all the reasons we were stuck here in the mountains of central Oregon in the first place.

"Kyra?" Simon stepped inside the doorway, and I felt my stomach drop when I heard the way he said my name, all patronizing, like I was too soft and needed coddling. As if he *pitied* me, and the very idea made me want to hit him all over again.

This whole situation was so hard to wrap my head around. Just twenty-five short days ago, my life had been so boringly normal. I was an ordinary small-town girl who wanted nothing more than to sneak behind the bleachers so I could make out with my boyfriend.

But the whole twenty-five-days thing was a lie—just smoke and mirrors used to disguise the fact that I'd been missing for five entire years. The truth was, that normal life of mine had vanished the instant I'd climbed out of my dad's car in the middle of Chuckanut Drive and had been carried away on a flash of light.

It was the stuff bad sci-fi was made of: a girl, a flash of light, and a missing chunk of time. Yet it was all true. Ridiculously-appallingly-*crazy* but true.

And I'd seen it happen again with my own two eyes— one of those "takings"—the night Simon and I had dragged Tyler up to Devil's Hole, hoping, because it was his very last chance in the world, that whoever they were would take him the way they had me.

And they had.

The fireflies had come, the way Jett had told me they would, as a precursor to the light. Except he'd made it sound like we'd see a small cloud of them, twinkling in the night sky to let us know we'd found the right place.

Instead, those fireflies had engulfed us, nearly choking

7

me. And when they'd gone, it wasn't just Tyler who was missing, it was my dad and Agent Truman too.

"I don't wanna hear it wasn't him," I countered before Simon even had the chance to start in on me. "Who else would know my nickname?" It was the same argument I'd used before, and I hazarded a sideways glance when Simon sat down on the twin-sized bed right next to me, the mattress dipping heavily beneath him.

He sighed and sagged forward, balancing his elbows on his knees. His broad shoulder brushed against mine, and it was impossible *not* to notice the way he restrained himself for my benefit, like he wanted to tell me all the reasons I'd been wrong about the message being from my dad, reasons I knew, really, if I'd just stop being too stubborn to admit it.

Instead of saying any of those things, he scrubbed his hand over his dark, closely sheared hair and said, "Maybe you're right. Maybe it was your dad. But I'm not here to talk about that. If it was him, he'll have to wait. At least for now. I want to talk about the other message. The NSA email." He sighed again. "If it really means that much to you, I think we should go there, to the Tacoma facility. I think we should find out if it's really Tyler they're holding." He faced me, his unusual eyes capturing my attention.

"I thought you said that's the kind of place the Returned should avoid." My voice was pinched and tight, but my chest—my lungs—filled fully for the first time as my heart crash-crash-*crashed*, making those crappy old windbags vibrate like crumbled parchment.

"True enough. But if it's important to you . . . ," he added, a smile slipping over his lips as he shrugged. "I just need to think. Come up with a plan . . ."

"You'd really do that for Tyler?" I bit my lip and lifted my eyes to his. "For me?"

"I know you don't believe this, but I want you to be happy, Kyra."

Regret over the way I'd behaved pricked me, and I had to stop myself from leaning into his arm, which was so much bigger than mine.

Then I grinned, because to borrow one of my dad's expressions, even though I shouldn't look a gift horse in the mouth . . . come on. "And what else? I mean, besides getting Tyler back, what are you hoping to gain, exactly? I know you, Simon. You must think you can get something out of going there, or you wouldn't risk it."

I expected him to give me some cock-and-bull story about bringing me into his fold, or about teamwork, or . . . I don't know, how it's *us* against *them*—the Returned versus the No-Suchers. Instead, he answered candidly, "If we're lucky, we're hoping we can scrounge up some classified documents, maybe get our hands on some alien technology they're hiding in there. Mostly, I wanna know more about these guys. What makes them tick. Figure out the chinks in their armor."

"What if they don't have any?" I asked.

Simon's smile turned up full blast. "Everyone has 'em."

In the end, it didn't matter to me what his reasons were. I

9

tried to tell myself not to get my hopes up, but it was almost impossible because I'd seen the email too. It might not have been *from* Tyler, but I'd already committed every word of the classified email to memory, and I was convinced it was *about* him:

> "Washington State Patrol reported an unidentified male between the ages of 16 and 20 years old at a rest stop just south of Olympia, Washington. . . . Subject was carrying no identification and refused to reveal his name to officials. Subject is currently being held at the Tacoma facility for my inspection."

But it wasn't the content of the email, it was the signature line—from NSA Agent Truman, the very same agent who'd ambushed us that night at Devil's Hole and then had disappeared himself—that had me convinced: the boy in question *had* to be Tyler.

We'd all been looking at that email right before my dad's message had popped up, and to say that I'd hoped it was Tyler the NSA email referred to didn't even begin to describe what I felt.

Because here's the thing: if I could dream, it would be of him.

Tyler.

But dreaming was one of those things only afforded to those who could sleep. And since I no longer needed much—sleep, that is—it meant dreaming was pretty much a thing of the past. Like the horse and buggy, or phone booths, or floppy disks.

But I missed dreaming so, so, *so* much. I missed the way you could dream about something you'd seen on TV or overheard during that day, even if you barely remembered noticing it. Or the way dreams could be completely-utterly-*totally* random and have nothing to do with anything at all. Like this one time when I dreamed I was dragged onstage during a Wiggles concert, and it was so embarrassing because *what was I even doing at a Wiggles concert in the first place*?

And just like all those million fireflies that had been there that night at Devil's Hole—appearing right before the flash of light, their sticky feet clinging to my skin and their wings tangling in my hair as they forced their way up my nose and invaded my ears and my mouth—that ache for Tyler crawled over me, making me itch and burn and want to scream for some sort of relief. Even seventeen days later, it was maddening. Exhausting. Every time the sun came up, I got this sharp ache in my gut like I was one day closer to something.

One day closer to missing him more maybe. Or to finding him possibly. Or to never seeing him again . . .

I didn't know what it was, but it was like a knife twisting my insides each and every morning, and each morning it was worse. As if each passing day the knife turned a notch, tangling into my viscera, becoming so enmeshed it was almost a part of me, and if I couldn't relieve it soon, it would eventually rip me apart.

All I could do was pray that finding Tyler would be the cure.

I was desperate to see him one more time. To touch him or taste the mint on his breath. Each night I prayed for sleep . . . just so maybe I could dream of him.

But even without the dreams, I still saw his face every time I closed my eyes, with every blink . . . blink . . . *blink*. It was like my own personal hell, torturing myself with what-ifs and what-could-have-beens. My dreams had been replaced by pacing and journaling and drawing, anything to find some way to extinguish my guilt.

I was haunted by what I'd done, and by all the unanswered questions: What really happened to Tyler the night he vanished? Where had he gone?

Had he even survived?

Except the thing was, if the NSA really did have Tyler the way their email said that they did, then they'd had him for weeks, because Jett had given me the numbers—the Returned always came back within forty-eight hours.

Well, everyone but me, of course. I had to go and be all different.

March to the beat of your own drummer, my dad always said.

Simon reached over and gripped my knee. "I need you to do one thing for me." He leaned closer so I could smell the peppermint on *his* breath. "I'll do everything I can to help you with this, but I need you to keep quiet about it for now. At least until I can talk to Jett and Willow and figure this thing out."

I nodded once, and he stood abruptly to go.

"Simon," I said, stopping him. His hand was on the door-jamb as he raised a dark eyebrow and looked down at me. I suddenly wished I hadn't been so hard on him all this time. "Thanks." It didn't seem like enough to say to someone who was about to risk so much for me and for Tyler, who he'd barely known at all, but it was all I had to offer him.

"If Tyler's really there, we're gonna find him, Kyra. I swear we'll get him back."

KYRA'S STORY CONTINUES
IN *THE REPLACED*

When Kyra intercepts a message saying that the shadowy government organization called the Daylighters might have Tyler, she and her friends must risk everything to launch a rescue mission to save him.

But what if it's a trap? And worse, what if the returned Tyler isn't the same boy Kyra lost?

Violet solves murders
by following clues only she can sense.

Read the entire BODY FINDER series
by Kimberly Derting.

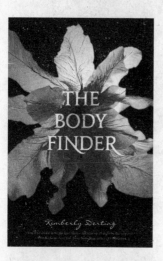